harvest dance

Bluestar Island, Book 2

Jennifer Faye

Lazy Dazy Press

Jennifer Faye/Lazy Dazy Press
P.O. Box 1736
Greensburg, PA 15601
www.JenniferFaye.com

Publisher's Note: This is a work of fiction. Names, characters, places, and incidents are a product of the author's imagination. Locales and public names are sometimes used for atmospheric purposes. Any resemblance to actual people, living or dead, or to businesses, companies, events, institutions, or locales is completely coincidental.

Book Layout © 2017 BookDesignTemplates.com

Harvest Dance: A Clean Small Town Romance/ Jennifer Faye. -- 1st ed.
ISBN 978-1-942680-15-4

To my father!
P.S. The apple cobbler is on the way!

Bluestar Island series:

Book 1: Love Blooms
Book 2: Harvest Dance
Book 3: A Lighthouse Café Christmas
Book 4: coming soon

Thanks & much appreciation to:
Content Editor: Trenda London
Copy Editor: Lia Fairchild

ABOUT THIS BOOK

A single dad, who's in over his head, and an event planner running from her past, are drawn together on charming Bluestar Island by a determined seven-year-old and her escape-artist goat. Event planner, Charlotte "Aster" Smith, has fled the only life she has ever known. The situation has left her questioning her own judgment as she cautiously tries to create a new life for herself on Bluestar Island. Taking the job of event coordinator for the small town is a step in the right direction. The only problem is it's currently a part-time position, but the mayor suggests with additional funding the position could transform into a full-time job. In the meantime, she needs a second job in order to stay financially afloat.

Farmer and single father, Sam Bell, is struggling to keep his aging farm from going bankrupt while raising his young daughter. And now that his daughter's babysitter is heading off to college, he needs help. So, when he finds Aster is in need of work, he thinks his problems are solved. But things aren't always what they seem.

In the lingering rays of a Bluestar Island sunset, Sam and Aster find themselves dancing upon the sand. As they help each other heal, the possibility of a future together becomes tangible. But will the ghosts from their pasts extinguish this budding romance?

Includes a delicious recipe for Aster's Amazing Apple Cobbler!

contents

Los Angeles, CA
January

Bang! Bang!

Charlotte Aster Smith's stomach knotted tight with nerves. She sat alone in the dark. With each pound on the apartment door, she jumped.

She didn't dare say a word. Perhaps if she remained quiet, he'd grow bored and move along. Though deep inside, she knew that wasn't going to happen. She couldn't be that lucky.

Bang! Bang!

"Charlie! Open up." Oz's tone was slurred. He'd been drinking again.

She resisted the urge to yell at him to go away. They had broken up. He had no reason to bother her. She remembered how his dark eyes had flared with anger when she'd dumped him after a few months of dating—a few months of him gradually trying to take control of her life.

In the beginning, Oscar, who preferred to be called Oz, had been thoughtful and a bit on the romantic side. Okay, maybe that was a stretch. But he'd been attentive and full of compliments. He'd reeled her in, and just when he thought he had her hooked, his mask had slipped.

He'd suddenly become needy and was constantly checking up on her. Where was she? What was she doing? At first, she'd told herself that was what people did who cared about you.

The truth was that she wasn't a good judge of people. She couldn't remember her biological parents and her foster families had been cold and distant. When her friends at work had spoken up and voiced their concerns about Oz, they'd solidified the nagging voice in Charlotte's head—he was trouble.

But breaking up with him had escalated things. At that point, he'd started leaving her threatening voicemails and harassing her at work. A restraining order had been issued against him. He ignored it. But all he ever received were warnings.

"Charlie! Open this door! Don't make me break it down."

He wouldn't. Would he?

She thought of her elderly landlord, who lived downstairs. Rosa Vega was the sweetest woman, but she was a little hard of hearing. Her television was turned up so loud Charlotte could hear it in her apartment. She probably wouldn't hear Oz. If someone was going to save her, it was going to be herself.

Charlotte reached for her phone. Her hands were shaking so badly she knocked it off her bedside table. It clattered to the floor.

Thud! Thud!

Her heart lodged in her throat. He was breaking

down the door.

She scrambled out of bed. In the dark, she ran her hand frantically over the hardwood floor. She only had seconds until he got to her. Until he made good on his promise...

You will never leave me. Not in this world.

Just the memory of his hissed promise sent a cold chill racing down her spine. She swiped her finger over the phone. It lit up.

She dialed 8. Erase.

She tried again. This time 9-1-1.

"Nine one one, what is your emergency?"

"Someone's breaking into my apartment," she whispered. "Hurry."

"What is your name?"

"Charlotte Smith."

She closed her bedroom door and locked it as she whispered her answers to their questions. All the while she prayed the police would arrive soon. But would they be there soon enough?

"Charlotte, are you still there?" the operator asked.

"Shh..."

"Is he in the apartment?"

"Yes." She whispered it so softly she wasn't even sure she'd actually uttered the word.

"Find someplace to hide."

Immediately, Charlotte's gaze moved to the window. It was her only escape. But she had a second-floor apartment, and it was a straight drop down to a concrete sidewalk. Even if she attempted it, she'd be certain to break a bone or two. And then he'd be sure to catch up to

her.

"Charlie, I'm coming for you." He was no longer yelling. Instead, his voice had a low, menacing tone.

Her heart hammered so hard it echoed in her ears. She rushed to her closet and climbed inside, sliding the doors shut behind her.

"Charlotte," the operator said, "hang in there. The police are almost there."

Bang! Bang!

"Charlie, are you hiding from me?" He let out a maniacal laugh.

Thud! Thud!

He was kicking down the bedroom door. Her heart thudded in the back of her throat. This door was a flimsy barrier compared to the exterior door. And then he was there in the room with her. The breath caught in her lungs.

Fury radiated off him. She shrank into the back of the closet. Her lungs burned, desperate for oxygen. In that moment, she sent up a silent, desperate prayer.

Charlotte promised herself if she made it through this nightmare, she would get as far away from Oz as she could get. She would run. Run fast.

"Beneath the harvest moon…
true love can bloom."

1

Bluestar Island, MA
August

he sun shone bright in the cloudless sky. The birds sang out their sweet tune.

Charlotte "Aster" Smith couldn't believe this was her first visit to Bluestar Island. Okay, maybe it wasn't exactly a visit. Perhaps it was more like an extended stay. For how long? Well, that she wasn't sure about. There were just too many variables at this point to make such a determination.

But while she was on the small New England island, settled just off the Massachusetts shoreline, she intended to soak up every bit of sea breeze and summer's lingering rays. It was almost Labor Day weekend—the official end to the tourist season on Bluestar Island. She wondered what the island would be like once all of the tourists returned to their lives on the mainland.

Something told her it would be even more magical.

Within a week of being on Bluestar, she had not only a roof over her head but also a part-time job and invitations to visit people and places. She honestly hadn't had a moment to sit still. There was always something going on—including evening strolls on the beach.

Now that her cuts, bruises, and fractures had healed, she was starting her life over. Everything was different, including wearing heavy makeup to cover the angry red scar trailing down her jaw. Not even her name was the same. Not exactly. In an effort to hide from Oz, she now went by her middle name, Aster. It was one of the many things about herself that she'd never shared with him.

And what did she want this new life to look like? She wasn't quite sure. She pondered the idea as she climbed into a golf cart and proceeded to make her way down Main Street.

Thanks to her college friend, Darla Evans, she had a roof over her head. And Darla's cousin happened to be the new mayor of Bluestar. Based on her prior experience, Mayor Banks had given her a job as his temporary assistant. It didn't pay much but she got by on it. And if she did a good job—no, an impressive job— she might gain a permanent position at city hall.

Still, she knew her future on the island, as idyllic as it was, was iffy at best. If her past caught up with her, it'd be all over. She'd once again have to move on and start over.

Aster shoved aside the disturbing thoughts. She centered her attention on the here and now. Today was her first day on the job, and she desperately wanted to

Jennifer Faye

make a good impression.

She navigated the mayor's blue golf cart slowly down Main Street. The wide roadway was lined on either side by green trees and black lamp posts. People smiled and waved at her. She returned the gesture, even though she couldn't remember all their names. If she stayed on the island long enough, she promised herself she'd learn all of their names sooner rather than later.

She came to a stop as people crossed the street. Most people were dressed in shorts and colorful T-shirts along with sunglasses and flip-flops. Tourists. It was as evident as if they'd had the word tattooed on their foreheads. She wondered if the locals thought the same of her.

The light ocean breeze rushed past her. She automatically moved her hand to her hair to smooth it, but her fingers touched her pixie cut. Her long brown curls were gone. They'd been replaced by bleach-blond locks cut short and bangs—something she'd never had before. The hairstyle had been a shock at first, but its easy management was growing on her.

She pressed the brake as another crowd of ten or so people walked into the street without bothering to check for traffic. But then again, Bluestar outlawed cars and trucks, unless they had a special day pass. Transportation on the island was either shoe-leather-express, bicycles, or golf carts.

She progressed farther down the street and finally arrived at her destination, the Hamming It Up Deli. The only problem was there weren't any available parking spots. She glanced up and down the block. Nope. Not a single available parking place anywhere.

She immediately spotted the problem. People were lined up out the door at the Elegant Bakery. She definitely had to make a visit there. But not today.

Not wanting to be late, she double-parked. It wasn't like she was going to be in the deli long. The order had already been placed and charged to the mayor's business account. All she had to do was pick up the food.

Birds in the trees lining the street sang out a sweet melody as she rushed by and pulled open one of the two white doors with long oval windows. She stepped inside the deli, but she didn't get much more than a couple of steps before she came to a halt. The deli was packed. Inwardly, she groaned.

How was she supposed to make a good impression on the mayor and the city council when she wasn't even timely? Lucky for her, the line moved at a decent pace.

In the meantime, she glanced around at the unusual décor. The floor was a gray slate, while the walls looked to be covered in reclaimed lumber with a collection of old black-and-white photos on display. Some were shots of the deli at its grand opening many years ago. Others were of people, presumably the prior owners and employees. It was a visual history of the deli.

On each side of the wide center aisle were tables for the patrons to enjoy their meals. Brightly lit display cases and white counters lined the back of the deli with three checkouts. It was a really cute setup. No wonder they were so busy.

Finally armed with a wide cardboard box of sandwiches, salads, and pickles, she headed out the door.

Honk-honk. Honk-honk.

Her gaze zeroed in on a man in a green golf cart. From beneath a ball cap, his face creased with frown lines as he gazed around for the person who had his golf cart hemmed in.

As he lifted his hand to press on the horn again, she called out, "Okay. I'm coming."

His blue gaze turned to her. He didn't smile. "You can't double-park here."

He was right. And she felt bad. "I'm sorry."

"Just get it moved. And don't do it again." He continued to frown as he looked away from her.

"I won't." This was not the way she wanted to start her time here in Bluestar. She'd made a mistake. She'd apologized. Maybe she should take a different approach. "Can I offer you a ham sandwich?"

He glanced at her. Surprise reflected in his eyes. "Are you serious?"

"Of course." She'd just run back inside and get another one.

He shook his head, but she couldn't tell if he was refusing her offer or shaking his head over her attempt at a peace offering. She shrugged it off.

She walked to her golf cart and secured the box in the backseat, which was easier said than done. She paused. How was she going to keep the box from tipping over?

She could feel the man's stare upon the back of her head. With the food at last secured behind the seat, she climbed into the driver's seat and attempted to start the cart. Nothing happened.

She turned the little key again. Nothing.

She inwardly groaned. *Please start.* She turned the key again. And again. And again.

"Is there a problem?" the grumpy man asked.

Heat bloomed in her cheeks. This just couldn't be happening. She turned the key once more. Nothing. She needed to make a good impression, and instead, she was about to do just the opposite.

"Do you need some help?" His voice came from so much closer to her.

She lifted her head and found he was standing next to her. She tilted her chin higher and higher until her gaze met his. "It won't start."

"Let me have a look."

"You can't. It's not mine."

Suspicion reflected in his eyes. "Whose cart is it? And do they know you have it?"

"You think I stole it?" The thought horrified her.

He arched a brow. "I don't know. You tell me."

"I didn't steal anything. I have permission to use it." She was nervously rattling on. The last thing she needed was to deal with the sheriff. "It belongs to the mayor. Call him if you want."

"You work for Tony?" When she nodded, he said, "Okay. Let's see if I can get it started."

"But…but you don't have to."

"I do if I want to get home."

That much was true enough. She moved from the seat, but in her rush, she tripped. The man reached out to her, grabbing her upper arms. In that moment, time seemed to stand still. She stared into his eyes—his blue eyes. They were the shade of the sky on a sunny, cloudless day. And she felt as though she were getting swept away in his stare.

In his eyes she saw pain—a deep pain—the kind you didn't talk about. She noticed the same thing about herself when she looked in the mirror. Sympathy welled up within her. She didn't know what he'd been through, but having been through her own trauma, she understood this stranger a little better.

The sound of approaching voices broke the time continuum, and suddenly everything sped up. The rush of it all swept the air from her lungs. Had that really happened? Or had she imagined it all?

"Are you okay?" The tone of his voice had suddenly changed to one of concern.

She nodded. "I am. My foot just got caught when I stepped out of the cart."

He let go of her, and suddenly the skin where he'd once been touching her felt chilled. She resisted the urge to rub her hands.

As curious onlookers ventured closer to find out the problem, Aster got pushed back toward the sidewalk. And that was fine with her. In fact, it was for the best. Because her reaction to this man's nearness had shaken her to the core.

It didn't matter how good-looking he was, how dreamy his baby blues were, or how his crusty exterior was a little bit of a turn on; she was not at all interested in getting involved with anyone. Not a chance. Not after what had happened to her in California. Just the scant thought of Oz left a sour feeling in the pit of her stomach.

The last she'd heard, they'd plea-bargained his case down to simple assault. Simple assault, really? It hadn't felt so simple to her.

There was no trial. No one would hear her harrowing tale or see the scars she had to live with for the rest of her life. The thought that no one seemed to care what he'd done to her—what he'd do to the next unsuspecting women—made her sick.

His sentence had been knocked down to a year of house arrest. Soon he'd be free, but she was gone and she hadn't left a trail. He was never going to find her on this small island. She hoped.

She shoved away the dark, troubling thoughts. They did not belong there on this sunny, carefree island. Bluestar was like a world unto its own. She glanced around, finding the crowd of onlookers had dispersed. She breathed a little easier. "What about the cart?"

He rubbed his hands on his faded jeans. "Just a lose wire, but you may want to let Tony know that he should take it to the shop to have someone go over it."

Hope swelled in her chest. "So, it's all good? Nothing serious?"

"It's fine. You can drive it now."

A smile pulled at her lips. "Thank you. How can I repay you?"

He lifted his blue-and-white ball cap and raked his fingers through his short, blondish-brown hair before replacing it on his head. "How about moving it so I can get out of this parking spot?"

"Oh. Yes. I will." She started into the street. She paused and glanced back. "Thank you again."

For a moment, he didn't say anything. Then he sighed. "You're welcome."

As she drove away, she couldn't help but regret that she hadn't gotten the man's name. She told herself she was trying to learn the names of all of Bluestar's residents and that learning his name was no big deal.

But she knew that wasn't the whole truth. There was something special about that mystery man. She was curious to know what had caused the wounded look in his eyes. That was exactly why she planned to stay as far away from him as possible.

2

er first day of work was over.

Aster had to admit, if only to herself, that it had been a lot harder than she'd been imagining. City Hall had some written procedures but not many. And the reason for doing certain tasks was stated to her as: *because that's the way it's always been done.* Which was absolutely no help to her.

Right now, she did not have a designated position. She got the distinct impression the mayor had taken her on as a big favor because Darla was his cousin. Aster felt bad about the imposition and knew she had to work extra hard to show the mayor that he hadn't made a mistake by hiring her.

"Are you still here?" The mayor came to a stop in front of her desk that was a makeshift office area in an alcove in the upstairs hallway. Not ideal but it would do for the moment.

She craned her neck to stare at him. The mayor was dressed in navy-blue pants. A blue-and-white-striped shirt was completed with a blue bow tie.

His bronze face lifted into a smile that made his blue

eyes twinkle. His dark-brown hair was trimmed very short. Everything about him said he cared about appearances. Having left most of her business attire in L.A., she'd have to splurge on some new clothes.

He looked at her expectantly, and she recalled his inquiry about her still being at the office. "Ah, yes. I just finished reviewing the town's calendar for the remainder of the year. I'm trying to get on top of things." She still felt awkward about his golf cart breaking down earlier and that grumpy man having to help her out. "I'm really sorry about your golf cart—"

He waved away her worry. "You have nothing to be sorry about. I should have had it looked at a while ago. In fact, it's in the garage as we speak." His gaze moved over her desk where she'd been researching the island. "I like that you're a go-getter. I am too. But it's after five now, and your day ended at noon. I wish I could pay you for a full day—"

"It's okay. I understand. I'm just grateful for this opportunity." She signed off of her computer and gathered her things.

"We're grateful to have you. You never know what the future holds. I have plans for Bluestar and you could be a part of them."

She stood and pushed in her chair. They started to walk toward the grand staircase. This city hall wasn't just a boring block building. It was situated in an enormous historic mansion that had belonged to one of the island's founders. It had been kept up over the years and was in immaculate shape.

"I'm looking forward to a future here," she said.

"That's good because I have a special project for you." He started down the wide wooden steps with a burgundy floral runner.

"Oh. What's that?" She hoped it was something exciting.

"I would like you to lend a hand to a dear friend of mine, Ms. Birdie Neill. It's not exactly city business, so this would fall under the heading of special projects that I'd previously discussed with you."

She nodded. He wanted to help the community with more than just the things approved by city council. It was more of an outreach project where the mayor helped citizens with their own community affairs.

She liked the idea. "I'd be happy to help."

He smiled. "That's good. It's a fundraiser for one of Bluestar's residents. It's all rather top-secret at the moment. But if you stop by Birdie's house tomorrow morning, she'll let you know what needs done."

"But what about my work here at city hall?"

"I want this fundraiser to be your main focus right now. The turnaround time is short as it will take place over Labor Day. Make sure this fundraiser is a big success."

Labor Day was less than two weeks away. With that short timeline, she hoped there wasn't a lot to plan.

She nodded. "I'll do that."

He paused just outside the double doors that led to the portico. "And if you need my input or assistance, you already have my cell number."

"Yes, sir."

He turned one way, and she turned the other way to

head to Darla's apartment. Her walk was short but then again, it was possible to walk anywhere on Bluestar Island, even from tip to tip of the crescent-shaped island.

She had no idea if her roommate would be home, but she was anxious to thank her again for this job and to tell someone about her great day.

Well, it had been mostly a great day. Her thoughts turned to the man in the green golf cart, who had been quite perturbed that she'd pinned him into a parking spot. But in the end, he couldn't have been that upset, as he'd helped her out. Still, it'd be best if they stayed out of each other's way. And there would be no more double-parking for her.

Aster used the key Darla had given her to let herself inside the apartment. It was a small efficiency unit with one bathroom and two bedrooms. Darla had rearranged her place just for her, and Aster didn't know how she would ever repay her.

The bedroom Aster was staying in was quite small. It had been Darla's office, but she'd removed her large desk and borrowed a twin bed from her parents. Who was that kind and caring? Darla and the rest of her family. They made Aster feel welcome, safe, and wanted. If Darla wasn't careful, Aster was going to adopt her family.

She'd just put her things in her room when she suddenly heard the front door squeak open. Her heart lodged in her throat. She quickly tiptoed over to the doorway and peeked into the living room, finding Darla standing there with a bag in her hand. Aster expelled a pent-up breath. Every now and then, she was still a bit

jumpy, usually when she was alone. But time was helping her heal physically and emotionally.

"Hey Charlotte…oops, I mean Aster. Sorry, it's taking me a bit to get used to the name change." Darla's heart-shaped face lifted with a smile.

"Imagine how hard it's been for me. There were a couple times today at work that someone was calling out Aster, and I paid no attention. When they finally got my attention, I had to explain that I was deep in thought."

"I'm sorry you have to go through all of this." Darla moved toward the counter. "Do you think you'll ever go back to being Charlotte?"

"I don't know." She thought of Oz and his threats. Eventually he'd forget about her. Maybe he already had.

"At least you're safe here."

"Thanks to you. I don't know what I'd do without you."

Darla removed her ponytail holder and finger-combed her shoulder-length blond bob. "I haven't done that much."

Aster rolled her eyes. "No, not much at all. Just put a roof over my head and helped me get a job."

"Okay, I might have helped with the housing, but you got that job on your own merits. You're the one that interviewed for it."

"But the mayor is your cousin. Of course, he's going to hire me."

"Apparently, you don't know my cousin very well. He doesn't do what people tell him to do. He does what he thinks is the right thing. And he thinks you could be good for Bluestar." She cleaned her hands and then opened the bag in order to remove two white to-go containers. She shoved one toward Aster. "I hope you haven't eaten."

"I haven't. I just got home."

Darla's brows rose. "I thought it was just a part-time job."

"It is but I want to do a good enough job so that it becomes a permanent full-time job."

Darla nodded in understanding. "Before I forget, I've been meaning to tell you that I have a bicycle, and you're welcome to use it any time you want."

"Thanks. I might take you up on the offer when I get a second job."

Concern reflected in Darla's eyes. "Don't push things. After all, you just arrived on the island, and you are already starting a new job."

"I know. I just don't want to sponge off you. I need to be able to take care of myself." It was one of those things that had stuck with her when her parents died, and she'd realized she only had herself to count on. And as she was passed from one foster family to another and then another, it only confirmed her belief that she had to be able to take care of herself.

"Stop thinking like that. You aren't sponging. I offered. I've missed our time together." Darla proceeded to grab utensils and napkins. "They had extra so I brought home dinner. It's nothing special. Just some extra dinners from the café."

Darla went to her bedroom to change out of her black-and-white work clothes, which smelled like diner food. Then they grabbed the food and headed for the couch. They sat on opposite ends with their legs curled up. It felt so much like their college days when they'd kick back and quiz each other before a big test.

Back in those days, Darla had a serious boyfriend, Will Campbell. He was also from Bluestar. Darla had been crazy in love with him and had followed him to California for school. He'd been a year older than her, and she'd been certain they would end up together. They didn't. To this day, Aster still didn't know what had gone wrong. Whatever had happened had been bad because after the breakup, Darla dropped out of college and headed back to Bluestar Island. It was the one thing Darla never wanted to discuss.

As they ate their burgers and fries, Aster talked about her first day at city hall as well as her first official assignment. "I'm supposed to assist a Ms. Birdie Neill with some sort of fundraiser. But I wasn't supposed to tell you because it's a secret."

"Don't worry." Darla nodded as she dunked two fries in ketchup. "It's one of those secrets where just about everyone in town knows about it except for the person they're trying to help."

"It would seem the person would find out if that many people know."

Darla shook her head. "Sam pretty much keeps to himself since his wife died."

"Oh. That's so sad. I'm glad to hear the town is stepping up to help him."

"That's Birdie's idea."

"Is Sam her son or grandson?" Aster tried to figure out why this woman would go out of her way for him.

Darla shook her head. "Neither of those. How do I explain this? Birdie is a bit of a busybody. But in the best way ever. She only pushes when she thinks it's for a person's own good. And I have to say from what I've witnessed, she's usually right."

Aster wasn't sure how she felt about working with a busybody. The very last thing she needed was for her past to catch up with her. She didn't relish packing up and moving so soon.

"I don't know." Aster's protective walls rose up around her. "Maybe working at city hall is too public."

"Stop worrying. It's a perfect fit for you."

"I don't know. What if Birdie finds out about my past? She'll tell everyone."

"No, she won't. Birdie is the sweetest. You'll see." Darla looked at her with sympathy reflected in her eyes. "Besides, even if everyone on the island finds out your real name and what happened to you, they'll pull together to protect you. The creep is just one guy. It's not like he's part of the mafia. I'm sure he'll forget about you, and when he gets released from house arrest, he'll move on to his next unsuspecting victim."

Chills rushed down her spine. "He should have a tattoo on his forehead to warn everyone he's a monster."

"Agreed. But don't worry. I know I said Birdie is a busybody but trust me, she won't badger you. She is sweet and kind. She only wants the best for people."

Aster's protective walls lowered a bit. She searched her friend's sympathetic gaze. "Do you really believe that?"

"I do. You're safe on the island. I promise. The creep

is in your past. Just relax."

It was easier said than done. She didn't think she'd ever fully relax. A part of her had changed during the month he'd stalked, tormented, and finally attacked her. Her finger traced over the uneven scar that trailed down her jawline. It was still red and took heavy makeup to hide from the rest of the world.

But Darla was right. She didn't have any reason to run from Bluestar. Not yet.

3

f it wasn't one thing…
…it was another.
The next morning, Sam Bell stood
on a ladder as he secured a window
shutter that had pulled loose in the storm the other night.
He'd just finished the repair work when he heard a
vehicle heading down the road. He glanced over that
way to see the little mail truck off in the distance. It was
one of the few vehicles allowed on the island. It bounced
as it hit a pothole.

Pam, the mail lady, waved at him. He waved back.
She rumbled on by on her way to the end of the island.
She always started at the far end and worked her way
back toward his farm.

He climbed down the ladder and set off toward the
end of his long driveway to meet her. He needed the few
minutes of silence to gather his thoughts. Everything felt
as though it were piling up lately—from the new barn
burning down to the fact he was about to lose his
daughter's babysitter. Even worse, he had yet to find a

replacement.

By the time he reached the main road, Pam was sitting there waiting for him. She held out a few envelopes to him. "Not much today."

"Sounds good to me." And if it was all junk mail, he'd be thrilled. The last thing he needed was another bill.

"How are things going?"

He shrugged. "They've been better."

"Any thoughts of rebuilding the barn?"

He rubbed the back of his neck as he recalled the fire that had destroyed the new barn he'd been building. "Some, but I'm not sure if I can make it work. Maybe next year."

He'd love to rebuild the barn now, but he knew there was absolutely no way it was going to happen. And if things didn't change soon, he'd be forced into parceling off farmland and selling it. Or worse yet, he'd have to sell the entire farm—though deep in his soul, he knew he'd never be happy anywhere else.

They bid each other a good day. Sam trudged back along the drive. He didn't want to look at the mail. He already knew what he'd find, but still it wasn't like he could just ignore the envelopes with his name typed out in black ink on each of them.

He lifted the stack to start examining them. The first envelope had a bright red stamp on it: Urgent. *Really? Was that necessary?*

It agitated him to no end. And because he was too responsible to rip it up out of spite, he instead rotated what was undoubtedly a past due notice to the bottom of the stack. It would just have to wait.

The next envelope was plain and unassuming. Still, he sensed it was another request for payment from yet another creditor. They'd been coming in a steady stream for years now—ever since his wife passed on—ever since he'd lost control of the farm while he'd wallowed in his grief. And now, he didn't know if he'd ever get back on solid footing.

"Daddy! Daddy!" Nikki, his seven-year-old daughter, ran up to him. "Have you seen Dash?"

Dash was one of their pygmy goats. His daughter had a special relationship with the little goat. He acted more like her puppy than a goat, which led to another set of problems.

He stifled a sigh. He knew the answer before he asked it, but he spoke the words anyway. "Why would I see Dash out here? Tell me you didn't let him out of his pen again."

"But he looked so lonely in there." Her big round blue eyes pleaded with him to understand.

Every time she planted her hands on her little girl hips and stared at him that way, he couldn't help but think of Beth. Nikki may have his hair and eye coloring but the rest was her mother's beauty.

He didn't want to take a firm stance. Not today. Still, he couldn't let Nikki get away with everything. Just like he was working harder to get a handle on his finances, he also had to work harder to be a bit firmer with his daughter.

He rested his hands on his waist and looked pointedly at her. "How many times do I have to tell you

it isn't safe letting him out on his own?"

"But he wasn't alone. He was with me."

"If he was with you, how come you can't find him?"

She swished the toe of her shoe around in the dirt. "Well, um…I had to go inside."

"You should have put Dash back in the pen before you went inside."

"But I was only gone a second."

He arched a brow. "Are you sure it wasn't longer?"

Her face scrunched up into a pouty face. "Never mind." She leveled her slender shoulders and lifted her chin. "I'll find him on my own."

When she turned to stomp off, a smile played at his lips. She was seven years old going on sixteen. With her mother gone, she was growing up faster than she needed to. He didn't have the time to spend with her like he wanted. Sure, when she wasn't in school or with the babysitter, they were together. But he was always working while she found something to occupy herself close by. She deserved more than he could give. The guilt weighed on him.

However, finding Dash was one problem he could solve. "Hold up, Nikki."

She didn't slow down, so he picked up the pace. "I didn't say I wouldn't help you find Dash. I just need you to be more cautious with him. He's still young and learning. We don't want him getting hurt, do we?"

As her short legs kept moving, she shook her head. "I didn't mean to lose him. He just ran off."

"Listen, he couldn't have gotten very far. We'll find him." He reached out and gently grabbed his daughter's arm. "Hold up a moment."

She reluctantly stopped and turned to him. "We have to find him. He's scared."

"How do you know that?"

"Because he's a baby and he's all...alone." She waved her hands around as she talked as though emphasizing every word just like her mother used to do.

Another wave of pain crashed over him. He missed Beth so much that sometimes he thought the pain would suffocate him. And just when he thought he was ready to move on with his life, the pain would come roaring back. At times like this, he wouldn't even see it coming. It would totally blindside him and steal his breath away.

"Daddy?" Nikki yanked on his shirt sleeve. "You aren't listening."

He blinked repeatedly. "Sorry, sweetie. I think you're right. Dash is still young, and he probably is scared when he's away from his momma so that means you shouldn't take him out of the goat pen."

"But it's just for a little bit. He likes me."

He couldn't argue with her on that part. His daughter had a way with animals, especially Dash, who would follow her to the ends of the earth and back again.

How did he make her understand what he was trying to say? He cleared his throat and began again. "Since he trusts you so much, you have to do what is best for him. That means making sure he doesn't run off—even if it means keeping him inside the pen."

Her bottom lip stuck out. "Okay."

"Let's go find him. Do you know which direction he went?"

Nikki's slim shoulders rose and fell as she gave a shake of her head.

Well, this should be fun. This wasn't a small farm, but something told him Dash wouldn't get far. He was a momma's boy, and he was Nikki's shadow.

Buzz. Buzz.

His cell phone vibrated in his pocket. "Hang on. Let me get this."

His daughter's face scrunched up. "But Daddy…"

"This won't take long. I promise." He was expecting a phone call about the additional crops he'd planted this year in hopes of saving the funds to rebuild the barn.

The truth of the matter was the old barn had taken a battering when the last hurricane skimmed up the Atlantic coast. Now with part of the roof missing as well as the back wall, it wasn't long for this world.

The one thing he'd learned the past few years was that he had to deal with problems as they came to him. Trying to jump ahead and solve a problem that hadn't quite happened, well, it just muddled everything. In the end nothing was fixed, and in some cases, it created new and unexpected problems. But, there were just too many immediate problems facing him.

4

ife on the island was different from
anything she knew.

It took a bit of adjusting. As did
going by her middle name.

And yet Aster found herself being drawn into the
close-knit community. Comparing Bluestar to Los
Angeles was something akin to comparing apples and
oranges. They were totally different in almost every way
imaginable.

But in the next breath, she told herself not to get too
comfortable there. Oz's threat echoed in her mind. She
had no doubt that sooner or later he'd be looking for her,
anxious to settle the score—his words not hers. The
question was, had she covered her trail well enough? She
hoped so.

In their brief time together, she hadn't revealed a lot
about herself, just general things about her job at the
local college. Her co-workers didn't know what had
happened to her. And for that she felt awful. Someday
she would apologize to them, but for now it was safest

for them and herself if she remained silent.

She turned her attention to the beautiful summer day. There wouldn't be many of those left as autumn was quickly approaching. And though most people enjoyed the summer months, Aster had always been partial to autumn. She loved its crisp mornings and warm afternoons.

And on this particular day, Ms. Birdie Neill tasked Aster with the job of retrieving some apples from a local farm for the fundraiser. The task seemed simple enough. Birdie had even loaned her a golf cart.

Aster drove the flamingo-pink golf cart out of town on a windy road that swept toward the coastline and then zig-zagged back inland. It was a very picturesque ride with the lush green foliage and glimpses of the ocean. It was her first time exploring beyond the town limits. She wondered how long it would take to reach the end of the island.

That thought didn't have a chance to take hold as she slowed to a stop next to an adorable mailbox that was painted with white and black spots just like a cow. She smiled. Her stop was 913 Sea Glass Drive.

She stared down the dirt lane. She could barely make out the roofline of a house but not much else. She'd been warned that you couldn't see all of the farm from the road.

She turned the golf cart down the lane. The ruts made the ride bouncy. Aster tightened her hold on the steering wheel. She clamped her jaw together to keep her teeth from rattling. Surely it couldn't be far. And she was right. Soon the rest of the farmhouse came into sight.

The two-story white home with red shutters wasn't anything special, and yet she couldn't help but think how homey it looked with two white wicker chairs on the front porch. Or perhaps that was just the way she wanted to see it. After running for her life, she was seeing things differently.

Just then an old truck drove around the house. It was robin egg blue, and Aster did a double-take at seeing a pickup on the island. Someone was being a rule breaker. Interesting.

The truck pulled to a stop and the driver got out. He was tall and thin. His short hair was covered with a blue and white ball cap. She got out of the golf cart and approached him.

As he drew nearer, she recognized him. *Oh no!* "It's you."

His eyebrows rose. "Don't tell me you're having golf cart problems again."

Heat swirled in her chest and rushed to her cheeks. "No. Uh… Thank you for helping me yesterday."

"Then you must be lost," he said. "If you're looking for the lighthouse, it's further down the road."

She shook her head. "No. I'm here to see you."

The man's brows lifted as his sky-blue eyes reflected his confusion. "I don't think so. We don't have any business."

The heat intensified in her cheeks. The sooner she could get this taken care of, the better. "I'm Aster. I'm here to pick up the apples."

Just then a young girl climbed out of the passenger side of the truck and slammed the door shut. A distinct frown pulled at her pretty face. Her pigtails fluttered in the breeze. "We'll never find him."

The defeated tone of her voice struck Aster. Sympathy welled up in her. She immediately wanted to help the girl, but she had no idea who was lost.

The man turned to the girl. He knelt in front of her and proceeded to tenderly swipe a tear from her pale cheek. "He'll turn up when he gets hungry."

Her chin wobbled as crocodile tears splashed onto her cheeks. "You promise?"

The man didn't say anything for a moment. "Why don't you go check in back? Maybe he returned."

Her eyes lit up with hope. "Okay."

When the little girl took off running around the house, he turned his attention back to Aster. "Sorry about that. Now what were you saying about some apples?"

It took Aster a moment to gather herself after watching that touching moment between father and daughter. "Uh...never mind. It's not a good time. I'll come back later." She turned to walk away.

"No. Wait." When she turned back, he said, "The thing is I never promised you any apples. I would have remembered that."

"Oh, no, it's not me who asked for them. It was probably Birdie. But then again, it could have been someone else. I didn't think to ask who had contacted you."

"Whoa. Slow down. I haven't talked to anyone about apples. At least not recently."

"But I was told to come here." When he still looked confused, she worried her bottom lip. This was not a great beginning to her assignment—her chance to prove herself. "Wait a sec."

"For what?"

She was already in motion. She didn't stop to say a word. Instead, she focused on rushing back to the cart where she'd left her purse on the seat. She reached inside her pink bag and pulled out a flowered notebook.

She rushed back toward him. She flipped through her notes until she found the right page. "It's right here. I need to pick up two bushels of apples from Frank Hornell."

A slow smile came over the man's face. "Right there's your problem. I'm not Frank."

"You're not?" How had she gotten that wrong? She stared at her notes, like the answer for the mix-up was suddenly going to jump out at her.

"No. He lives at 931 Sea Glass Drive. This is 913 Sea Glass Drive."

She blinked. "It is?"

He nodded.

"Daddy! Daddy!" The little girl came running up to him and didn't slow down until she plowed into him.

He stood there like a sturdy oak tree that had withstood the test of time. He absorbed her energy without a grunt or a stumble. It was as though he was used to this sort of behavior, and it didn't seem to faze him. Aster instantly liked the man. Sure, he might have been grouchy in town, but she had been blocking him in. But now she was seeing a totally different side of him. And she liked what she saw.

But she knew not to go with her initial assessment.

After all, look how that had turned out for her in the immediate past. Her gaze moved to the little girl, who stared up at the man as they discussed the situation. He worked so hard to soothe her worry, and the little girl looked at him with such trust and love. Aster may not be able to trust her judgement any longer, but perhaps she could go by the girl's unwavering faith in her father.

"Can I do something to help?" Aster asked before she even considered that this might be a family thing.

Both the man and the little girl turned to her. Surprise was written all over both of their faces.

"Have you seen Dash?" the girl asked.

"Is this a person?" Aster's gaze moved between father and daughter.

"No, silly. It's my goat." The little girl said it so matter-of-factly that for a moment Aster felt silly for not knowing the answer. The little girl studied her.

The child's stare was so intense that Aster wondered if she'd detected the scar on Aster's jaw. It was ugly and she didn't want to scare the child. But she vividly recalled layering on her special makeup that morning. Her fingers tingled with the need to touch her face and confirm that the makeup was indeed hiding the evidence of her past, but she resisted the urge.

"Do I know you?" The girl's voice drew Aster from her thoughts.

"No." Aster knelt down to make direct eye contact with the girl, just like she'd seen her father do when he spoke to her. Then Aster stuck out her hand. "Hi. I'm Char..erm, Aster." She was having a hard time with this name change stuff. But it was necessary for now. "And what's your name?"

The girl glanced at her father, who nodded. Then the girl shook her hand. And it wasn't some dainty little shake. She had a firm grip for a child her size and a solid shake. "My name's Nikki. Can you help me find my goat?"

"I... I don't know." She quite honestly didn't know the first thing about goats. "But I can try." And then she straightened and looked at Nikki's father. "If that's all right with you?"

"The name's Sam. Sam Bell. And you don't have to help."

"Oh no. I don't mind. I'd like to meet Dash."

She'd never met a goat before, but she'd dubbed this year as an adventure. And the important element of adventures was trying new experiences. She never thought it would include goats, but why not?

Nikki grabbed her hand and started pulling toward the back of the house. "We have to start back here."

"Nikki, slow up," Sam said. "I have an idea. Your grandmother dropped off some ginger snap cookies yesterday. Grab a couple of those. Dash loves them."

The girl's blue eyes, which were so much like her father's, lit up. "Okay." She turned to Aster. "Stay here. I'll be back." And then the girl took off running as fast as her legs would carry her.

Sam turned to Aster. "You can leave now. I can explain things to Nikki."

Aster shook her head. "I said I'd help find Dash and I meant it." She glanced around from the big old farmhouse to the red barn in the distance. "Where should

I start?"

"You could start by checking all of the goat houses in the pen."

"Goats have houses?" She was intrigued. Then she couldn't resist adding, "Do they have kitchens and televisions too?"

He smiled. It wasn't just any smile. It was one of those slow smiles that just kept growing until his mouth was upturned at the corners and his blue eyes twinkled. The vision made her heart flutter. As soon as she realized the reaction he had on her, she glanced away. Men were off limits—so far off limits. A gentle sigh of regret slipped past her lips.

"Shh… Don't give Nikki any ideas." His deep voice drew her from her meandering thoughts. "They're back in the meadow behind the house."

When he turned in the other direction, she called out, "Where are you going?"

"I have to go check the barn. Dash is the curious sort. Instead of sticking close to home, like the others, he likes to wander. I just hope he hasn't gotten himself into trouble."

Aster nodded in understanding. It was then that her gaze strayed across a patch of land where the grass had been burned away. At least that's the way it looked to her.

As she took in the scene, she realized what she was staring at—the site of the barn that had burned. Birdie had mentioned it in conjunction with the town's intention to build Sam a new barn. She wondered how Sam would feel about the town's generosity.

Just then Nikki came out the back door, letting the screen door shut with a loud *whack-whack!* "I have cookies."

"You go check the houses with Aster," Sam called out.

"But I checked there," Nikki replied.

"He might have come back. Check again." Sam trudged toward the barn.

"Come on." Nikki grabbed Aster's hand and pulled her along.

Aster wished she had been more like the little girl with the big personality when she was young. Instead, Aster had been very quiet. After her parents died when she was six, she'd become a ward of the state. To lose her parents—her loving parents—at such a tender age and forced to live with strangers had been traumatic for her.

She hadn't been open to people. She had closed down, lost in a world of her own pain and the fear of losing someone else she cared about. In her child's rationality, it was best not to care for anyone than risk being hurt again. As she grew older, she became angry and rebellious. Not exactly the combo that foster families are looking for when considering taking in a child. And so, she'd been bounced around from one home to the next.

Now being older and dare she say it, wiser, she could look back on those times and realize that her childhood would have been so different if she had been more like Nikki, who wasn't afraid to show her emotions or to act on them.

They started on one end of the fenced in meadow with lush green grass and a few shade trees. The goat houses—six to be exact—were painted red like the old barn and had white trim with a slanted shingled roof. A ramp led up to the doorway. And best of all, there were suspended bridges between the houses. Some sort of webbing was attached to the sides of the bridge to keep the goats from falling off.

A short distance away was what looked like a playground for goats. There were old tires. Some were partially buried in the ground so they stood up and others were lying flat. There was an old plastic playground set that she guessed might have belonged to Nikki once upon a time. There were hay bales stacked up. And even a trampoline. Wait. A trampoline for goats? Aster smiled as she took it all in.

Nikki walked up the first ramp and stuck her head inside the first house. "I can't see. I have to go in."

Aster wasn't so comfortable with that idea. "Wait." She reached into her pocket for her phone to use the flashlight app and then realized she no longer owned a phone.

Just like so much of her life, it had been a casualty of her dating the wrong guy. Not wanting Oz to be able to track her, she'd ditched her beloved phone. And now she felt lost without it. But day by day that feeling was subsiding… Until she automatically reached for it, like she'd just done.

"What?" Nikki sent her an anxious look.

"Um. Be careful."

Nikki's little girl face scrunched up into a frustrated

46

look. Aster resisted the urge not to smile because that look was one they had in common.

"He's not here." Nikki didn't even bother walking down the ramp; instead, she jumped off and headed toward the next house.

Just then Aster's gaze met that of a white goat, who was staring right back at her. And it didn't look happy to have them in its area. Perhaps this wasn't such a good idea. After all, she didn't know the first thing about farms, animals, or most especially goats. She swallowed hard and took a step back.

And then the goat started to run toward her. Nikki stepped between her and the goat. This wasn't good— not good at all.

"Nikki, watch out." Aster moved quickly, pulling the girl out of the way.

The goat came to a stop as though Aster's sudden action had startled him. But he was still staring at her. Aster didn't dare take her gaze off him. She didn't trust Mr. Goat in the least.

Aster spread out her arms in an effort to shield Nikki. "Just stay there."

"But why?" Nikki glanced around Aster. "That's just Billy. He won't hurt you."

Aster hesitated, not so sure about the girl's assessment. But when Aster lowered her arms, Nikki marched right past her.

Billy's ears perked up. His little tail swished back and forth. Aster didn't know much about goats, but it would appear he was excited to see Nikki.

He let the girl pet him, while his attention returned to

Aster. His ears lowered. His tail slowed. Aster's mouth grew dry. He didn't like her. That much was perfectly obvious. She was an intruder. And he wanted her gone. It was starting to sound like a very good idea.

"Come here." Nikki motioned for Aster to step up beside her.

"I... I don't think that's a good idea." Nikki's feet felt as though they were cast in concrete. She couldn't move if she wanted to.

"Come on, Billy." Aster took a couple of steps forward and then paused to look back at the goat. "Billy, come on. Aster is our friend."

As though the goat actually understood her words, he started toward her.

Aster's heart pitter-pattered faster as her palms grew damp. She was a city-mouse, not a country-mouse. Maybe she should have made that clear. She opened her mouth to say so, but her vocal cords failed her.

Nikki approached her with Billy by her side. It was as though he was some sort of puppy instead of a miniature goat. Thank goodness for his small size.

"You can pet him." Nikki looked at her expectantly.

Aster didn't want to do it. Billy didn't like her. Not one little bit. "He'll bite me."

The girl giggled. "No, he won't." She wrapped her arms around his neck and hugged him as though he were nothing more than one of her stuffed animals. She whispered something in his ear. Then Nikki turned back to her. "See. No big deal."

Aster shook her head. "He doesn't like me."

"He doesn't know you." Nikki moved toward her,

grabbed Aster's hand, and pulled her toward the little goat. "Don't worry. He won't hurt you. Janie used to be afraid of the goats, too, but now she loves them."

"Is Janie your dad's girlfriend?"

Nikki broke out in laughter. She pressed her little hand to her mouth. Aster could only assume her guess had been wrong. She felt a sense of relief.

"No, silly. She's my babysitter."

"Oh, okay."

She didn't have time to think about their conversation as they neared the goat. She wasn't sure what to do. The girl was so certain this was going to be fine with Billy. Was she right? Or would he bite her hand?

Aster's gaze darted toward Billy's mouth. Goats had teeth, right? Sure. They must. Little ones? Or great big teeth? As luck would have it, Billy's mouth was firmly closed. No chance for her to see the choppers that were about to sink into her flesh.

But Nikki was so sweet, so confident that Aster had a difficult time saying no to her. Plus, Nikki was distracted from losing her beloved goat, Dash. But being bitten by a goat seemed like a stiff price to pay for all of that. She shouldn't do this.

Before she could put her thoughts into action, her finger tips touched the coarse fur. Billy looked at her but he didn't move—didn't even bare his teeth to her. She expelled a deep breath that she hadn't known she'd been holding.

"See." Nikki beamed up at her. "I told you he was nice."

Aster reserved judgement until she ran her hand over his back a few times. This wasn't so bad after all. A tiny smile pulled at her lips. "You were right."

"And he likes you."

"How can you tell that?"

"Because if he doesn't like someone, he runs away. He's always running from Daddy. And Daddy gets so mad. His face turns red and then he has to chase Billy."

"And what do you do during this?"

"Laugh." If nothing else, at least she's honest.

As she continued to pet Billy, Aster smiled at the image Nikki had painted of her father. "And who wins in the end?"

"Daddy, of course." Her tone was one of matter-of-fact.

They continued checking all of the goat houses, but Dash was nowhere to be seen. This wasn't good. Aster knew nothing about goats, but she had to reason that a curious animal could stray quite a ways. Thankfully, automobiles weren't allowed on the island without special permits, but there were other dangers, including seaside cliffs. The thought sent a chill through her body. She quickly dismissed the horrid thought.

Once they stepped outside the goat pen, she knelt down to Nikki. "Where was Dash when you last saw him?"

"By the porch." Nikki frowned as though she were replaying the events in her mind. "I'd run back in the house to get a drink. I was so thirsty. But I was only gone for a second."

Aster subdued a smile. Something told her that

Nikki's second and that of a clock's were totally different things. Time to a child was so different to that of an adult. She vaguely recalled the feeling of time stretching out forever. These days, she didn't have nearly enough time to do all of the things she wanted to do.

But coming to Bluestar Island was a step in the right direction. If only the circumstances behind her visit were different. Still, since she'd heard about this small island while in college, she'd wanted to see it for herself. And to her surprise, it was even better than she'd imagined.

The townspeople were quite welcoming. And the views were absolutely amazing. The fact she could walk on the beach every time she had a free moment amazed her. Who got to live a life like that? She certainly hadn't dreamed it possible for herself. But how long would she get to enjoy this little sliver of heaven?

5

"I've got him!"

Aster jumped. Her heart pounded. She turned around to see Sam trudging through the field with his arms full of a black goat. She hoped no one had noticed her startled reaction.

Sam moved with such ease that it made it appear as though Dash was light as a feather. Even Aster knew that wasn't the case, which left one alternative—the handsome farmer was very strong.

It was a good thing for Sam that it was a small goat because Dash didn't like being carried, not one little bit. He wiggled and squirmed, trying to work himself free. And he cried out his utter indignation at being carried.

But it was the man holding onto the angry goat that caught and held her attention. Sam held his head high as though to keep it away from the thrashing goat. She noticed his thick brows above his mesmerizing blue eyes. A straight nose that wasn't too big and not too small. And then there was his strong jawline and dimples. He was quite a looker. His shoulders were broad. And his biceps were quite muscular as they strained against the sleeves of his light blue T-shirt.

Nikki's face lit up with excitement. "Dash!"

The girl ran faster than her feet could keep up with, and she stumbled. Nikki's arms flailed about much like a windmill. Aster started forward, but then Nikki regained her balance.

The goat was too worked up to hear her. Sam didn't stop to let his daughter pet the animal; instead, Sam marched directly toward the goat pen.

He called over his shoulder, "Can you get the gate?"

Aster wasn't sure if he was speaking to her or Nikki, but Aster moved quickly to do as he asked. And it was a good thing because Nikki was so intent on Dash that she hadn't seemed to have heard her father.

With the gate securely closed, Aster stood on one side of the fence with Sam and Nikki on the other side. Sam gently set the goat on the ground but he didn't release him. He glanced over his shoulder and looked around. His gaze eventually settled on her.

"Aster, could you give me a hand?"

Her gaze moved from him to the unhappy goat and then returned to him. Her refusal hovered at the back of her throat. She'd been around enough goats for one day. She was good right where she stood.

"I can do it, Daddy." Nikki held out her arms to take the goat.

"Not this time, Nikki. He's putting up too much of a fight."

But then he looked at Aster. "Please. I need to look

him over."

The worried tone of his voice spurred Aster into action.

She had to turn her back to them as she made sure to secure the gate to keep Dash or any of his goat friends from making a run for it. But in her mind, she could imagine Nikki with her bottom lip sticking out as she crossed her arms. And when she turned around, that was exactly what Nikki was doing.

By then, Sam had placed the goat on the ground. The animal seemed a little less upset now. But Sam still wore a worried expression on his face.

"Over here," he said.

Aster moved next to him. "I have no idea what I'm doing."

He glanced up at her. "I just need you to hold him." As though he noticed the fear on her face, he said, "Don't worry. He's all bluster and no action."

She wasn't so sure she believed him. "You mean if I hold him, he's not going to chew off my arm."

The worry lines eased from Sam's face as he let out a deep, hearty laugh. It broke the tension that had been building in everyone since he'd found the little black goat. He shook his head. "No, he won't." And then he took her hand and guided it to the front of the goat. "Wrap your arm around his chest like this. And then put your other arm over his lower back." When she did as he instructed, he said, "That's it. See, he already likes you. He's not even fighting you."

And then Sam set to work examining the goat from front to back. All the while, Nikki fretted, wanting to know if something was wrong with her goat. Aster had never seen anyone care so much about a goat. But then again, she'd never known anyone who owned a goat…until then.

"Just a little nick," Sam said. "I'll go get my medical kit and be right back."

At which point, Nikki plunked down in front of the goat and frowned at him. "Dash, you can't run away." She waved her little finger at him. "Now you're hurt." She reached forward and wrapped her arms around the goat to hug him.

To Aster's utter amazement, the goat didn't move or in any way resist the girl's attention. It wasn't like Aster knew much about goats; well, she knew nothing about them, but she'd swear the little goat loved the attention Nikki lavished on him.

As Nikki pulled back and continued talking to the goat, Aster turned her head to glance around at the other goats. None seemed to be paying them any attention. Some were lying down, and others were munching on weeds.

Sam quickly returned from the house with a first aid kit in hand. He cleaned up the small gash and determined that it was minor, but he'd keep an eye on it.

Once she followed Sam out of the pen area, Aster said, "I should be going. I hope things go well for Dash."

"He'll be fine. Nikki will see to it." He nodded to where his daughter was fussing over the little goat.

"They seem to really like each other."

He sighed and nodded. "She's never taken to a goat quite like she has with him. I'd swear she'd take him to

bed with her, if I'd let her."

"You wouldn't, would you?" The question was past her lips before she realized it was quite improper—especially with a man that was practically a stranger.

To her great relief, he let out another laugh. "No. I wouldn't. I might spoil my daughter, but there are some lines that even she can't cross. Not even if she begs."

As Aster took in the sight of the little girl hugging the very patient goat, she smiled. "I can imagine her tucking Dash under the covers."

"Shh… Don't give her any more ideas. Trust me, she has enough of her own."

Nikki let herself out of the pen and made sure to secure the gate. "Will he be okay, Daddy?"

"He'll be fine."

"That's good. I love him." And then Nikki leaned into her father's side and hugged him.

The sight of the tender moment between father and daughter left a lump in Aster's throat. It was something she'd witnessed on television but couldn't remember ever personally experiencing. Those two were so lucky to have each other—though she did wonder what had happened to her mother.

Aster swallowed hard. "Well, I should be going—"

"But you don't have the apples you came here for," Sam said.

"Oh. But this isn't the right farm. I mean I got the address mixed up." Heat of embarrassment warmed her cheeks.

Sam smiled, making her stomach flutter. "Come on. The orchard isn't far. And picking some apples is the least I can do after you helped us this morning."

Aww... Her heart swooned just a little. The more she got to know him, the harder it was becoming not to like him more than was wise. No wonder the residents of Bluestar were set on helping him.

Still, she didn't want him going out of his way for her. "But I really didn't do anything."

Sam and Nikki were already in motion. "I have some baskets on the back porch."

"I'll get them." Nikki ran ahead.

Aster followed them. "This really isn't necessary."

"You never said what you need so many apples for," Sam said.

That was true. She hadn't told him because he wasn't supposed to know about the fundraiser. And yet she was a miserable liar so she spoke the truth, just not all of it. "They're making a batch of apple butter."

His brows lifted. "Apple butter?" When she nodded, he said, "I remember my grandparents used to make that every autumn. I can still remember the delicious aroma. It never tastes as good as when it's prepared outdoors in a great big kettle." A smile settled over his face as he appeared to be lost in thoughts of days gone by. "Back then life seemed so simple—like nothing bad could ever happen." The smile slipped from his face and when he glanced at her, sadness had dimmed his eyes. "Let's get you those apples."

Nikki joined them at the old blue pickup. She handed her father the baskets, which he tossed in the back, and then they climbed into the cab. He started the engine and with Nikki in the middle, they set off.

"I didn't think you were allowed to have vehicles on the island," Aster said.

"You aren't. At least not without a special permit. But agricultural equipment is exempted. It'd be hard to run a farm with nothing but a golf cart. There are certain rules for operating those vehicles in town but if you abide by them, there aren't any problems."

She nodded in understanding. Bluestar was like a world unto itself. At first, she'd been shocked by the lack of traffic, but she'd come to find the alternate forms of transportation had their own charms.

It was trying to figure out all of Bluestar's little nuances that kept tripping her up. Like why was the town keeping the fundraiser from Sam? And why was the town taking on the responsibility of rebuilding his barn?

The questions kept collecting in her mind, one after the other. And yet she had no answers. Perhaps she needed to have another chat with Darla. If she was going to help the town and in turn, hopefully earn a full-time position at city hall, she needed to know how the town operated because it wasn't like anything she was used to back in California.

The truck hit a rut in the dirt path, bouncing Aster's attention back to the present. The truck's engine groaned a little as they climbed a small hill. Another thing she'd noticed about the island was that it was not level. The flattest area was the town. It was probably why they built it there. To the north and south of town were a series of rolling hills. She couldn't wait to have more time to explore the island.

The farther they went, more trees appeared, but as

they crested the hill, she wasn't expecting to find row after row of apple trees. They were all so neat and orderly. With their green leaves fluttering in the breeze, it was a picture-perfect sight.

"Wow! How many trees are there?" Aster took them all in.

"You know, I'm not quite sure," Sam said. "I've never counted them."

"I'll count them!" Nikki turned to Aster. "I'm really good at math."

Aster smiled. "You are?"

Nikki nodded. "I like it."

"Me too." Her smile broadened. She liked the little girl. And then her gaze moved to Nikki's father—he wasn't bad either.

Sam pulled up to a row of apple trees and got out of the pickup. "We should pick the apples here. These are gala apples. My grandfather planted these trees before I was born. Since I took over the farm, I've been expanding the orchard each year."

"Are they all galas?"

He shook his head. "I also have Red Delicious and Granny Smiths, but they won't be ready to pick until next month. I'm planning to expand the orchard with some honeycrisps."

"Where are the ones you planted?" Aster asked.

"They are over that way." He pointed to the left.

"And what's that way?" She pointed in the opposite direction, where the trees had greatly thinned out.

"That would be the family cemetery."

"Oh."

"Mommy's there," Nikki said it as a matter of fact.

And it broke Aster's heart. It was as though the girl had never known anything else. Aster knew what that felt like to lose her mother. She'd been killed, along with her father, in a car crash when Aster was six years old. And she'd been searching for her place in this world ever since.

Aster resisted the urge to reach out to the girl and hug her tightly. After all, she was a stranger to Nikki, and she didn't want to scare the girl with a sudden outpouring of emotion.

Sam handed them two baskets each. He told Nikki to pick apples from the ground—to search out the good ones for the basket and to place the bad ones in a pile. While Nikki did as he instructed, Sam told Aster to pick the apples she could reach while he used a wooden ladder to pick some apples from higher up in the tree.

Aster had never picked apples before. She was probably the only person on the island who hadn't done such a simple task. She'd always lived in the city and never had the opportunity. And that made her feel a bit uncomfortable.

She swallowed hard and avoided his gaze. "Do I just pick any apple?"

He shook his head. "You'll need to make sure the apple is ready to be picked." He moved closer to the tree. And then he gestured to her to move up next to him. "Stand closer so you can see what I'm doing."

She hesitated to get so close to him. What if he noticed her scar? How would she explain it? Her pulse raced as her palms grew damp.

Jennifer Faye

When she didn't move, he sent her a questioning look. And so, she did what he'd asked her. As she stood next to him, she realized just how tall he was—almost a foot taller than her.

To her relief, he focused his attention on the tree. And when he reached out for an apple, she noticed his tanned arm was corded with muscles. Something told her he didn't have a gym membership. He did his exercising the old-fashioned way, with lots of hard work.

"First, you'll want to check the skin color around the stem. If it's green, it's not ready to pick. It needs to be yellowish. Then you'll want to grasp the apple and lift it up toward the stem. Give it a twist. It should come off the limb easily. If it doesn't and you have to yank at it, it's not ready for picking and you can move on." Then he demonstrated what he'd just told her. The apple easily came off in his hand. "Do you want to give it a try?"

She nodded and then stepped up to check the skin color, finding it yellowish. She reached out and followed his directions, but the apple didn't fall off into her hand as his had done. "Did I do it right?"

He nodded. "Try another one."

She did. And this time the apple easily fell into her hand. She smiled. She'd picked her very first apple.

And so, they set to work. Aster couldn't help but marvel over the way Nikki ran around as though she had the energy of ten people. She never seemed to slow down.

Sam worked quietly from his perch on the ladder. She wondered what he'd be doing if she hadn't interrupted his day. Would he be out there in the

orchard? Or would he be tending to the animals?

She hadn't seen any cows out and about, but from what she'd seen so far of the Bell farm, it was quite big. The cows must be off in a distant field soaking up the sun and enjoying a mouthful of green grass. At least that was what she thought they ate, didn't they?

The question teetered on the tip of her tongue, but then she bit it back. She'd shown enough of her ignorance of farming ways for one day. But as the silence drew on, she felt the urge to say something to fill the void.

"Have you lived here long?" she asked.

"Almost ten years. Before that it belonged to my grandparents. And before that it belonged to my great grandparents."

"Wow. So, what you're saying is that this has always been the Bell farm?"

"Yes. My ancestors were one of Bluestar's founding families."

"That's great." She didn't know much about her ancestors. Perhaps one of these days she'd join one of those online ancestry sites. When Sam didn't say anything, she asked, "Do you plan to hand this farm down to your daughter?"

"It was the plan." He climbed down the ladder and proceeded to position it beneath another tree.

She'd noticed his use of the word *was. "It was the plan."* Did that mean it was no longer an option? And if so, why not?

It seemed like the more she learned about the gentleman farmer, the more she wanted to know. She told herself it was a natural curiosity that she'd have about anyone she'd just met.

"How long have you been on Bluestar?" Sam's question drew her attention. Was he truly interested? Or was he diverting the questions away from himself? If anyone was an expert on diversionary tactics, it was her. Still, he'd shared a little of his life with her. The least she could do was reveal a bit of herself.

She gave another apple a twist. It fell into her hand. She placed it into the basket. "I've been here for a week."

"And how do you like it?"

In truth, part of her was homesick. She missed her tiny apartment, but what she missed most was her landlord, Rosa Vega. She'd grown quite close to the older woman. So many times she'd been tempted to phone her, but she'd resisted the urge. She didn't want to endanger Rosa's life if Oz or one of his goons came around.

But she couldn't share any of that so she forced a smile on her face. "I love it. I might stay forever."

"Do you know someone on the island?"

She hesitated to answer. Pre-Oz she wouldn't have thought a thing about answering the question but post-Oz she was extremely uncomfortable when a man asked too many questions.

Still, she'd learned quickly that there weren't many secrets on the island. If Sam wanted to know where she was staying, he'd merely have to ask someone in town.

She swallowed hard. "I'm staying with Darla Evans." And before he asked the inevitable question, she said,

"We were roommates in college."

"Well, welcome to the island."

After that they worked in silence until apples filled all of the baskets. Sam graciously carried his baskets to the truck, and then he carried hers. It was very sweet of him. And then they both helped Nikki finish filling her baskets.

The ride back to the house was filled with Nikki chattering on about the goats before she abruptly shifted gears to talk about school starting soon. She was very excited to be starting first grade.

Aster was quiet as she listened to the exchange between father and daughter. Though she noted that Sam didn't have to say much as Nikki talked practically nonstop. Aster wondered if she'd been the same way with her father. She wished she could remember those times.

The pickup pulled to a stop. Aster was happy to get out. Being around Sam was making her think too much about her past, which was better off left alone.

"Can I go see Dash?" Nikki asked her father.

Sam walked over to the back of the pickup. "Aren't you going to tell Aster goodbye?"

Nikki turned to her and waved. "Bye."

Aster was touched by the girl's good manners. "It was so nice to meet you."

"Will you come back?"

"I... I don't know." Aster moved her gaze to Sam, not sure how to respond.

He averted his gaze. "I'm sure Aster is very busy."

As the girl's happy expression dissolved into a

frown, Aster said, "But I can always make time for a friend. Would you like to be my friend?"

The smile returned to Nikki's face. "I would. And Dash would like to be your friend too."

Aster couldn't help but laugh. "I'll see you and Dash again."

"Soon?"

Aster nodded. Bluestar was a small town. She was certain they'd bump into each other soon enough. And she was looking forward to it. There was something special about Nikki...and her father.

"Okay. Bye." With a quick wave, Nikki ran off toward the goat pen.

Aster turned to find Sam placing the last basket of apples in her cart. "Thank you. The apples are much appreciated."

A slow, easy smile lit up his tanned face. "It was my pleasure. Stop back if you need anymore. And soon I'll have pumpkins."

"I wouldn't know what to do with a pumpkin."

"You could make a pie with it or roast the seeds. Nikki likes to make jack-o'-lanterns."

She was impressed by the pumpkin's versatility. "I'll keep all of that in mind." She glanced around. "You must grow a lot of things."

He nodded. "Earlier in the summer, I had a small garden, and I would take produce to the farmer's market in town."

"You must be busy." It was then that she noticed the faint shadows under his eyes.

"It keeps me going."

"Well, I've taken up enough of your time. Thank you for the apples."

She sat in the cart and started the motor. "Bye."

He gave a nonchalant wave.

When all was said and done, she couldn't remember the last time she'd enjoyed herself quite so much. All of her worries and fears had slid to the back of her mind.

Maybe it was time to let go of her worries about Oz. After all, it wasn't like he was going to find her there. As it was, he was paying for his crimes, even if it wasn't the punishment she'd been expecting.

She'd much rather think about the beautiful morning she'd spent on the farm. She'd learned that first impressions weren't always accurate—certainly not in Sam's case. He was kind and generous, not to mention a loving father.

She smiled as she drove down the lane. She felt as though she'd made a new friend—correction, two new friends. She thought about including Dash and his four-footed cohorts but decided that would be pushing things.

6

*I*t was not the morning he'd been anticipating.

It had actually turned out better.

Sam stopped walking. He stopped breathing. He stopped everything as that startling thought sank in. He surely hadn't meant it the way it had sounded in his head. Of course not.

He meant he'd had a much better time with his daughter picking apples in the sunshine than checking on the irrigation lines out in the fields. And the fact that Aster had been there, well, that had absolutely nothing to do with the pep in his step or the fact that he'd smiled more this morning than he had since—since Beth was alive.

The air whooshed out of his lungs. Guilt soon followed. Here he was enjoying himself and the day with his daughter, and Beth wasn't here for any of it. And if he'd have made a different decision on that long-ago day, his daughter's mother would still be here. Nikki would be able to see how wonderful her mother was instead of having to imagine her through his words and the pictures in the house.

Because when it came down to it, he was no replacement for Beth, not even close. He couldn't give his daughter the gentle nurturing that she should get from her mother. The best he had to offer her was his own mother, who filled in as often as she could. But his mother had a job at the visitors' center and a social life, so she couldn't be at the farm all of the time. Nor would he want his mother to be there constantly. It wouldn't be fair to her. After the traumatic loss of his father, his mother appeared to have found a way forward.

It was just him and Nikki. And the babysitter.

"Hey, Mr. Bell. Sorry I'm a little late." Janie Simpson smiled at him as she slowed her bicycle. Her long, straight ponytail fell over her right shoulder.

She was late? He hadn't noticed. And that wasn't like him. He didn't like tardiness because he always had too much to do and never enough time to do it. But he was in too good of a mood to ruin it by admonishing Janie.

"No problem," he said. "I was just heading out to the fields. Nikki is with the goats. Do you need anything before I go?"

"Don't forget that I leave for college not this weekend but the next." Beneath her bangs, worry lines came over the eighteen-year-old's face. "You did find another babysitter, didn't you?"

The truth was that he'd been putting off finding a replacement because bringing someone else into the household wasn't easy for him. Whomever he hired had to be fiercely independent and a good influence on

Nikki. Above all, Nikki had to approve of them. Where was he supposed to find someone like that?

Janie had been recommended to him a couple of years ago after his wife's death. At first, he hadn't been sure about her. After all, she was a teenager. But he'd quickly learned that she was smart and reliable. In addition, the high school was cattycorner from the elementary school. So, Janie would hang around doing her homework and then escort Nikki home. He'd never find anyone like her again.

Still, he didn't have a choice. He had to pick someone to look after Nikki while he worked. A while back he'd put a notice in the local paper, and he'd gotten a number of applicants. The problem was choosing one.

He cleared his throat as he pressed his hands to his sides. "I have some candidates."

Janie smiled. "That's great. I didn't want to leave you guys in a lurch." Then the smile slipped from her face. "I should go check on Nikki." She started to pedal toward the house.

Something was wrong. He could sense it. "Janie, wait."

She paused and turned back to him. "What do you need?"

"I sense there's something on your mind, but you're not sure about telling me."

She shook her head. "It's nothing. Don't worry."

Any time someone told him not to worry, that was exactly what he did. "Tell me."

"Well, it's just that my mother wants to head to college a week early. She says we can look around New

York City and do some shopping. But it's okay if you don't have someone to watch Nikki. We can tour the city another time."

"No." This was his problem—his fault for procrastinating for so long. "You should go with your mother and have a good time. I know it would mean a lot to her. And you've definitely earned it." In fact, he was planning to put a bonus in her last paycheck. "Don't worry about Nikki. I've got everything covered."

"You do?" Her eyes lit up with excitement. "That would be great. My mom will be so excited. I'll call her as soon as I get to the house. You're the best, Mr. Bell." With a smile on her face, she pedaled away.

He sure didn't feel like the best. If he was the best, his wife would still be with them. There would still be cows on the farm as there had always been until these last couple of years, and his old barn wouldn't be falling down while the new one had burned to the ground.

He sighed. But the one thing he'd gotten right so far was Nikki's happiness. Through it all, her smile lit up his heart with overwhelming love. Her love for him and this farm was what kept him trying to get things right—to make the farm prosperous once more.

How had the time gotten away from her?

Aster navigated Birdie's cart back to her house, fully loaded with apples from front to back. When Mr. Hornell learned that Sam had donated six bushels of apples, he'd insisted on doing the same. Aster had never seen so many apples, and they smelled amazing.

Still, she'd been gone longer than she should have

been. She knew they couldn't start making apple butter without the apples. But there was something about the Bell farm that had drawn her in. Nikki was so sweet and even the goats weren't so bad, but they took some getting used to. She couldn't tell what they were thinking, and that bothered her. With a dog, you could tell whether they liked you or not by a glint in their eyes or a swish of their tails, but for her, goats weren't that easy to read.

All of a sudden Aster broke out in laughter. Only a couple of months ago, she'd been worried about getting notes for a meeting typed up for review, and now she was tasked with picking apples and figuring out goats. Oh my, how her life had drastically changed.

And though she wanted to blame Oz for her having to lose the home she'd worked so hard to make for herself and having to start all over again in a different part of the country, in part she was thankful. Not that he'd attacked her. Definitely not that. Perhaps her life had been in a rut. And now she was able to discover Bluestar Island. It was calming and happy. The residents were welcoming, and maybe this was where she was supposed to end up after all. Could Bluestar be her destiny? Or was it a bunch of wishful thinking?

She didn't have a chance to come up with an answer to those questions as she pulled the cart to a stop in front of Birdie's little bungalow. Birdie was on the front porch, sitting in a white rocker, and she wasn't alone. Her orange and white cockapoo, Peaches, was by her side. Darla was there as well.

Peaches stood and greeted her with a friendly bark.

"Sorry I'm late." Aster rushed up the walk. When she reached the porch, she paused to fuss over the dog. Then she turned to Birdie. "You'll never believe what happened."

Birdie used her cane to gesture to the cart. "It looks like you've been picking apples all morning."

"I have."

"But you were only supposed to pick up a few bushels." Birdie frowned as though trying to figure out what they were going to do with the surplus.

Aster launched into an abbreviated story of how she'd mixed up the addresses and wound up at Sam's farm. She assured both Birdie and Darla that she hadn't given away anything about the fundraiser. They still looked a bit worried, but they didn't press the subject. The last thing Aster wanted to do was let them down. Darla had been instrumental in giving her this fresh start, not to mention a new job, even if it was only part time... For now. And Birdie, well, she was a very special lady with a big heart and the ability to organize all of Bluestar from her front porch.

"We better get going. They already have the fire going for the kettle," Birdie said. "Everyone is wondering where we are."

"What should I do with all of the apples?" Aster asked.

Birdie's brows drew together as she thought over the situation. "I know. You can take half of the baskets for the apple butter. And I'll phone Hannah and let her know that I have some apples in need of pie shells."

"Who's Hannah?" Aster asked. She was still working

hard to learn the names of all the Bluestar residents.

"She owns The Elegant Bakery, and she's Sam's younger sister."

Aster's mouth formed an O. "I was in her bakery once to pick up an order for a breakfast meeting at city hall. It was amazing. And don't get me started on how good the muffins were. I had the blueberry. It was to die for."

Darla laughed. "Now you know why I take a wide birth around the bakery. I can only indulge once in a while, or I'd never fit in my clothes."

"Not me," Birdie said. "I'm at the stage in my life where I plan to take in as many of life's indulgences as I can." She winked at them. "There have to be some privileges in getting to my age." Her expression grew serious. "Are you sure Sam didn't suspect anything?"

"Only that I'm not good with directions since I ended up at the wrong farm."

"That's my fault," Birdie was quick to say. "I should have been clearer with my instructions." She stood and headed toward the walkway. Peaches followed her. Birdie paused at the edge of the porch and stared at her golf cart filled with apples, leaving no room for anyone but the driver. "We should do something about those apples now." She glanced at Aster and Darla. "Would you ladies mind putting the baskets for the apple butter in Darla's cart?" Upon their agreement, Birdie continued. "And then Aster would you mind delivering the apples over to the bakery before meeting us at Betty's?"

"Betty?" She sent Birdie a confused look.

"Oh, I'm sorry, dear. I keep forgetting that you're new to the island. You just fit in so well. Betty Simon is my best friend, and we're making the apple butter in her back yard." Birdie proceeded to give Aster detailed instructions on how to get to her house.

She was relieved to find Birdie wasn't upset about the extra apples.

"Okay. I'll see you there shortly."

With Darla's help, they quickly moved the heavy baskets. While Darla drove Birdie to Betty's house, Aster drove into the heart of Bluestar. Luckily at this time of the morning, the roads weren't too crowded with tourists. She was even able to find a parking spot.

She climbed out of the golf cart and turned to head into the bakery, when a young woman wearing a white cloth cap, a bright white shirt, and black apron stepped outside the bakery. They hadn't been introduced but by the look of her, she had to be Sam's sister.

Aster walked up to her. "You wouldn't happen to be Hannah, would you?"

She smiled and nodded. "And you would be Aster?"

She also smiled and nodded. "It's nice to meet you."

"Nice to meet you too." Hannah's gaze moved to the apples in the cart. Just then an older couple stepped up to the bakery, causing Hannah to move to the side. Once they passed, she said, "Would you mind driving the apples around back?"

Another person exited the bakery with a big white cake box in their hands. It was certainly a busy place. And the cinnamon and butter scent wafting from it made Aster's mouth water.

"Sure," Aster said. "No problem."

"I'll meet you around back." Hannah headed back inside the bakery.

Aster drove to the rear of the bakery. She was already out of the golf cart and unloading the first basket of apples when Hannah opened the back door.

Hannah rushed forward. "Here. Let me help you with those."

Hannah took one handle on the basket. "These apples look really good."

Aster gripped the other handle. "They should. This basket came from your brother's farm."

Hannah's eyes widened. "How did that happen?"

Aster told her about the mix-up with the address as well as their search for the goat. "Your niece is adorable. And from the looks of it, she has your brother wrapped around her little finger."

Hannah didn't say anything as they placed the basket just inside the entrance to the kitchen, and Aster started to worry. "I'm sorry if I said something wrong."

"No, it's fine." Hannah sent her a smile as though to emphasize her words. "It's my fault. I was just thinking that I've been so wrapped up with the new bakery that I haven't spent as much time at the farm as I'd like to." She turned and held the door open. "Does Sam know what we're up to?"

Aster shook her head. "I didn't say a word."

"But surely he must wonder what we're doing with all of these apples."

"He did and between you and me, I'm not a good liar so I told him the truth."

"So, he does know."

Aster once more shook her head. "He knows that we're making apple butter, but he just assumed it was for the Labor Day weekend celebration. He has no idea it's to raise funds to rebuild his barn."

Hannah sighed. "That's good. Because if my brother knew, he'd put a stop to it. You have no idea how stubborn he can be—even when it's for his own good." They lifted the next basket out of the cart. "So, you're a friend of Darla's?"

"I am." She had a feeling that title was going to stick with her. She would always be known around Bluestar as "Darla's friend." Not that she minded. She was lucky to have such a good friend. "We were roommates in college."

"And so, you came out here to visit her?"

"Something like that, but Bluestar is growing on me. I'm thinking of sticking around for a while."

Hannah sent her a bright smile. "That's great. This is the best place to live. Not that I'm partial or anything."

They unloaded the last basket of apples while discussing Bluestar's merits. It was a lengthy list. And if Aster hadn't already been convinced that she could be happy staying there, Hannah's description of the town and the island was enough to sway her.

"I love how the town pulls together," Aster said. "That doesn't happen in a lot of places."

Hannah nodded in agreement. "Bluestar is unique. I hope you'll decide to stay."

"Right now, that's the plan." But she knew not to get too comfortable with that idea. "But we'll have to see how things go."

"I understand. Island life isn't for everyone."

Aster arched a disbelieving brow. "Really?"

"It's what I've heard. I just think they don't know what they're missing."

"Granted, I've only been here for a week, but I have to agree with you. There's just something special here. I mean look at what everyone is doing for your brother. I just wish I could do more."

Hannah glanced her way. "How are you at baking pies?"

Aster shook her head. "I wouldn't have a clue where to begin. I'm afraid I've never baked more than a frozen pizza."

"No problem. Would you like to learn?"

She hadn't really thought about it before. She'd always gotten by with picking up store-bought baked goods. What would it be like to broaden her horizons? After all, wasn't this the year to try new things?

She glanced past Hannah and into the kitchen where someone was rolling out a pie crust. She watched as they sprinkled flour on the dough, rolled it out, and then turned the dough. They made it look so easy, but she knew it wasn't easy—especially when you'd never even held a rolling pin.

"Okay. But only if it's something easy." She really didn't want to fail on her first try.

Hannah smiled. "That can be arranged. Let me give it some thought. I'll have these apples stored in a cool, dark spot. And then how about we meet here the Sunday before Labor Day?"

Labor Day was more than a week away. "What time?"

"At six." When Aster felt her mouth sag, Hannah laughed. "Okay, how about eight?"

It wasn't great but it was better than six. What could she say? She wasn't a morning person. Then she once more reminded herself of her theme for the year—try new things.

Though it went against everything in her, she said, "Okay. I'll see you at eight."

Hannah was still smiling. "Don't worry. I'll have the coffee on. I'll see you then."

And then Aster made her exit. She wondered what had come over her. She'd never shown an interest in baking before. But then again, she'd never been given an opportunity to learn how to work in the kitchen.

She realized that she might be perfectly awful at it. As she started the golf cart to head off to Betty's, she hesitated. Maybe she should go back inside and let Hannah know that she'd made a big mistake, and she didn't want to waste Hannah's time. But if she didn't try, she'd never know.

And so, she pressed down on the accelerator. She had to admit, even if only to herself, that all of this new stuff was a bit stressful. Well, maybe not all of the new things in her life—her mind rewound to meeting Sam and his daughter. She'd made new friends today. A smile pulled at her lips.

7

e couldn't get her image out of his mind.

Sam kept busy the rest of the morning from checking the irrigation lines in the pumpkin patch to securing the entrance to the old barn. He didn't want Dash getting in there again. There were too many things for a curious goat to get hurt on.

It was becoming evident that what he needed to do was tear down the barn sooner rather than later. But then where would he store his equipment? Even though part of the roof had blown off, it still provided a modicum of protection for the equipment. Perhaps if this year's crop was good and the prices held, he'd be able to either repair the old barn or get a loan to build a new barn. It was his goal.

The only problem with that lofty goal was that with an old farm, there was always something that needed repaired from a leaky roof to a broken window. If it wasn't one thing, it was another.

He checked the time on his wristwatch and found it

was almost time for Ethan to arrive. His sister's boyfriend was a contractor on the island. If Sam had the money, he could keep Ethan very busy around the farm. As it was, he could only afford to tackle the most urgent problem. The old window had accidentally been broken when he had been teaching Nikki how to play softball. Needless to say, the lesson hadn't gone according to plan.

Ethan was a good guy. He made Hannah happy and that in turn made Sam happy. He knew if his father were still alive, he'd approve of the firefighter-turned-contractor. And Sam was happy to have another guy in the family. Even though Ethan and Hannah hadn't said anything about a future together, Sam knew it was just a matter of time.

He had just stepped out onto the front porch with a cup of coffee in hand when he saw a golf cart headed down the lane. He waved to Ethan, who waved back.

Sam gulped down the rest of the still-warm brew. He knew he was going to need the caffeine as there was still a lot to do that day. He hustled down the steps to the cart, which had a great big sheet of cardboard protecting the new glass.

"I'll take the glass," he said.

"Thanks. I just have to grab some tools." Ethan reached over to the passenger seat and grabbed a black toolbox.

As they made their way to the porch, Ethan glanced at the broken front window. "So how did this happen?"

Sam moved off to the side of the porch and gently laid the glass flat on the floor. "I was teaching Nikki how to play softball."

Ethan nodded. "She wanted to learn."

He shrugged. "Not really. This was my idea. With her dance and gymnastics classes, I just thought maybe some sports would be a good balance."

Ethan smiled. "And then she hit the ball through the window—"

"No. That was me too."

Ethan's mouth opened, but then he seemed to think better of saying anything and wordlessly closed it.

"It's okay. You can say it. I'm a total klutz." He sighed. Lately, he'd been overextended and as a result making mistakes.

"No. What I was thinking is how do you manage to do everything? Do you sleep at night?"

He nodded. "I get five hours a night, whether I need it or not."

"Five? Ouch. That's not much."

He shrugged. "I've been doing it so long that I'm used to it."

At least that's what he kept telling himself, but if it wasn't for the coffee, he might end up falling asleep standing up. This was just a rough patch and he'd get through it.

"What you need is some help?"

"I do have help. I have Janie, the babysitter, but she's about to head off to college."

"Do you have someone else lined up?"

"I had advertised for a new babysitter, but none of the applicants seem like the right fit." He knew he was being picky about whom he wanted to watch his

daughter. But Nikki was full of energy and without a mother, she needed someone to interact with her and not sit and watch television or read a book but to be totally present while watching his daughter. He hadn't thought he was asking too much but perhaps he was. "Maybe I should advertise again."

"Did you put a notice up at the café? I think everyone who lives in Bluestar makes a visit there at least once a week. Your sister put up a notice for her spare apartment, and that's how we got to know each other."

"I don't think so. I don't need a love connection."

Ethan laughed. "That wasn't what I meant. When my aunt was in the hospital, I had breakfast, lunch, and dinner at the café. I've tried almost everything on the menu. Your sister says she's starting to think I like the food at the café better than what she makes."

He paused from retrieving a screwdriver. "Hey, my sister's a good cook."

"I agree. I tell her that all of the time. But now with the bakery starting to take off, she's working long hours. That's the only reason I still eat at the café. That and I can't cook anything. If it were possible to burn water, I'd do it."

Sam nodded. "I used to be that way. Beth was always the cook, and I did the dishes. But now, well, there's just me. I had to learn to cook."

"And how's that working for you?"

He sighed. "In the beginning, Nikki and I ate a lot of burned food. But I was determined to do the best I could for my daughter, so I just kept trying. Some recipes come out better than others. Thankfully, Nikki isn't picky."

"That's impressive. She's lucky to have you."

"I don't know how lucky she is. I still burn an occasional dinner now and then. I get distracted with the laundry or vacuuming, and forget I have food on the stove."

Ethan nodded in understanding. "You really do need some help around here. I hope you find someone that fits in."

"I don't have any choice. Janie is leaving a week early for college." He was so tired of thinking of all of the problems facing him. "We better get this window repaired."

"Agreed. I have a kitchen to start working on for a friend of mine."

"You mean Greg Hoover?"

Ethan's brows rose. "How did you know?"

"It's a small town, remember? Not much goes on around here without everyone knowing. And he's so excited about the remodel that he's telling everyone and anyone that will listen. I think he's your biggest advertising."

"I might have to give him a discount if he brings in more business."

"Trust me. If someone needs some work done on their house, they'll know to call you."

As they continued to work, Sam decided that this afternoon he'd write up a new ad for a babysitter. Maybe he'd be more specific about what Nikki needed such as someone not afraid of goats. Immediately, Aster's image came to mind. A smile tugged at his lips as he recalled

her nervousness around the goats, but he'd give her credit; she didn't run away. In fact, in the end he thought she might actually like Dash—at least a little bit.

♥♥♥

The scent of burning wood and simmering apples wafted through the air.

Aster inhaled deeply. It wouldn't be much longer now until the apple butter was done. She couldn't help but wonder if there would be some taste-testing. She'd definitely be the first to volunteer.

At the moment, she was the designated stirrer. While the apples simmered over an open fire in a giant copper pot, they had to be constantly stirred with a wooden paddle with a long horizontal handle. It was really quite unique—at least it was from Aster's perspective.

Darla strolled up to her. "You seem to be fitting in just fine. I told you, you would."

"This island is amazing. The only run-in I had was the other day."

"You mean outside of the deli. Did you ever figure out who the guy was?"

She nodded. "I ran into him again."

Worry reflected in her eyes. "Oh no. How did it go?"

"Better than I'd have imagined."

"You mean this time he wasn't grouchy."

"Well, he wasn't exactly happy to see me at first."

"I'm not following."

Aster glanced around to make sure no one was close enough to overhear. "The grouchy guy was Sam."

"No way!"

"Shh…" Heat rushed to her cheeks. There were a

couple glances her way, but then they returned to their prior conversations. "I don't want everyone to know."

"If they don't know already, they will soon enough."

"No, they won't. Unless you tell them. Because I'm sure not planning to tell anyone else." The very last thing she needed was to be the center of small-town gossip. She needed to keep a low profile in hopes of staying in Bluestar and not having to move on.

Betty Simon, who was Birdie's best friend and the hostess of this gathering, strolled over to them. She was on the petite side with short, curly, dyed-red hair and a big warm smile. "How are the apples coming?"

"I think they're almost done." At least she hoped so because her arms were growing tired from stirring.

Betty moved closer to the pot and peered in at the bubbling apples. "I think it needs a little more." She turned back to Aster. "You poor dear. Your arms must be tired. I'll find someone else to take over the stirring."

The idea was appealing, but being anxious to fit in, she said. "That's okay. I've got it."

"Thank you, ladies, for joining us." Betty smiled at both her and Darla. "The turnout today is wonderful."

Chime. Chime.

"Sorry," Darla said. "I've got to get this." She stepped away to answer her phone.

"What do you think of Bluestar?" Betty asked.

It wasn't the first time she'd been asked that question, and she was pretty certain it wouldn't be the last. "I really like it here. What's not to like?"

Betty smiled and nodded. "I've lived here my whole life. I've visited other places but none could compare to

Bluestar. Do you think you'll stay long?"

"It depends."

"On?" Betty wasn't bashful as she prodded for more information.

On whether Oz finds me. On if I can ever afford my own place. On whether or not I eventually feel like moving on.

She went with the answer that would create the least number of questions. "On whether I get a full-time job."

They went on to discuss her part-time work for the mayor. And how he'd volunteered her services to help with the Labor Day picnic. So far, it consisted of a picnic in the park and some booths with items for sale, but she couldn't help but think there could be more—a greater sense of community.

She didn't want to admit it to Mayor Banks, but she knew nothing about small towns—about what the citizens enjoyed. The only thing she could draw on was her prior experience working for a college. They'd organized quite a few events to keep the student body occupied. It wasn't quite the same thing, but it was something.

A few minutes later, Darla returned and Betty moved on to have a word with Birdie. "Sorry about that."

"No problem." By that time Aster's arms were aching from constantly moving the big wooden paddle. "Would you mind stirring for a little bit? My arms really do need a break."

"Sure." She moved next to her and took over. "You should have accepted Betty's offer to find someone to take over for you."

"I didn't want her to think I wasn't willing to do my part." Aster rotated her shoulders, feeling the pain of her stiff muscles. "So, what do you want to do this evening?"

Even though she'd been on the island for a week now, they'd both been so busy that they hadn't had much time to catch up with each other. When she'd been in California, they'd texted each other and had the occasional phone call, usually for a birthday or holiday. It wasn't that they didn't want to keep in touch; it was that life kept getting in the way. When one was free to talk, the other was busy working or dating or something.

And then there was the east coast time of Bluestar and the west coast time zone of L.A. But it never meant the friendship they'd formed in college had slipped away. It was one of those relationships where time could pass but when they finally got together, it was as though time had stood still.

Darla sighed and then she looked guilty. "The phone call was from my boss. I need to cover for someone this evening. I'm really sorry."

Aster couldn't deny she was disappointed. She had intended to ask Darla more about Sam—from a work standpoint. Since he was the reason for the fundraiser, she thought the more she knew about him, the more it would help her plan the community picnic.

But there was no reason it couldn't wait until another time. After all, they shared an apartment… It was just like old times. They would find time to talk.

"No problem." Aster sent her a reassuring smile.

"I know. Why don't you meet me at The Lighthouse

for dinner? Maybe a late dinner. I won't be as busy then, and we can talk some."

"Are you sure? I wouldn't want to get you in trouble."

Darla shook her head. "You have nothing to worry about. Pete's really laid back as long as you get your work done."

Well, she didn't have any other plans. The only thing that bothered her was spending some of her meager funds on food. Until she gained full-time employment, she needed to watch where she spent her money.

"And dinner's on me," Darla added.

It was as though she had been reading Aster's mind. "No. I can afford my own meal."

"I know you can. I just feel guilty because I had to back out of our plans."

"You're going to work, not going out on a date or something fun. Stop worrying." And then feeling bad for upsetting her friend, who was generous enough to take her in, she said, "I'll be there."

Darla smiled. "Great."

"Now I do have a question for you. Is your ex on the island?" She'd been curious about him since she'd arrived on the island.

Darla shook her head. And then she lowered her voice. "Will doesn't come back very often. Maybe once or twice a year to see his father, Chief Campbell. And when he's here, I'm not."

"You aren't over him?" She knew it. They'd been so in love while Darla had been in college. And when they'd broken up, Darla had never wanted to talk about it.

"Will is so far in my rearview mirror that I can't even see him." She gave the pot an extra fast stir, and some of the bubbly apples rushed to the rim of the pot but didn't spill over. "It's just easier. We don't have to have that awkward moment when we see each other again. And he doesn't have to stress about visiting his family."

"I understand." Aster didn't believe her reason for avoiding Will. There was more to it than making things easier for Will, but that wasn't the time to push things. "Well, I'm looking forward to dinner."

A little later, Darla left to get ready for work, but Aster stayed to help out. Once the apples were sufficiently cooked, they were portioned out into canning jars and then sealed. The whole routine was new to her, and she found it all fascinating. With so many women helping, it didn't take as long as Aster had imagined.

She just wondered if Sam would appreciate everyone's efforts. She hadn't known him long enough to get a read on him. And with him living on a farm outside of town, she didn't think their paths would cross all that often. A sense of disappointment came over her.

8

ow was Dash? Had he run off again? And how was the gentleman farmer?

It was just after lunch the next day when Aster found her thoughts drifting back to the Bell farm. She told herself it was just a general curiosity. After all, it was her first experience with goats. She smiled as she thought of Dash and Billy.

She cleaned her lunch dishes and returned them to the cabinet. Now she wasn't sure what to do with her time. She wasn't used to this feeling. When she'd been in California, she worked all day and when she was done, she'd played on a beach volleyball team as well as a softball team. She was always busy.

Now her life had totally changed in more than one way. Not only was she on the opposite coast, but she had time on her hands—too much time. This gave her time to think—think about what had led her to this point. And thinking about Oz was something she didn't want to do.

So instead of sitting around, she grabbed her purse

and headed out of the apartment. As the afternoon sun warmed her face, her thoughts returned to the Bell farm. Nikki was adorable. Her connection with the goats fascinated Aster.

She'd never been exposed to many animals growing up. None of the foster homes she'd stayed in had animals. In one place, they said the kids were problem enough for them. Yeah, she hadn't stayed in the best homes. Probably in part because she'd been a problem child, full of anger over losing her loving parents, not understanding why it had happened and never feeling as though she belonged anywhere. Maybe if someone had taken the time to talk to her—to help her understand—to help her grieve.

As the warm, late-August breeze rushed past her, she continued walking. She had absolutely no destination in mind. The only thing she wanted to do was learn more about her surroundings. And then she realized she needed to purchase a few more outfits for work.

She started by exploring the shops located on Main Street. She had some money, not a lot, but with only a part-time job, she couldn't afford to squander it. She didn't know when she'd have to move on.

Window shopping was inexpensive…that was until you saw the cutest item and had to step inside to take a closer look. Aster promised herself that wouldn't happen.

She moved from one end of Main to the other. There were clothing boutiques: men's, women's, and children's. There were shoes stores that appeared to specialize in sandals and brightly colored flip-flops.

In between the shops were restaurants, from a Mexican flair at Katrina's Kantina to Little Moon Hibachi Grille. The aroma wafting from each place made her mouth water. If she stayed on the island long enough, she'd make it her mission to eat at each establishment.

However, she had a special fondness for The Lighthouse Café. Maybe it was because it was where her best friend worked. Or maybe it was how they'd designed it to look just like a lighthouse with a black-and-white tower. And she'd already seen the rotating white light at the top of the tower shining at night. Someone had quite and imagination but it was most fitting on Bluestar Island.

She paused at each storefront and admired their contents…even the men's shop just because she could. If she was going to get a full-time position at city hall, she had to be on top of her game. She had to know the ins and outs of Bluestar. And she had a lot to learn.

Not anxious to spend a lot of money, she entered one of the women's boutiques and headed straight for the back where stores kept their clearance rack. She tried on outfit after outfit, mixing and matching pieces. In the end, she checked out with four outfits that were all marked down sixty percent. A victorious smile lifted her lips as she made her way out the door. *Today is a good day.*

And then she moved on to Seashell Drive. There were even more souvenir shops on this street than she'd previously noticed on Main Street.

When she reached the candy shop, she just couldn't resist going inside. The chocolate car as well as the gumball spiral race track drew her in for a closer look. If she had visited this place when she was a kid, she would have thought it was the best place in the entire world.

The shelves of candy on the walls reached clear up to the ceiling. They really had that much candy, from marshmallow puffs to jellybeans in every color. By the time she walked out of the shop, she had a little white paper bag full of chocolate-covered cherries, caramel chews, and some of the jellybeans. It was an unnecessary splurge, but what was life without a few indulgences?

And she intended to find herself a second job. She just didn't know what that job would be just yet. In part that scared her, but she forced herself to think about it as a new adventure. She had the chance to reinvent herself. She could be anything or do anything. Not everyone had that opportunity. A lot of people became stuck in a rut, and before they're able to get out of it, life had passed them by. But that wouldn't happen to her.

She glanced up to find the sign for the next shop consisted of a big green lily pad with *The Lily Pad* and a dragon fly scrolled out on it in black paint. She smiled as she took in the sign. She definitely had to find out what was in this shop.

She headed straight for the bright red door. She pulled it open to find she wasn't the only one that had been drawn in. The aisle ways were narrow as there were so many crafts on display. And there were ceramics in many shapes and sizes.

Some of the items were completed but there were other items for creating your own crafts. She couldn't resist exploring each aisle. She found so many things she'd like to buy, but with her tight finances and not having a place of her own, she'd had to pass on them. But if her circumstances were to change, she'd definitely be back.

She made her way to the last aisle, and it was there that she stumbled across dog accessories from scarves to collars. She didn't have a dog yet, but she had been thinking about getting one when she was settled someplace for good. But she couldn't resist looking at all of the accessories.

And then she happened upon a red collar with a brass bell attached. She picked it up and jingled it. She smiled. For a smallish bell, it gave off a loud jingle. This was something Dash needed to help Sam and Nikki keep track of him. Something told her that hadn't been his first escape nor would it be his last.

She held up the collar with both hands. It looked to be about the right size. And as she looked back at the shelf, she saw brass name tags that could be engraved. Wanting to help Sam and overcome by its cuteness, she carried the collar and name tag to the counter.

"Could I get this engraved?" Aster asked the young woman behind the counter.

"Sure. What name would you like on it?"

"Dash. D-A-S-H."

The woman's eyes widened. "Is this for the Bell farm?"

Heat swirled in her chest. She was hoping to do this without anyone noticing. "Um...yes."

The woman smiled. "They're going to love it. By the way, I'm Lily."

Aster smiled back. "I'm Aster."

"At last we meet. How are you enjoying Bluestar?"

"So far I really like it."

"Good. Well, let me engrave this. I'll be back in just a moment."

Aster passed the time by looking at all of the little doodads at the counter. This shop was filled from front to back. And there were so many things to like.

Her gaze moved back to the red collar, but she'd found the best item. She couldn't wait until she saw Nikki's face. The girl would love it. She just hoped Sam would like it too.

♥♥♥

There wouldn't be many more summer-like days.

Sam had spent all morning out cultivating a field in order to plant his winter wheat. It was hard to believe it was already that time of the year again. It seemed like he'd just planted the spring crops. Did this quick passage of time mean he was getting old? Or was he just not taking time out of his busy schedule to appreciate the passing days?

He drove the tractor back to the old barn. It was time to take a break and grab some lunch. His stomach rumbled its agreement.

He was just making his way across the yard to the house when he noticed someone biking up the lane with a cloud of dust behind them. He wasn't expecting anyone. Maybe they were here to see Janie.

He continued on his way. He'd almost reached the house when the bike came to a stop nearby. He glanced over to find Aster waving at him. He automatically

waved.

"You're back," he said.

She walked toward him. "I hope you don't mind."

"Not at all." He surprised himself by truly meaning it. "What can I do for you?"

"Well, I was in town, doing a little window shopping, when I found something. And I just had to buy it. I hope you don't mind."

"Mind?" He was confused. Was she saying she'd bought him a gift? He wasn't sure how he felt about that. "What are we talking about?"

"Oh yes." Color flooded her cheeks as she held out a brown paper bag. "It's just a little something."

For him? He didn't know what to say. Outside of his family, he wasn't used to people buying him gifts, certainly not beautiful women.

"Go ahead." Her voice jarred him from his thoughts. "Take it."

And so, he did take it because curiosity was eating at him. What was it that she just had to buy him? And then she'd made a special trip out here to give it to him. Suddenly, he got a bad feeling about this.

He hesitated. "Um… This was thoughtful and everything but I'm not really into dating or anything."

"What?" Her eyes widened. "You think I'm hitting on you?"

"Well, um…" Did he have this wrong? He glanced down at the gift in his hand. *No.* He was pretty certain this was headed someplace he wasn't ready to go. "You did show up at my place with a gift for me."

A smile lifted the corners of her glossy pink lips. "I

think you better look inside the bag."

He held it out to her. "I don't think so."

"No. You really need to see what's in it."

It appeared she wasn't going to leave until he did as she asked. No matter what she'd bought him, he wasn't going to accept it. He didn't want to give her the wrong impression—that he was ready to start over—to move on.

He opened the bag and stared inside. At first, he wasn't sure what he was looking at. He pulled it out and the bell jingled. Then he noticed the little round nametag with Dash written on it.

Nikki came running out to him. "What's that, Daddy?"

He swallowed hard as embarrassment made him warm and uncomfortable. "It's a collar for Dash."

"Can I see it?" Nikki reached for it.

He let his daughter take the collar. Then his gaze moved to Aster. Amusement was written all over her face. How had he jumped to the wrong conclusion? It wasn't like him. Was it possible he'd been hoping she'd bought him a gift? *No.* Romance was the last thing on his mind.

"I, uh, guess I owe you an apology." He shifted his weight from one foot to the other.

"It's okay. It was rather amusing."

He grew a bit warmer. "Glad I could entertain you."

"Can we put it on Dash?" Nikki asked.

"Aren't you going to thank Aster first?"

Nikki glanced at her. "You bought this?"

Aster nodded. "I saw it when I was in town, and I

thought it might help you keep track of Dash. You know, in case he gets out again."

"I love it. Thank you." Nikki's smile beamed.

"You're welcome."

Nikki turned to her father. "Now can we put it on Dash?"

"Yes." He turned to Aster. "It was very thoughtful."

"Come on." Nikki grabbed Aster's hand and pulled her toward the goat pen.

He watched them walk away hand in hand. Nikki was talking a mile a minute while Aster was nodding and agreeing. Aster had only happened into his life a couple of days ago, and she was already fitting in. Now if he could stop from jumping to conclusions where she was concerned, maybe they'd end up being friends. The thought made him smile.

9

hat was wrong with him?

Why would he think Aster would buy him a gift?

Two days later, Sam had no answers for those questions. He'd never before jumped to such an amazingly wrong idea. Now what must Aster think of him?

None of the answers that came to him made him feel any better. In the end, he chalked it up to not getting out and socializing much.

And that was why after dropping Nikki off at dance class, he didn't rush home to do some chores until it was time to pick her up. Instead, he left his golf cart parked and began walking because everything in Bluestar was within walking distance. He turned toward The Lighthouse Café.

He'd put off putting up a new notice for a babysitter for too long. And now that Janie was about to leave for college, he couldn't afford to be as particular as he'd

been the last time he'd taken applications.

Because if he didn't have a babysitter, there was no way he could keep the farm going. And with harvest time almost upon him, he'd be busier than ever. And the thought of him letting the Bell farm fail after being entrusted to pass it on to future generations was unacceptable.

After speaking with Ethan the other day, he'd typed up a new ad and printed it out. He headed for the one place where locals always searched for news, whether it was a rental, sale items, or job listings. Maybe that had been his mistake the first time around—he'd listed the babysitter ad in the local paper. He wouldn't make that mistake again.

He stepped inside The Lighthouse Cafe and found the dinner rush was over. He moved to the bulletin board that took up most of one wall in the vestibule. The only problem was the board was crowded—very crowded.

He wasn't even sure there was a pushpin available. He scanned the edges of the board until he spotted a red one on the left side. He immediately reached for it. Who would have thought leaving a little piece of paper on the board would be so difficult?

At last he spotted a flyer for a yard sale from two weeks ago. He immediately took it down and put up his notice. Problem solved.

He was about to turn and head into the restaurant for a cup of coffee when the outer door swung open. He turned, wondering if it would be someone he knew.

"Hello." Aster smiled at him as she stepped inside. "What are you doing here?" Then she caught herself and let out a little laugh. "Of course, it's a restaurant, so you're here to eat. What I meant to say is, are you coming or going?"

It would be best to just forget the coffee and be on his way. Because there was something about being around Aster that left him feeling off kilter. But when he opened his mouth, he said, "I was just going to grab a cup of coffee. Would you like to join me?"

Her smile broadened. "I'd like that, but I just need to look over the bulletin board first."

"If you're looking for anything on the island, that board will have the information," he said.

"So I was informed." She turned and started to peruse the board.

"Maybe if you tell me what you're looking for, I can help you." It wasn't like he had anything else to do until Nikki was done with her class.

"I'm actually looking for a job." She lifted her chin in order to view the notices at the top of the board.

"A job? But I thought you were working at city hall."

"I am. But it's only part-time. At least for now. I need to find another part-time job."

"I see." The wheels in his mind started to turn. But just as quickly, he dismissed the idea of hiring her. It would never work out. "And how part-time does the position have to be?"

She shrugged. "I finish my work at city hall by lunchtime so anything after that."

Then again, maybe this was a possibility. After all, he didn't mind getting Nikki off to school in the morning. He already had the animals fed by the time

Nikki woke up. And then Aster would be able to meet Nikki after school. As he started working out the logistics of the arrangement, he stopped.

What was he doing? There was no way Aster was the right person for the job. None whatsoever. He was letting his desperation rule his thinking. That was all.

Aster scanned the board, pausing to read the few job listings. She hadn't made it to his posting—not yet. He couldn't help but wonder what she'd say when she saw it. Would babysitting even be something she was interested in?

And there was the fact that if he were to ask her, she might think he was pressuring her into wanting the job. That wasn't the case. When he hired someone, he wanted it to be someone anxious to spend time with his daughter. He needed it to be someone who would find joy in his daughter's accomplishments, cheer her up when she was feeling down, and to be present in her life for whatever hours they were at the farm.

He knew it was asking a lot. He also knew he had been lucky when he'd found Janie to babysit for him. She had been like Nikki's big sister. They did their hair together, nails together, and he'd even heard them giggle over boys once. Thankfully, his daughter still found boys to be icky. He hoped it would stay that way until at least college.

"Here's a listing." Aster's voice drew him from his thoughts. "Oh, never mind. They want morning help."

He stuffed his hands into his pockets and rocked back on his heels. "Well, I should leave you to it."

"Here's another one." Her voice rose with

anticipation. "And it's for afternoon and evening help."
She reached for the slip of paper.

He watched where her hand went to see if it was his
job listing. His muscles tensed as an inner struggle
ensued between wanting her to take the job and not
wanting her to do it. Seeing Aster's bright, cheerful
smile around the farm would be nice. But he wasn't sure
how long Aster was going to be in town. What would
happen to Nikki when she got close to Aster, and then
she left?

Her heart pitter-pattered.

Could this be the job she'd been searching for?

Aster tried to remain calm, but there was just
something about being in close proximity to Sam that
made her pulse spike. As her gaze scanned the very full
bulletin board, she had a hard time concentrating. She
felt him glancing her way.

Before she could get a closer look at the job listing,
people exited the restaurant. Aster moved out of the way
to let them through. The passersby spoke briefly to Sam
and then smiled at her before stepping through the
doorway.

She turned back to the bulletin board. Hope swelled
in her chest. The position was for a babysitter. She had a
lot of experience watching children while living in her
foster home. She reached up and pulled off a tab with the
phone number. It didn't say how much they were paying,
but she'd find out.

She turned to find Sam still standing there. His brows
were drawn together as though he were in deep thought,

but he didn't say anything.

She held up the paper tab. "I found a possible job."

"You don't mind babysitting?"

She smiled and shook her head. "Not at all. And I'm highly qualified."

She immediately pressed her lips together. She'd said too much. The smile slipped from her face. Keeping quiet about what was now her past life was harder than she'd ever imagined.

"That's good to hear," he said.

Her gaze met his. "Why is that?"

"Because that ad is mine. I'm looking for someone to watch Nikki."

"Oh. I thought you had a babysitter." She tried to recall the name Nikki had used but after meeting so many new people, names and faces were starting to get jumbled.

"Janie is leaving for college." He didn't sound happy about it. "And I need to find someone suitable as soon as possible. Maybe we should get a coffee and talk about it."

She hesitated. Perhaps this wasn't such a good idea. What if he started asking her questions about her past? What was she supposed to tell him?

She'd already made an exception with the mayor, but Darla had sworn Aster could trust him. Thankfully, Darla had been right. Tony Banks was a standup guy. But what about Sam?

A part of her said to trust him. But her brain reminded her of how that had worked out when she thought she could trust Oz. That had been the single biggest mistake of her life.

Still, this was about a job, not dating. Definitely not dating.

"That sounds like a good idea." Did it sound like a good idea? She had to admit that getting paid to spend time with Nikki definitely was a bonus. Nikki was fun and charming.

He opened the interior door for her, and she passed by him, catching a whiff of spicy cologne mingled with his own masculine scent. She may have slowed down ever so slightly and inhaled deeper this time.

Her heart fluttered in her chest. It was an odd feeling, not something she'd experienced before. And she absolutely refused to acknowledge what it might mean. She had priorities to attend to, and none of them had anything to do with having a crush on the gentleman farmer. None at all.

As she stepped into the diner, she was surprised to find so many people seated at the tables and booths. It was past the dinner rush but people seemed to like sitting and chatting over coffee and a slice of apple pie with a dollop of vanilla ice cream on top. As she glanced around, she noticed there was a lot of pie being eaten by more than half the crowd.

So far Aster had held out on trying the selections of pie that were so prominently displayed in glass domes on the counter and in the glass display case. There were apple, cherry, coconut cream, banana cream, and a couple cream pies that she didn't know the name of. It didn't matter. They all looked so delicious.

"Sam," a female voice called out. "Aster, hi."

Aster turned her head until she located Hannah waving at her. "Hi."

Hannah waved her over to the table. Aster glanced back at Sam, wondering if he would wander over. His face was devoid of expression. Aster turned back to his sister and two other women seated with her. The one woman she recognized from the craft shop where she'd purchased Dash's collar.

When she approached Hannah's table, Sam ended up behind her. "Hi, Hannah."

"Hello." Hannah's gaze moved to her brother. "Would you two like to join us?"

"Thanks," Sam said, "but I can't stay long. I have to pick up Nikki after her dance lesson." He turned to Aster. "How do you like your coffee?"

"With cream and two sugars."

He nodded and then moved to the back of the diner, where he placed the order.

Aster turned her attention back to the three ladies, who were watching him and her with amused expressions on their faces. Aster smothered a sigh. Why did everyone think when they saw two single people together that they were interested in each other? Nothing could be further from the truth where Sam and her were concerned.

Even though it was late in the day, Hannah looked bright-eyed and energetic. Or maybe that was just happiness radiating off her. "I don't think you've met Josie and Lily. Josie works at the Brass Anchor Inn and Lily owns—"

"The Lily Pad." Aster finished Hannah's sentence for

her. "I know. We've met."

"How did Dash like his new collar and bell?" Lily asked.

"As far as I know, he didn't put up a fuss."

"Wait," Hannah said. "You bought a collar for my brother's goat?"

Heat tinged Aster's cheeks. She rushed to explain how Dash had escaped. Why did everyone make a big deal of her buying the collar? It was for the goat, not for Sam.

"I, for one, think it was thoughtful," Josie said.

"Me too," echoed the other two.

She smiled at the ladies and hoped they would be good friends. Being alone in a new place, even one as nice as Bluestar, was a bit disorientating. And though she did have Darla, she still missed her friends from California—the ones she'd known for years, especially Rosa. And the only way she could think to deal with that sort of loss was to start making new friends.

"So, what are you two doing here?" Hannah's gaze flickered between her and Sam.

Heat rushed to Aster's face. "We're not together."

"Really." Hannah let the word slowly roll off her tongue.

"I stopped by to see Darla, but then Sam and I ran into each other. I was looking for a part-time job, and he came in to get a coffee." As she spoke her face grew warmer. All three of the women looked at her with bemused expressions. "It's not what you're thinking. We, um, barely know each other."

"We weren't thinking anything." Lily elbowed Josie.

Josie leaned forward. "Um, that's right. We weren't thinking anything at all."

She didn't believe them. Not at all. The best thing to do was to part ways. "I should let you all get back to your meal."

"Aster, wait," Hannah said. "I wanted to let you know that Josie and Lily will be joining us on Sunday to bake."

"That's great," Aster said. "But you should know that I don't know how much help I'll be, since I don't know how to bake."

"No worries. You'll learn." Hannah sent her a warm smile while the other women agreed.

Aster was touched that they were going out of their way to make her feel included. "I'm looking forward to it."

"I've got your coffee." Sam stopped next to Aster with two to-go-cups in his hands. When he handed her the one cup, their fingers brushed. There was this static charge that arced between them. It made all of the nerves in her body tingle and her heart beat faster. It was a feeling that she'd never experienced before.

Just as quickly as it had happened, Sam pulled his hand away. The sudden disconnect brought a sudden end to the strange sensation. Her gaze lifted to his. He didn't know what she expected. Did she want him to say something? Or did she just want confirmation that she hadn't been the only one to feel something.

But he blinked and glanced away. His gaze landed on the women seated at the table. "I should be going."

He turned and headed toward the door. What in the

world had happened? Had he changed his mind about discussing the job with her?

"Don't leave on our account," Hannah called out to her brother.

Or was he feeling uncomfortable being with her in front of his sister and her friends? She could understand that. After all, Hannah and her friends were working hard to make something more of what was going on between her and Sam than there was.

Aster turned to Hannah. "I'm sorry but I need to talk to him." And then realizing how that might sound, she clarified. "About the babysitting position."

Hannah was smiling like she knew something Aster didn't know. "Good luck. I hope you get the job."

Josie and Lily piped in their encouragement as well.

Aster rushed toward the door, hoping to catch up with Sam. She couldn't let this opportunity slip through her fingers. As she passed through the first set of doors, she noticed he wasn't in the vestibule. She kept going. Out on the sidewalk, she looked to the right. It was tough to see through the crowd of tourists, but with his six-plus-feet height, it helped him stand out. She didn't see any sign of him.

She turned her head to the left, and then she spotted his blue and white ball cap. She took off race-walking, weaving through the crowd, careful not to spill her coffee. Trying to catch up to him wasn't as easy as she'd hoped.

"Sam!" She raised her voice louder. "Sam!"

This at last got his attention. He stopped and glanced around. She waved her hand, hoping even with her five-

foot-three-inch stature that it would gain his attention.

And then she was there next to him. "I was hoping we could continue our conversation."

He glanced at his watch. "I don't have much time."

Someone bumped into her, launching her toward Sam. She quickly regained her balance but realized this was not the place to have a job interview of sorts.

"Then we'll have to make it quick. But not here. How about…" Her voice drifted away as she considered a nice place to converse. Beyond the delicious scents of garlic and onion from a nearby restaurant was the sea breeze. It beckoned to her. "Why don't we go for a walk on the beach?"

"I don't know." Just then someone bumped into him, and his coffee sloshed over onto his hand. He moved the cup to his other hand before drying his hand on his jeans. "Okay. Let's go."

And so, he set off at a fast pace. She had to take almost two steps for every one of his long strides. But she didn't complain. She kept pace with him, even if she ended up doing a little huffing and puffing. She really needed to get out and exercise more. Maybe she could try doing a couch to 5K on the beach. The idea appealed to her.

As they neared the beach, the crowd thinned out. It appeared now that the sun had sunk low in the sky, a lot of the tourists had gravitated into town for dinner and entertainment.

Side-by-side they descended the steps that led from the parking lot to the beach. Aster paused on the bottom step to slip off her tennis shoes and socks. She loved the feel of the sand beneath her feet.

They headed toward the water. She wasn't sure if she should start the conversation or wait for him to say something.

"How do you feel about crafts?" he asked.

That wasn't a question she'd been anticipating. "I like them."

"Nikki loves them. She'll try them all. She loves to work with her hands."

Oh. Now she understood the question. "No problem. We'll find some projects to work on together."

"And there might be times when you'll need to feed her. It doesn't have to be anything elaborate. Maybe a sandwich and a can of soup. Or a frozen pizza. I'll make sure there are some easy-to-make foods in the house. Will that be a problem for you?"

She shook her head. "Not at all."

"I usually work until six or seven. There will be occasions when I have to work later than that. Will that be a problem?"

"No. At this point, I don't have any other obligations."

"Perhaps I jumped too far ahead. You mentioned something about having babysitting experience."

She nodded. "I did a lot of it when I was younger."

"Are you sure you want to babysit again? I mean there are probably other things you'd rather be doing with your time."

"I would love to spend more time with Nikki. She's very sweet, and I have a feeling that life doesn't get boring with her."

He shook his head and gave a little laugh. "Life is never boring with my daughter. Before she's finished with one thing, she's onto the next. And if you do decide to take on the job, I have to warn you that the goats are a big part of her life." He paused as though gathering his thoughts. "I think in a way they've helped fill the empty spot in her life."

Aster knew he was referring to his wife's death. "I understand."

His head turned her way. "You do?"

"My parents both died when I was around Nikki's age. So, we have something in common."

"I'm sorry. That had to be rough."

"It was." She wasn't going to lie or sugar-coat it. "I lost the two most important people to me in an instant. I didn't take it well, but Nikki is fortunate to have you and your family."

He raked his fingers through his hair. "I don't know about that. Most of the time, I have absolutely no idea what I'm doing. Like thinking that teaching her to play softball would be a good idea. And then breaking the window."

"She broke the window?"

He shook his head. "No. I did that."

"Oh." A little smile pulled at her lips. "But you don't have to know what you're doing. You just have to keep showing up and trying to do your best."

He stopped walking. His gaze met hers. "Do you really believe that?"

She nodded. "If one of my parents had survived the car accident... If I had one of them to help me through that difficult period, it would have made all of the difference. You are that rock for Nikki."

Without a word, he turned and resumed walking. It was though he were absorbing her words and making sense of them.

She knew their time was limited, and she didn't want him to be late to pick up Nikki, so she circled the conversation back around to the babysitting position. They discussed some of the details, including her pay. It all sounded acceptable to her. "If you are open to the idea, I could start working tomorrow or Monday. I'm not sure. Do farmers take the weekends off?"

"It all depends on the season. I just didn't think you'd want to start working so soon."

She shrugged. "I need to find another job. Working at city hall is great and everything, but with it being a part-time job, I need to supplement my income. But you need to know that this will only be temporary. You know, until I have a full-time position at city hall."

"When do you expect that to happen?"

"Not very soon. The mayor has to justify the need for the new position, and then city council has to vote to add it to next year's budget."

He nodded. "I understand. So, you should be able to babysit until the end of the year?"

"Yes. However, I can't start working until lunchtime. Will that be a problem?"

He shook his head. "That's fine. After Labor Day, Nikki goes back to school, so you won't need to pick her up at the school until three twenty-eight. But you can't be late."

"I understand."

He was quiet for a moment as though rolling everything around in his mind. "All right. How about starting Monday at noon, we do a trial period?"

"Okay." She really wouldn't expect anything else. After all, he barely knew her. "That sounds fair to me."

"Good. How about we give it a two-week trial period, and then we'll talk again?"

She stopped walking and turned to him with her hand extended. "Shall we shake on it?"

His gaze moved to her hand and then back to her eyes. He placed his hand in hers. His large hand engulfed hers. As his grip tightened, she could feel the roughness of his calluses rub over her skin. It sent a wave of goosebumps racing up her arm.

When his gaze met hers, their connection lasted longer than was necessary. Her heart skipped a beat. She should glance away. But she couldn't move. It was as though the world faded into the background and just for a moment, it was just the two of them.

The laughter of a passing couple startled her out of the trance Sam had over her. She pulled her hand away, and she suddenly missed the warmth of his touch. She swallowed hard, hoping when she spoke, her voice didn't betray her.

Sam held out his hand. "Let me have your phone."

Her pulse accelerated. She didn't have a phone—at least not since she left L.A. "For what?"

"So, I can put my number in it." He stared at her with his brows scrunched together as though he didn't understand her worry. "What else would I do with it?"

"I… I don't know."

With his hand still outstretched, he said, "Can I have it?"

She continued to hesitate. "I don't have one."

Surprise reflected in his eyes. "You don't have a phone?"

She knew how strange that must sound in this day and age where just about every human had a mobile phone. How was she going to explain this to him without creating more questions?

"I… I lost it when I was traveling." Not exactly the truth. But then again, not exactly a lie.

"Oh. That must be rough. You know, not having immediate access to the numbers of your family."

She nodded in agreement. The truth was that she hadn't talked to her foster parents since she had turned eighteen and had been turned out on her own.

"Well, you can give me the number when you get a new one."

"Yes, I'll do that." She would eventually have to buy a new one. "I'm looking forward to Monday." She was still gazing into his dreamy blue eyes. She blinked and glanced away. That may not have come out the way she meant it. "I mean I'm looking forward to spending time with Nikki."

"And you're sure the goats won't be a problem for you?"

She shook her head. "I think Billy and Dash are starting to like me."

Sam let out a laugh. "I don't think Billy likes anyone but my daughter. But he's harmless."

They continued to walk and talk for a few more minutes. She admired Sam's due diligence where his daughter's well-being was concerned. Her first impression of him outside of the deli had been so far off target. Deep inside, he was warm and caring. Not that she was thinking of starting anything with him.

10

ad he done the right thing?

Sam had been questioning his decision to hire Aster ever since they'd parted on the beach. He'd called Darla for a reference and character check. Darla couldn't say enough good things about Aster.

He'd been so picky about hiring a babysitter for so long and all of a sudden, he picked someone he didn't know all that well. Or did he know her better than he was willing to admit? He recalled that day when they were picking apples. And then he thought about their conversation while they were walking on the beach.

He didn't know what it was about Aster, but it was like he'd known her much longer. Or maybe he was a lot lonelier for adult companionship than he was willing to admit.

"I'm so excited." The happy lilt of his daughter's voice was a welcome distraction.

He glanced at the clock on the wall above the kitchen sink. Aster should have been there by then. Maybe she

was having a problem finding the house. No, because she was there before. Maybe she had to walk from town. Still, it wasn't far. He wasn't sure what was keeping her, but he hoped she wouldn't be much longer. He had a lot to do this afternoon.

Nikki finished the last of her peanut butter and grape jelly sandwich with the crusts cut off. She was about to get up from the table when he glanced over to make sure she'd finished her lunch.

"Don't forget to eat your grapes. And finish your glass of milk."

"Oh, yeah. I forgot." She scooted up to the table and popped a green grape into her mouth. "I can't wait until Aster gets here. We can go out and see Dash."

He didn't know about Aster's willingness to visit the goats, but he did know they were going to have a talk about punctuality. This was unacceptable. Maybe she had forgotten this was her first day to babysit. Maybe she had to work late. Even so, she should have called.

He reached for his phone to call her but then realized he didn't have any way to contact her. He would remedy that as soon as she got there…if she got there.

He moved to the kitchen sink and started cleaning off the dishes and placing them in the dishwasher. There weren't many, just a couple of bowls and a bunch of utensils.

Once the dishes were placed in the dishwasher, he wiped off the counters and the table. He was getting anxious to get outside. This nice weather was supposed to turn rainy later in the week, and he wanted to get as much tractoring done as he could before that happened.

He checked the clock again. She was now sixteen minutes late. He glanced out the window, down their long driveway. There was still no sign of her. She wasn't the first babysitter to bail on him. He didn't know why he thought Aster would be different—why he thought she'd actually connected with his daughter. Obviously, he'd been all wrong about it.

"I'm just going to call Gran and see if she can come."

Nikki marched up to him and crossed her arms. She frowned up at him. "Aster's coming. You just have to wait."

He glanced at the clock again. And then he observed the sad expression on his daughter's face.

He felt bad for her. She had a big heart and wanted to believe in people. He subdued his frustration. "Maybe something came up and she can't make it."

"She'll be here. You'll see."

He sighed. Nikki wasn't going to let this go. She really wanted Aster to show up. "Okay, we'll give her five more minutes, and then I'm calling Gran."

He just hoped if Aster showed up that she had a really good excuse for worrying Nikki. And then he was letting her go. He needed someone reliable.

Things were working out.

Aster smiled as she quickly pedaled Darla's powder-blue bike toward the Bell farm. She had to admit that in the beginning she'd worried about taking the job and spending so much time around the gentleman farmer who made her heart beat quickly.

But she realized the error of her thoughts. Sam was going to be out working the farm when she was there. She'd hardly spend any time around him. The thought should have made her feel better but it didn't.

There was a movement out of the corner of her eye.

A blur of reddish-brown fur ran right in front of her.

Aster squeezed the brakes.

Her heart slammed into her ribs. The animal stopped and looked at her. She tightened her grip on the brakes. She yanked the handles to the right. The front tire dropped from the pavement.

Aster was tossed from the bike.

Her hands and knees took the brunt of the fall. The ground was hard and rocky. When she caught her breath, she turned over and sat there for a moment, making sure she hadn't broken anything.

Other than scraping her palms and being a bit dirty, she was all right. She got to her feet and dusted herself off.

This couldn't be happening.

She righted the bike and crouched down on the side of the road. Her stoved fingers fiddled with the bike chain but no matter what she did, she couldn't get the gears to move so that she could hook the chain back over the gear attached to the pedals.

A gust of wind rushed past her, sweeping her hair into her face. She swept aside the loose strands. Sam was going to think she'd forgotten about their arrangement. Or worse, he was going to think she didn't want the job. Neither were at all correct.

She only had one option—to walk. Quickly. Very

quickly.

And so, that's what she did. She ignored the throbbing in her right knee. With grease all over her fingers and bloody cuts on her palms, she began pushing the bike. Thankfully there wasn't far to go.

And to think that not long ago, she'd thought this was a good day—a pretty great day in fact. That morning when the mayor mentioned he'd wanted a special event for the Labor Day picnic—something that would draw the island's residents together—he'd tasked Aster with coming up with that special something.

She'd organized a lot of events back at the college where she'd worked but most of those had taken money. The mayor had specified that whatever she came up with would have to be free—free to the participants and free to the town.

She'd immediately started scouring the internet for something that could be set up on short notice and wouldn't cost anything. And then she'd recalled her walks around town, hoping she'd have noticed something that would help her. It was after searching her memories that she stumbled across her last talk with Sam on the beach. He'd said something that had stuck with her.

He had been trying to teach his daughter to throw a ball when he broke the window. That was it. They could have a ball toss tent to knock over pop bottles. But would that bring the people together? Not really.

But what if she went with something more basic? What if she went with a softball tournament? It could be a slow-pitch game so most anyone could play. And those who couldn't or wouldn't play could cheer on the players. After all, there were three baseball diamonds at the far end of Beachcomber Park, and she was certain she could round up some bats and balls. The teams didn't have to wear uniforms. They could arrange to wear certain colors. The more she thought about it, the more she liked the idea. But with it being so close to Labor Day, did she have enough time to get people to sign up? She hoped so.

She'd run the idea past the mayor, who in the end loved the idea. But he, too, had worries about whether there was enough time for the sign-up. And so, she'd printed out sign-up forms and distributed them throughout Bluestar at all of the local businesses. She'd collect them on Friday and hope they had enough people to make up a few teams.

She kept walking as fast as she could. At last she spotted the cute cow mailbox with the little black tail fluttering in the breeze. One thing she'd noticed about the island, it was almost always windy. Sometimes it was gentle but once in a while, it was quite gusty. She knew she'd never again smell the salty ocean breeze without thinking of Bluestar Island.

She turned onto the driveway. It was rough with stone chips and potholes. Still, she kept pushing Darla's bike. Not only had she broken it but now she was going to have to repair it, and she'd most likely lose her new job. All in all, it was turning out to be an awful day, even if the bright sun and puffy white clouds begged to differ with her.

Before she made it the whole way to the house, Nikki

came barreling out the door, letting the screen door swing shut with a loud whack-whack. "Aster, you're here!"

She couldn't help but smile. Nikki was so enthusiastic as she ran up to her with a great big smile. "I'm sorry I'm late."

"Daddy isn't happy. What happened to you?"

"I had a little accident. My bike, well my friend's bike, broke on the way here. I tried to fix it but I couldn't do it."

Nikki's eyes widened as she took in Aster's disheveled appearance. "Are you all right?"

Aster sent her young friend a reassuring smile. "I'll be fine."

"Oh." Nikki stepped up beside her. "Come on. Daddy's waiting."

They walked together to the back of the house, where Sam stepped out on the back porch. He was frowning as he crossed his arms. This wasn't the first time she'd seen him angry. But she had the distinct feeling it would be the last time because she was about to be fired before she'd even had a chance to start the job.

He arched a brow but he didn't say anything. Somehow that made everything feel even worse. It would be better if he just got his feelings off his chest and told her that she was fired.

"I'm so sorry I'm late," she said. "I had a bike problem."

"She wrecked," Nikki said. "Look at the chain. It's just hanging there. And...and I think she's hurt."

For a second, Sam's gaze diverted from her to the

bike. But then he was back staring directly at her, making her feel like she was back in a foster home, being disciplined for breaking curfew or for not doing the dishes exactly as they'd wanted. Sometimes it was her fault and sometimes they just looked for things to blame on her—at least it was the way it had felt.

But she wasn't that little girl anymore—the one who didn't have anywhere else to go and was stuck dealing with a crappy situation. No, she'd grown up and she could make choices. And she chose not to have him look at her with disapproval reflected in his eyes.

"Listen," she said, "I'm fine. I will understand if you want me to go—"

"No!" Nikki tugged at her arm. "You have to stay. You have to see Dash wearing his new collar. He really likes it."

She glanced down at the little girl. "I'm so sorry this didn't work out. I should go."

"Don't." Tears gathered in the girl's eyes.

Guilt stabbed at Aster's heart as she knew she was responsible for those tears. And she would have to live with that. Sam had expected perfection, and she was so far from perfect. It was best that things ended there.

She turned the bike around as Nikki begged her not to go. She'd just started to walk away when she heard Sam call out to her.

"Wait. You don't have to go."

She knew it was better for her if she just kept going. She knew sooner or later she would disappoint him. But she also knew there was a little girl counting on her to stay and keep her word.

In that moment, it didn't matter what she felt or what she wanted, she was going to do what she thought was best for Nikki. And right then, Nikki needed to know that people wouldn't let her down.

Aster straightened her shoulders and turned back to Sam. "Are you sure?"

He made his way down the steps and approached her. "It's what Nikki wants." When he reached out to her, she stepped back. "Hold still. You have some grease on your face." His fingers brushed over her forehead. "There that's better. Now let's see your hands."

She did as he said. Her palms faced down. He took her wrists and drew her closer for a better look.

By then her heart was beating so fast and loud she could barely hear her own thoughts. "I, uh, got grease on my hands when I was trying to fix the chain."

He turned her hands over. Angry red cuts marred her palms. They burned more now than they had right after the accident.

"We need to get these cuts cleaned up. Come on." He let go of her as he started toward the house. "Nikki, can you run upstairs and grab the first aid kit from the bathroom?"

Nikki ran ahead of them.

"You really don't have to do this," she said.

"Of course I do." He showed her inside the house and over to the kitchen sink, where he started to gently clean her wounds. "So, what happened?"

She tried to focus on the conversation and not the sensations zinging through her body from his touch. His hands were rough and callused from the many hours

working on the farm, but his touch was light. He was being so caring and kind. In that moment, it'd be so easy to fall for him. But she couldn't do that.

She swallowed hard. "Something stepped into the road in front of me. I think it was a fox. Or maybe a dog with a long tail."

"There are a few foxes in the area."

She was glad to know that she hadn't been imagining things. "I swerved to miss it and this is what happened."

"Are you hurt anywhere else?"

"My knees. But they're just bruised."

After her wounds were cleaned, medicated, and the deepest cuts bandaged, she felt better. "Thank you."

"You're welcome." At last he smiled at her. "But you really do need a cell phone in case of emergencies.

"I agree." It had moved to the top of her list of things to do.

"You'll stay now, right?" Nikki gripped her hands together. "Please."

Her gaze moved to Sam. He nodded. So, they were both going to try to make this arrangement work for the same exact reason—it was what Nikki wanted.

How could anyone possibly turn her down? "Yes. I'll stay."

"Yay!" Nikki bounced up and down on the balls of her feet.

"I'll be working in the barn this afternoon if you need anything."

"We won't," Aster said a little too quickly. "I mean, we'll be fine."

"Yeah, Daddy, we'll be fine." Nikki went to take her

hand and hesitated as though not wanting to hurt her. "Let's go see the goats."

Aster hesitated. "I should do something with my bike."

"I'll take care of it," Sam said.

"You don't have to. You've already done enough."

He turned to Nikki. "Let Aster rest for a bit."

"Oh. Okay." Nikki's brow scrunched up as though she were in deep thought. "We could watch a movie."

"That sounds nice." Aster smiled at the girl.

As she turned to go into the living room with Nikki, she knew this arrangement wasn't going to work out. Though Sam had his good points, especially his devotion to his daughter, he also had expectations of the way things should be, and he didn't leave much room for flexibility. She wasn't like that. She wasn't rigid.

Or maybe she was just making up with excuses to keep her distance from the handsome farmer who made her heart race every time he was close to her. She stifled a sigh. She was so confused.

11

hings were definitely looking up.

A couple of days later, Aster was surprised to find the arrangement with Sam was going quite well. In fact, the first day he'd taken the time to fix her borrowed bike. She had been surprised by the kind gesture. He'd lubricated the gears, greased the chain, and had it all ready for her when it was time for her to leave.

But the closer they became, the more she worried about her scar. As hard as she worked each morning to temporarily erase it with makeup, she worried that the more time they spent together and the closer they got, he'd notice her disfigurement.

Did it make her vain that she wanted to be seen the way she used to be—before a broken shard of glass from her assault had slashed her face. Lucky for her—was lucky even the right word—she'd moved her head and Oz had cut down her jaw. She was certain he'd have done worse if the police hadn't pulled the monster off her battered and broken body.

But if Sam had noticed her scar, he hadn't let on. As such, the more time that passed, the more comfortable she became around him.

Maybe this babysitting job was going to work out after all. She hoped so because she was really fond of Nikki. She was a ball of energy and always had a smile to share. And in some ways, she did remind Aster of herself.

Aster had let Sam know that she was going to be a little late. Since she'd received her first pay check, she needed to stop in town while the shops were still open to pick up a phone. As most of the stores closed at five, she needed to do it before heading out to the farm.

And she immediately found what she wanted. With a phone in hand, the first person she thought of was her landlord, Rosa Vega. She missed her friend dearly and she'd promised that she would let her know when she was settled and safe.

Although when she'd made that promise she hadn't thought of the danger it might put Rosa in with Oz. But maybe she was letting her imagination get the better of her. Would Oz really take the time and effort to track her down across the country?

His threat echoed in her mind. But he'd only meant to scare her. Hadn't he? After all, he had bigger problems than her since he'd been sentenced to house arrest. She had months until she had to worry about him.

And she did know Rosa's landline number by heart. Back when she'd still lived in California, she'd called it many times to ask her if she needed something from the grocery store or to let her know when she would be late after work. They'd watched out for each other.

Aster made her way to one of the benches lining Main Street. Once she had the phone activated, she punched in Rosa's number. The phone rang and rang. Rosa didn't move as fast as she used to—her words, not Aster's—and she figured if it was important, the caller would wait for her.

Ring. Ring. Ring.

Eventually the line was picked up. "Hello."

A big smile pulled at Aster's lips at the sound of her dear friend's voice. "Rosa, it's me."

There was a moment of silence. "Charlotte, is it you?"

Aster paused. It seemed like forever since anyone had used her given name. "It's me. How are you?"

"I'm fine. But it's you I'm worried about. Are you safe?"

Aster nodded but then realizing Rosa couldn't see her, she said, "I am. I've found a great place to stay."

"It sounds noisy there. Is it noisy?"

Aster smiled. Her friend had finally gotten some hearing aids. "I'm sitting along a busy street. I'm on my way to a new job."

"I'm so glad you called. I've been so worried about you."

Rosa was the first person in Aster's life since her parents' deaths to worry about her—truly care about her welfare for no other reason than she meant something to her. The breath caught in Aster's throat as unshed tears gathered in her eyes. She blinked them away and took a deep breath followed by another one.

Aster cleared her throat and went on to fill Rosa in on the generalities of her new life. She didn't want to give Rosa too much information just in case Oz gave Rosa a hard time.

Their talk went by far too fast as Aster reminded Rosa to make sure and go for a walk each day and to make sure she checked her calendar so she didn't forget any of her doctor appointments.

In that moment, she realized that not only had Oz physically hurt her and made her doubt herself, but he'd also taken away something, or rather someone, very precious from her life. Her heart ached. Rosa had been so much more than a landlord and neighbor.

Aster realized how Rosa had become her family and she hers as neither of them had anyone else. If she could have, she would have brought Rosa with her. But not sure where she would end up living or how long she'd be able to stay, she'd given up on the notion.

"I need to make this short." Aster tried to hide the emotion in her voice. She didn't want to hang up. It was the very last thing she wanted to do. "Make sure you don't mention this conversation to anyone. As far as you know, I skipped town one night. All right?"

"Yes, dear. But please promise that I'll hear from you again. I couldn't bear it if we never spoke."

"I promise." She knew the promise would put them both in more danger.

"And that I'll see you again someday." Rosa's voice cracked with emotion.

The tears splashed onto Aster's cheeks. "I promise." She didn't know how she'd make that happen, but

she'd learned a long time ago that if there was a will, there was a way.

"I love you." Rosa let out a muffled cry.

This time Aster didn't even try to hide her emotion. "I love you too."

Aster reluctantly disconnected the call. She swiped the tears from her cheeks and then started down the sidewalk. She had a happy little girl awaiting her. And she was so thankful because she needed a distraction. A big distraction.

12

The holiday weekend was almost upon them.

It was Thursday afternoon, and Aster was at the Bell farm. She could see when she arrived that Sam was having problems staying on top of everything. She felt sorry for him.

She couldn't imagine how hard it must be for him to run the farm, the house, and be a single father to an active seven-year-old. And yet he didn't complain. He just kept on trying his best.

Though it wasn't part of her responsibilities, she started the laundry for him. It wasn't a lot but it was something.

"What would you like to do today?" Aster joined Nikki at the kitchen table.

Nikki shrugged her slim shoulders. "I don't know. I wish Daddy didn't have to work."

"It's important. This is a big farm and there's a lot to do."

"Is that why you're here?"

Aster nodded. "Is that a problem?"

Nikki shook her head and then she smiled. "I like having you around. You're fun."

"I am?" She wasn't used to being called fun. For so long she'd been serious about her education and then her job. But Nikki reminded her that there was more to life than work.

Nikki's smile broadened as she nodded. "You always think of things for us to do."

It was true. She did work hard to think of activities, but last night she'd been so tired after her repeated attempts to bake cookies with the aid of an online video that she'd stumbled into bed and fell asleep with her clothes on. There hadn't been any time for her to do an internet search for ideas.

"How about today we do something different?"

"What does that mean?"

"How about you come up with something for us to do?" She wanted to know what interested Nikki.

She held up her palms. "I don't know. We could play with my dolls."

They'd done that yesterday and the day before. It was time for a change. Her gaze moved to the window. The September sun was shining brightly, and there was a light breeze fluttering the leaves in the tree.

"I was thinking maybe we could do something outside."

"We could play with the goats."

Play with the goats? Aster wasn't so sure that was possible or what it would look like. And though she had warmed up to Dash, she was still hesitant about the other goats, most especially Billy. He had this way of looking at her like she was the enemy. She didn't think he was ever going to like her.

It appeared Nikki was going to need some help thinking of some activities for them. "What sort of fun things do you do with your father?"

"Feed the goats."

"What else?"

"Pick apples."

That was fun? Okay. "What else? Maybe something you haven't done for a long time. Think really hard."

"He showed me how to make paper boats."

This was more like it. "And what did you do with the boats?"

"We took them to the beach and let them sail in the water." Her eyes twinkled with excitement. "Could we go to the beach?"

"I don't know." She hadn't talked about it with Sam. And at that moment, he was out on the tractor. "We would need to talk to your father."

"He'll let us. He likes the beach. I'll go get the paper." Before Aster could say a word, Nikki ran out of the kitchen. Her little feet stomped up the stairs. And then her footsteps could be heard overhead as she ran into her bedroom.

It looked like they were making paper boats. She just hoped Sam would like the idea and agree to let them go sail them. He would, wouldn't he?

Aster had her phone out and was searching for instructions on how to construct a paper boat when Nikki returned with a big box of crayons in one hand and colorful construction paper in the other hand.

"What's all of that?" Aster slipped her phone back into her pocket.

"It's what we need to make the boat. The last time Daddy and I made them, mine floated longer."

"That's great. Are you going to share your secret?"

"Crayons. Daddy says that it keeps the boats afloat longer. I must have colored mine better than him."

"That's wonderful. You must be very artistic."

Nikki shrugged. "Not really. I just like to color a lot."

Aster nodded in understanding. "I've never made a paper boat before, at least not that I can remember so would you mind if I use the instructions on my phone?"

Nikki shook her head. "I can't remember exactly how you put it together. I just remember about the crayons because I colored faster than Daddy." Then her nose crinkled in revulsion. "And he colored his black. Yuck!"

Aster laughed at the girl's horrified expression. She made a mental note not to use the black crayon on her boat.

"Okay." Aster read the instructions on her phone. "The first thing we should do is color the paper. It doesn't say if we should color one side or both." She looked at Nikki, who already had a pink crayon out of the box. "What do you think?"

She shrugged. "I can color both. I'm fast."

"Is that a challenge?" She noticed that Nikki excelled when it came to challenges.

Nikki swiped her crayon across the paper. Her hand moved back and forth quickly. "I'm going to finish first."

Aster grabbed a peach crayon and started coloring. "Not unless I catch you."

And so, they carried on coloring one side and then the other. Aster had forgotten how much she loved to color. There was just something so relaxing about it. Or maybe it was being there in that big old farmhouse that just oozed with a warm, comfy aura.

She wondered if that was part of the reason Sam struggled so hard to hang onto the place. What he needed was some help—more than a babysitter. He needed farm hands to help him with everything.

But since she couldn't help him with any of the big stuff, she decided to help him with the relaxing part. And as soon as her paper was colored, she would put the rest of her plan in motion.

♥♥♥

Sam had a long day.

All he wanted to do was shower, have a nice dinner, and sit in his favorite chair in front of the television. It was such a tempting thought, but he knew it wasn't going to happen because as soon as he stepped in the door, he needed to start the laundry. It was stacking up and soon he'd be out of clean underwear. The thought had him hurrying toward the house. The sooner the laundry was started, the sooner he could get a hot shower to ease the sore muscles in his neck. And then it'd be time to start dinner.

He stepped in the back door into the mud room, where the washer and dryer were kept, and he found the dryer was already running. That was odd because the

housework wasn't part of Aster's duties. He couldn't help but wonder if there had been some sort of accident in the house that she was cleaning up.

And then he noticed not one but two baskets of fresh laundry, all folded and ready to be taken upstairs. What had prompted this very kind gesture?

He yanked off his boots and socks. "Aster?"

"In here." Her voice came from the kitchen.

It was then that he inhaled the scent of… Wait. Was that fried chicken? He inhaled again. Sure smelled like it. He hadn't had home-cooked fried chicken since Beth. His heart clenched as though it were trying to fill that empty spot that Beth had left. But he noticed it didn't hurt quite as much as it used to.

He stepped into the kitchen and found Nikki sitting at the table while Aster stood at the stove. "What's going on?"

Nikki's face lit up. "You have to get showered, Daddy. Hurry."

"Hurry? Why?"

Nikki huffed. "It's a surprise and you're going to ruin it."

A surprise that didn't include him cooking dinner was fine by him. He wasn't about to argue. "Okay. I'm off to the shower."

Aster stirred something in a pot. "I hope you don't mind that I started the laundry for you."

"Uh, no. Thanks. I was planning to get to it this evening." He glanced past her to the steaming pot on the stove. "I don't know what you're making, but it sure smells good."

"Let's just hope I don't burn it. I called your sister, and she assured me this was pretty easy to make."

"You called my sister? You mean Hannah?" Since when had Aster and his sister become such good friends? It was apparent that he was missing a lot, which wasn't surprising since he'd been in the fields a lot lately.

Aster nodded. "She's going to show me how to bake. Well, you know, some easy stuff."

Before he could ask her more about this friendship, Nikki said, "Daddy hurry. We have to get going."

"Get going? Where?" So, there was more to this surprise than clean clothes and a home-cooked meal. He was intrigued.

"Daddy, it's a surprise."

"Okay. I'm off." He made his way to the stairs.

Step by step, he couldn't help but think of how good it felt to come in from a hard day's work to find his two favorite ladies waiting for him. He found himself smiling as he grabbed some clean clothes and headed for the shower.

What else did they have planned for this evening? Whatever it was he had a feeling that he'd enjoy it. Very much so.

A picnic at the beach.

This was the sort of stuff that movies were made of. At least that's what Aster had always thought because who took time out of their busy day to do something so frivolous?

Was it frivolous? The old Aster would have thought so, but the new Aster was learning there was so much more to life than her career. Did she love what she did for a living? Absolutely. Being paid to organize events to make people happy was amazing.

But having a personal life—a family—was equally important. She'd watched Sam this past week. It didn't matter how long he'd worked. When he came through the doorway at the end of the day, his face lit up when he spoke to Nikki. And no matter how tired he was, he made time for his daughter. That was love.

It was something that was missing from her life. She'd found it for a time with Rosa. They'd become family. But that connection had been stolen away. She hoped someday to get it back.

They spread a big blanket on the sand as the sinking sun reflected off the sea water. They each wore a light jacket because now that autumn was close, evenings were a bit on the cool side. But it didn't stop them from enjoying each other's company.

And surprisingly, dinner hadn't turned out so bad.

Oh, who was she kidding? This was the best meal she'd ever prepared. Aster smiled proudly. And she hadn't burned a thing. Although, the macaroni and cheese was a little overcooked and mushy. And the baked chicken was a little dried out. Still, she was going to call this a victory because it was all edible. And best of all, Sam had eaten everything on his plate and he'd asked for seconds. That was the highest praise she could hope for.

"It's time." Nikki clapped her hands together as she smiled brightly. "Let's sail our boats. Come on, Daddy."

"I don't have a boat," Sam said. "But I'll gladly

watch both of yours."

"Yes, you do." Nikki moved to the smallish box where they'd put their boats for safe keeping. She took off the lid and removed the boat they'd both worked on for Sam. Nikki rushed back to him and held out the boat. "Here you go."

"Nikki says your favorite color is black," Aster said.

He nodded. "It's all of the colors combined."

"I don't know about that, but we compromised on the colors," Aster said.

"I used the black crayon," Nikki said.

"And I used the blue." Aster watched as he examined the paper boat with wide stripes of black and blue.

Nikki rushed back to the box. She withdrew her pink one and Aster's peach and aqua boat. They took off their shoes and rolled up their jeans. Then they carried their boats to the water's edge where they placed them in the water—each giving theirs a little push.

The three of them stepped back. They quietly watched as the little boats weaved and bobbed against the breeze. As the water rushed on shore, it swept over their bare feet. The boats drifted toward them before being pulled farther out to sea.

There wasn't anything particularly astonishing about the moment. In the grand scheme of things, it was a rather mundane thing to do. And yet Aster knew she would always remember this day.

There was something so peaceful, so touching, about watching their three paper boats gliding over the top of the water with the last of the sun's rays splashing over the surface. She wondered if she was the only one who was touched by this moment. She was probably overthinking things and letting herself get a bit too sentimental.

But then Sam's fingers brushed over hers. At first she thought the touch had been accidental. But then his fingers slid down over hers until their palms touched. Then his fingers slipped between hers, lacing them together. He gave her hand a gentle squeeze.

Her heart pitter-pattered in her chest. And for a moment, she didn't question his action. She just took in the tranquility of the moment and savored it. If a slice of life could be deemed perfect, it was then. And she didn't want this day to end.

Her gaze lowered to their entwined fingers. She found a strength in that union. Maybe she should tell him about Oz. What would he think? What would he say?

"It's sinking!" Nikki rushed toward the boats.

Sam let go of Aster's hand. Her fingers remained outstretched as though longing for the return of his touch. But as Sam followed his daughter into the tide water, the distance between him and Aster lengthened.

And just like that the moment was gone—washed out to sea—never to be captured again. Or maybe it was never meant to be their moment. A disappointed sigh slipped past her lips and was carried away in the breeze.

1 3

ad that really happened?

Aster had been asking herself that since her moment with Sam at the water's edge. Her heart skipped a beat at the special memory. The touch of two hands—the entwine of fingers—the beginning of something?

Aster's breath hitched. Was it the start of something? Did she want it to be the beginning of something? She didn't have an answer for those questions.

She was making too much of things. Sam just got caught up in the moment. Right?

Aster exhaled. It wasn't like Sam had acted any differently toward her the rest of the evening. It had been an innocent moment. Nothing more.

And now she had to concentrate on her work. Because today she would learn if there was enough public interest in having a softball tournament. There would be lots of signups, wouldn't there?

She really needed this to go well. She needed to prove that her position at city hall was useful. If not, she'd have to consider leaving the island.

"Good morning, Aster." Mayor Banks stopped next to her desk, drawing her from her meandering thoughts. "How's your special project for this weekend coming?"

"I checked with the parks and rec department, and they have all of the equipment we'll need for the tournament. The sporting goods store offered to donate a trophy for the event."

"I like it. We can engrave the winning team's name each year—well, if we get enough interest. What are we doing for team names?"

"Since we don't have money for uniforms, I was thinking we'd just assign colors to each team and they could wear a shirt in that color."

He ran his fingers over his clean-shaven jaw. "I like the idea. It would be better if we could afford to order shirts but the budget just won't allow it. Now about the names?"

"I was thinking we'd name the teams after the color of their shirts. Just to keep things simple since there won't be any sponsors."

"So, the orange team and the red team?"

She nodded. "I'm hoping we'll have enough sign-ups to make four teams."

"When will you know?"

"This morning." She checked the time. "The businesses should be opening right now. I'm about to head out and collect the sign-up forms."

He nodded. "Good. Make sure and add me to the list." He arched a brow. "Did you pass a sign-up sheet around city hall?"

She inwardly groaned. "I hadn't thought of it. I'll just print one out."

"I'll make sure it's passed around while you are out collecting the other forms. I'm thinking we'll have enough people for at least four teams."

She handed over the sheet to him. "I hope so."

And then she set off, visiting all of the shops on Main Street from Hamming It Up Deli to The Elegant Bakery to the other side of town at Sea Gems Jewelry. At each stop, she was thrilled to find signatures and contact information on each form. Some forms had more sign-ups and others had less, but every single sheet had at least one name on it. And that was just the businesses on Main Street. She still had other shops to visit.

It was closing in on the lunch hour by the time she'd rounded up all of the forms. She headed back to her desk with a smile on her face.

"Aster, wait up." The mayor strode toward her with another sign-up form in hand. "Here you go."

"Thank you." She beamed at him.

"I take it there's a lot of interest."

She smiled and nodded. "All of the forms have at least one signature on them."

"Great. Now are you sure you don't mind working on this tonight and tomorrow?"

"I don't mind. I can't work on it until after dinner, but I'll get it done."

"Next year we'll arrange it with more advance notice. Just let me know your hours and I'll make sure you get paid."

"Thank you. I appreciate it."

"Then I'll leave you to it."

Aster couldn't stop smiling. Things were really starting to look up. The only thing that would make it better was if Rosa was there on Bluestar. Her friend loved to watch baseball on television. She'd love to cheer on the teams in the softball tournament.

Thinking of her dear friend made Aster homesick. It was funny how she was fine for a time. Then something would remind her of home, and she got that uneasy feeling in the pit of her stomach. In her mind, she'd walk through her old apartment. She could envision her tiny kitchen with the small window above the kitchen sink. The window had a small ledge where she kept a couple of silk plants. They were the only kind she could keep alive.

And then she imagined going down the exterior steps and knocking on Rosa's door before letting herself inside. Everything in Rosa's place was older, but it gave the place a homey charm. Aster couldn't even count the number of hours she'd sat at Rosa's kitchen table. Sometimes she'd help with dinner, and other times they'd play cards.

She worried about Rosa all alone in California. Maybe later she'd call her again just to make sure she was doing okay and staying on top of her doctor appointments. After all, what were the chances that Oz would bother her?

Aster pulled out her new phone and dialed the familiar number. And just like before it rang and rang.

"Hello."

Tears gathered in Aster's eyes at the sound of her

dear friend. "Rosa, it's me."

"Is something wrong? Did he find you?" Worry laced Rosa's voice.

"No. I'm fine."

"But you weren't going to call again."

"I know. And I probably shouldn't have but I got to thinking about you and missing home." Her voice wobbled as her emotions bubbled up.

"I miss you too. I wish I could be there with you."

"You'd love it here." Aster stopped herself before she revealed her exact location. She swallowed hard. "How are you doing? Are you still going to bingo every week?"

They chatted for a little while about nothing in particular. It was just so good to hear Rosa's voice. Maybe in a year or so, when she was certain Oz had moved on and forgot about her, she could go back and visit her dear friend. She clung to the wish, as it was the only thing that could quell her homesickness.

This was working out.

Sam hadn't been sure about hiring Aster in the beginning. After all, she was new to the island and new to him. But all he had to do was see her with Nikki to know he'd made the right decision.

It was a different relationship than Nikki had with Janie. Nikki looked up to Aster. And Aster worked hard to not only keep Nikki entertained but also to teach her things—small things such as helping with chores.

At first, he found himself looking for all of the reasons this arrangement wouldn't work out. Other than

the problem with her bike and being late for work on her first day, he hadn't been able to find a reason to let Aster go. She'd brought a happiness to the house that it'd been lacking since Beth died.

Aster had gone above and beyond the work he requested of her. And she didn't expect anything in return. And maybe that was what he and Nikki needed right then—a helping hand. It allowed him to stay focused.

If he could get through this year... If he could have a good crop... If the prices held... Then next year would look better. Next year he would be able to rebuild the new barn. Next year he could hire help for the farm so he could spend more time with Nikki. They just had to get through the rest of this year without any other big incidents.

And if Aster were to stay on... His thoughts spiraled back to their picnic on the beach. The memory of looking at her smile as the ocean breeze played with the short strands of her hair made his heart beat faster—in a way it hadn't in a long time.

He refused to acknowledge that he'd felt anything when their hands had touched. It was just a friendly gesture—a thank you for making such a magical evening for him and his daughter. It was nothing more.

After all, it wasn't like he was planning to move on. He was still too busy blaming himself for his wife's unfortunate death. How was he supposed to move beyond that?

He shoved the troubling thoughts to the back of his mind because there was no banishing them. The memories of how his beautiful family had fractured and broken one sunny afternoon was always lurking at the edge of his thoughts.

Whack-whack.

The sound of the screen door closing alerted him to Aster's arrival. He needed to have a word with her. He approached her in the kitchen. She had a stack of papers in her arm.

"What's all of that?"

"What?" She looked a bit flustered. And then she followed his gaze to the papers. "Oh. These are sign-ups for the softball tournament this weekend." Then her eyes widened. "Would you like to sign up?"

He shook his head. "I don't have time for that."

"But surely you're coming to the picnic, right?"

"We have to go to the picnic." Nikki rushed into the kitchen, looking all sorts of energetic. "I love picnics."

"You're going with your grandmother," he said. "I have to work."

"But it's a holiday." Nikki's bottom lip stuck out just the way Beth's used to do when she was trying to talk him into skipping out on work to go have dinner with his family.

And the very last thing he wanted to do was disappoint his daughter, but he knew if he didn't keep pushing, the chance of losing the farm increased. And he couldn't let that happen.

He knelt down in front of his daughter. "I'm sorry but I promise I'll be there next year. This year I have to work on clearing some of the older fields and getting them ready for fall planting."

Nikki crossed her arms as dark clouds of anger gathered in her eyes. "You're always too busy."

"Nikki, you don't understand—"

She turned and ran for the steps that led to her bedroom. Her feet stomped up the steps.

"Nikki!" He sighed as he raked his fingers through his hair. "Nikki, come back."

He took off after his daughter but she was too fast. Before his foot hit the second step, there was a slam of the bedroom door. That wasn't going to stop him. It wouldn't be the first time he'd had to speak through a closed door.

When he reached her bedroom, he paused. He drew in a deep breath and then blew it out. He needed to do better. But what did better look like? Spending more time with his daughter at the expense of the farm? Or hoping his daughter would forgive him for working hard to turn things around and save the only home she'd ever known?

He raked his fingers through his hair. This was one of the times when he needed Beth. She would know what to do—the right words to say. He missed her soothing ways and her knack for soothing their daughter.

But now, there was just him. He couldn't stop trying to get through to his daughter because he loved her like crazy. She was his baby girl.

He rapped his knuckled gently on the door. "Nikki?"

"Go away!"

"Nikki, please. I want to talk."

"No!"

"Nikki, honey, you don't understand."

Jennifer Faye

"You have to work. I got it."

"It's important or I wouldn't miss the picnic. I..." He struggled to find the right words. "I'm sorry."

Silence.

He tried the doorknob but it was locked. This wasn't the first time she'd shut him out. He consoled himself with the knowledge that when she calmed down, things would go back to normal. Thankfully she didn't hold grudges.

With a deep sigh and a heavy heart, he walked away. He had to get better at this parenting stuff or they would never make it through her teenage years. And he didn't even want to imagine what that would be like when she started dating. He banished the thought from his mind. One problem at a time.

When he re-entered the kitchen, Aster said, "Just give her a little time. She's been so excited about the picnic. It's all she's talked about this week. And I think she's a little nervous about going back to school."

"Nervous? About what?"

Aster shrugged. "Fitting in. Doing her best. Who knows? School isn't always the easiest. But Nikki is so easy to like that I'm sure when the first day rolls around, everything will work out."

He nodded as though he understood but he didn't. Not really. "What can I do?"

"Just keep doing what you're doing. You're a great father."

"I think Nikki would disagree."

"As she gets older, she'll understand that you did what you had to in order to care for her."

His shoulders drooped. "I hope you're right."

"I am." She gazed into his eyes. Compassion and understanding showed in her hazel eyes. Then she glanced away. "You better get going. Don't worry about Nikki, I'll talk to her."

"Thanks." He started for the door. His hand was on the doorknob when he realized he'd forgotten what he'd wanted to speak to her about. He retraced his steps into the kitchen. "I forgot to mention that I'm giving you a raise."

She shook her head. "You don't have to do that."

Who turned down a raise? And then he realized she didn't want to take the money because she felt sorry for him. He'd said too much, and now she thought he didn't have the money to pay her.

"I insist. You've earned the raise. By doing the laundry and cooking dinner, you've made my life so much easier."

"I don't mind it. I like to stay busy."

"And you've earned the raise." When she went to argue, he held up his hand, stopping her. "It's not a lot. So don't make a big deal of it. I just wanted you to know how much I appreciate you—the work you do." On his way to the door, he called out, "I might be a little late tonight."

"No problem. I have this." She sent him a reassuring smile.

He noticed that day by day he was starting to count on Aster more and more. He didn't know how he felt about that. He knew he should be happy that he had someone reliable and caring to help him keep his life together, but he couldn't help but feel that he could get too used to this—more than was wise. It wasn't like Aster was going to stay forever—just until she had a full-time position at city hall.

14

*S*unday morning arrived sooner than she'd expected.

Aster let out a yawn and then another. She'd been up late working on the upcoming softball tournament. It had been a lot more work than she'd been expecting. Eighty-two people had signed up for the tournament. Eight-two. *Wow!*

The mayor was happy with the response. She was thrilled with the turnout—especially since this whole tournament had been last minute. She arranged the sign-ups into eight teams. Then she calculated that each game would last for approximately ninety minutes. Instead of using all three fields, they could use two of them and not have the area so crowded.

Four teams would play and then the other four. Then those winners would play each other. And then it would be the championship game. Aster estimated that it would take seven or so hours to play, including breaks. She sent out the email with all of the pertinent information, including the fact that the tournament would start at 9:00

a.m.

She checked the time. It was a quarter till eight—almost time for her foray into baking with Sam's sister. She pressed *send* on the mass email and then she headed for the door. She said a brief hello to Darla but kept going. She didn't want to be late for her baking lesson.

She had to admit that she had second and third thoughts about agreeing to this. She didn't like to fail at things. And that's fully what she expected to do. She might be able to plan events and organize teams but when it came to baking, she was totally out of her element.

Still, it was to help Sam. And though she'd wanted to pitch in before she knew him, now she was even more determined to do her part. She couldn't let her fear of failure keep her from doing her best.

She walked to the bakery. With it being a holiday weekend, the town was abuzz with activity. The tourists were out and about, buying last-minute mementos and trinkets. She couldn't blame them. If she had to leave here, she'd want to take something with her that would remind her of the island—of her time with Nikki and Sam, definitely Sam.

What was she saying? She gave herself a mental shake. She was not falling for Sam. No way. She wasn't ready to be more than friends.

But if she was open to a relationship, Sam would be an ideal partner. Not only was he a good guy but he had a heart of gold where his daughter was concerned. Aster had observed how his eyes lit up when Nikki was around. She was his whole world. And he worked so

hard as a single parent. How he was able to do so much was beyond her. She doubted she could do that good of a job if she were in a similar position.

And the fact that she didn't know where she was going to live a year from now or a month from now meant she couldn't get too close to him. She couldn't have Sam come to rely on her and then disappear from his life, not after he'd already lost his wife.

What am I thinking? It's not like he's into me.

And I'm not into him.

Aster walked faster. She needed to get to the bakery and get to work. All of this walking was giving her too much time to think. Because in the end, even though Sam was nothing like Oz, the thought of starting a new relationship—any romantic relationship—scared her.

"Aster? Aster, are you all right?"

Aster blinked her eyes and focused on the worried looks of Josie and Lily. "Um, what?"

Lily stepped forward. "Is everything all right?"

Aster nodded. "Yes. Of course."

Josie moved to her side. "You looked like you had something weighing on your mind. If you need someone to talk to, we're"—she gestured before herself and Lily—"good listeners."

Aster sent them a reassuring smile. "I'm sure you both are great listeners, but I'm good." She needed to change the subject and quick. "I just finished organizing the softball tournament. I noticed you both signed up."

"Are you playing too?" Lily asked.

"Afraid not. Someone needs to make sure everyone is where they need to be."

"I'm sure someone else can do it, if you want to join us," Josie said.

"Maybe next time." Aster was touched by their effort to include her.

They made small talk as they approached the front door of The Elegant Bakery. Aster had been in the shop once before to pick up an order for city hall. It had been bustling that day and she'd been in a rush. As such, she hadn't had a chance to really take in the decor.

Today the bakery was closed. According to the sign on the front door, it was the only day they were closed. Aster stopped just inside the doorway and took in the black and white décor. In some ways it reminded her of stepping back in time with the brass fixtures and the giant gold-framed chalkboard behind the counter. And then there was the gorgeous, giant, crystal chandelier over a beautiful wood pedestal table. In the center was a nine-tier gold cupcake holder filled with finely decorated cupcakes. Aster couldn't help but smile as she took in the elegant view before her.

"This place is amazing," she said to no one in particular.

"It is." Lily pointed to the chandelier over the table. "And that helped bring Hannah and Ethan together."

"Really?" She was trying to figure out how a chandelier could bring two people together.

"It was their first date, though both of them will still argue that it wasn't a date, but I beg to disagree. And, well, they disagreed vehemently over the purchase of that chandelier. But it got them talking and the rest, as they say, is history."

So, buying a fancy light could be the start of something serious? Interesting. "Are they married now?"

"No," Josie said. "But we're all waiting for Ethan to pop the question."

"Or Hannah could do the asking," Lily said. "There's no reason a woman can't propose."

"But it's still so romantic when the man does it." Josie sighed. "Especially when he has a beautiful diamond ring to go with the proposal." Josie turned to Aster. "What do you think? Should the man propose? Or the woman?"

Aster immediately put up her palms. No way was she getting between these two friends with their disagreement. "I don't have an opinion."

"But you must," Lily said. "Haven't you ever daydreamed about that big moment?"

She gave a vehement shake of her head. "I don't think marriage is in the cards for me." She didn't want to let someone get that close to her—close enough to hurt her. "I like my freedom too much."

Josie frowned as though she were taking this information into consideration. "But if you were to get engaged, how do you imagine it would go down?"

Now what was she to say? No matter how she answered, she would upset one of her newfound friends and that was the last thing she wanted.

"Why are you asking her about getting engaged?" Hannah approached them. She arched a brow at her two friends. Then Hannah turned to Aster. "Are you and my brother an item?"

Aster gave a vehement shake of her head. "No. No.

No."

Hannah pursed her lips together as she turned back to her friends. "You wouldn't be talking about Ethan and I getting engaged, would you?"

Immediately, both Josie's and Lily's gazes lowered as they shrugged their shoulders.

"We were just talking," Josie said.

Lily lifted her head. "And you know that you and Ethan make the perfect couple."

Hannah let out a laugh. "I don't know about perfect, but we don't do too bad. But *if* we get engaged, it'll be on our timeline."

Aster felt sorry for Hannah. Maybe they didn't want to get married. She could understand that. Or maybe they had another reason for not getting engaged yet. Whatever it was, it was their business.

She decided to intervene. "So, I hope you're prepared to deal with someone who doesn't know her way around an oven."

Hannah smiled at her. "I have the perfect project for you. How do you feel about apple cobbler?"

"I, uh…" Would Hannah hold it against her if she told her she'd never had it? She hoped not. "I don't have any feelings about it. I, uh, I've never eaten it."

"Then let's get started." Hannah waved at them to follow her back to the kitchen. "I've got everything ready to go."

When Aster stepped into the kitchen, she was reminded of just how many apples they had to peel. This was going to take much, much longer than she'd imagined. She just hoped she was a help and not a hindrance. And so, she set to work, carefully following Hannah's detailed instructions.

15

Labor Day had arrived without pomp or fanfare.

At least that's the way it felt on the Bell farm.

Sam got up at his usual 4:30 a.m. To him, the day didn't feel like anything special. To him, it was another Monday—another work day. And with the harvest season almost upon him, he didn't have time to waste.

Nikki had slept over at his mother's house because they were going together to the Labor Day picnic. His daughter had repeatedly begged him to go with her, and each time he had to turn her down. It tore at his heart. He just couldn't be everywhere at the same time.

He could hear the echo of Beth's voice telling him to go to the picnic. The work could wait. But this year was different. This year he'd lost a ton of money on the new barn that had burned down. This year he had to work to make up for his mistakes that led to the fire—not thoroughly checking that everything was off in the barn before calling it a night. If he'd have just done one more walk through that night—if he'd have just followed his routine—he'd be going to the picnic with Nikki and Aster.

Wait. And Aster? Since when had she become such a big part of his world? It wasn't like she'd been in his life all that long and yet he looked forward to seeing her each day at lunch. And now that school was about to start on Tuesday, he wouldn't see her nearly as much. A sense of disappointment came over him.

He sighed. He reminded himself that seeing less of Aster was for the best. He wasn't ready to let someone into his life—to care about someone. He'd been hurt in the worst way possible when he'd lost Beth. He couldn't go through that again.

With determination, he set off to get as much done as he could that day. With Nikki otherwise occupied, it was his chance to get ahead.

He worked the tractor that day, cultivating another field. Since he'd sold the cows to pay some of the bills, he could keep expanding his crops. Next year, he planned to have his biggest planting year ever.

The day had been long but rewarding when the last two fields were turned. Now he should be able to get the planting done before the weather grew wet. It was well past noon when he pulled the tractor into the old barn. He checked the time. Two thirty. Hadn't he heard from his sister or was it his mother that the softball tournament was going to run until past four? Yes, he was certain of it.

Almost a half hour later, a freshly showered Sam drove his golf cart through town. Parking was hard to come by. It appeared the picnic this year had a bigger turnout than usual. He wondered if it had anything to do with the softball tournament Aster had planned.

It took him a bit to locate an available parking spot near the Purple Guppy Pub, and then he walked to the other end of the park. As he searched for his family, he walked past the food and craft booths that had been set up. He noticed a large sign showing the contributions to this year's fundraiser. They had exceeded their goal. He felt as though he should contribute, too, but when he stepped up to the table for the apple butter, he was informed they'd just sold their last jar. He was bummed because he really enjoyed a toasted bagel with melted butter and apple butter in the morning. He hadn't had that since last autumn.

Just then his stomach rumbled its complaint at missing lunch. He'd been in such a rush to finish his work early that he hadn't stopped to eat. He glanced around at the food booths. Most were in the process of closing up. Then he spotted one that was serving apple dumplings as well as apple cobbler. He hadn't had apple cobbler in years. It was something his grandmother would often make in the autumn months. His mouth watered at the memory.

He stepped up to the counter and hoped they would still have some as well as vanilla ice cream. And he was lucky because they did. He got a bowl of warm cobbler topped with a scoop of ice cream. The bowl was full, and he had a feeling since they were closing up for the day that he'd been given an extra-large piece. Lucky him.

The aroma of cinnamon and apples caused his

stomach to rumble with eagerness. He dunked the plastic spoon into the fluffy crust. He scooped up some biscuit, baked apples, and a bit of ice cream. He took a bite, and he was swept back in time to his grandmother's kitchen table.

He took another bite to be sure. And then he was certain this was his grandmother's recipe. His sister must have made it. Hannah was so talented. He'd have to let her know that she'd outdone herself.

On his way to the softball fields, he finished off the cobbler. He tossed the empty bowl and spoon in one of the many trash cans.

It didn't take him long to locate his family. Nikki, his mother, Chief Campbell, Hannah, and Ethan were all seated together. Aster was seated nearby with a clipboard and pen in hand. It looked like she had things under control.

He climbed up in the stands and had a seat next to his daughter. Nikki turned to him and smiled. "You came."

"Better late than never." He gave her a little hug. "Hey, Mom, what did I miss?"

"The most delicious lunch." His mother and the chief went on to tell him all about the things he'd missed. He noticed how they'd started to finish each other's sentences. It was like they'd been together for years. He wondered what his father would think of his mother moving on.

When the chief said something funny, Sam watched as his mother laughed. With her eyes lit up, she leaned toward the chief before placing her hand on his arm. They were so comfortable with each other. He hadn't seen his mother this happy in a long time.

He wondered if she still missed his father like he missed Beth. Of course she must, but somehow she'd found her way forward. He was still trying to figure things out.

"And now you're in time to see the last innings of the championship game," Chief Campbell said, drawing Sam from his thoughts.

Sam looked out at the two teams. The team at bat was dressed in blue shirts, and the players in the field were wearing orange. Easy enough to keep them sorted. And stepping up to bat was Mayor Banks, as he liked to be called. He wore navy dress shorts with a blue polo shirt. Sam smiled. He wondered if the man knew how to dress casual. Did he even own jeans or a T-shirt? Sam thought back to high school. Even then, Tony liked to dress up. Maybe someday he'd loosen up, but Sam highly doubted it.

The first pitch was a strike. The mayor hit the second pitch, sending it soaring into the outfield where Darla caught it. Sam wasn't surprised to see her playing since she was such good friends with Aster.

In the end, the orange team won and Aster, hesitant to get up in front of everyone, presented them with a trophy. He was happy for her that the tournament had been so well received. In fact, next year he hoped to participate.

Sam followed the crowd of people as they exited the bleachers. He moved over to where his sister Hannah and her boyfriend, Ethan, were standing. "Hey, Hannah, I had some of the apple cobbler when I arrived. You did an excellent job with it. It was just like Granny's apple cobbler."

"Thanks. But I didn't make it."

"You didn't?" How could that be? He was confused. "But it tasted exactly like her recipe."

"It was her recipe, but I didn't make it."

"Hi, everyone." Aster stepped up to their group. "Did everyone have a good day?"

His whole family plied her with compliments over how well the tournament had gone. He noticed how well she got along with his sister and mother. And then there was Nikki, who moved to stand right next to Aster. She gazed up at her with admiration.

"I want to be just like you when I grow up," Nikki said to Aster.

"You do?" Aster knelt down to talk to Nikki on her level. "Why is that?"

"Because you're good at everything."

Aster let out a laugh. "I wish that was true, but there are a lot of things I'm not good at."

"But she is good at making apple cobbler." Hannah's gaze moved to him.

He mouthed, "Really?"

Hannah smiled and nodded.

He clearly recalled Aster saying she didn't bake. Something told him his sister had a hand in teaching Aster. He just hoped she'd make apple cobbler again for him...and Nikki, of course.

Before Sam got a chance to vocalize his compliment, the mayor stepped up to Aster. "Do you have a moment? I have a couple members of the town council for you to meet."

"Ah, sure." Aster turned to Sam's family. "Excuse me."

And then she walked away with the mayor. Sam's gaze followed her. She'd obviously impressed the mayor, and now he was moving forward with his plan to make her position at city hall a permanent one.

It'd happened much sooner than Sam had expected. It used to be that things at city hall moved as a snail's pace. Not so anymore.

His mother announced that no one wanted to go home and cook, so they were stopping by The Lighthouse Café for dinner. He told them he'd catch up with them. He wanted to let Aster know what an amazing job she'd done. He was certain she was going to get the promotion at work that she'd been longing for. It filled him with mixed emotions.

He stood off to the side of the bleachers as he waited for Aster. A few people stopped by and chatted with him. They asked about the farm, and he did his best to gloss over the problems he'd recently experienced. No one wanted to hear about those on such a nice day.

In the distance, he heard, "Aster, did you hear? We did it."

Sam couldn't put a name to the female voice, but he'd heard it before. They must be talking about the success of the tournament.

"We did?" Aster asked and then there was a pause. "That's awesome." He was about to step around the bleachers when Aster said, "Sam is going to be so surprised."

He froze. *Surprised about what? Aster getting the full-time position?*

"I know. And he owes you a big thank you."

"Not me."

"Yes, you. You're the one that came up with the softball tournament. It drew out a lot more residents. More residents means more money raised for the new barn. This is just what he needs to get everything back on track."

New barn? Money raised? Things back on track?

The muscles in his body tensed. Today had been all about him. That fundraising sign he'd seen when he first arrived had represented the pity money people had donated because they thought he was a failure, first as a husband and now as a farmer.

He stepped back. Aster knew about this all along? The breath hitched in his throat. Why hadn't she warned him?

In the background, he heard the drone of the women's voices. Were they still talking about him? He wasn't sure. He took another step back. And then he turned.

He strode away from the park. He kept his head down and didn't make eye contact with anyone. He didn't want to speak to anyone. He was ashamed that the town thought they had to bail him out. What had Aster been telling everyone?

Had she used his situation to her advantage? Had she told people how badly he needed help in order to get them to turn up today?

When he reached his golf cart, he texted his sister

telling her that something had come up at the farm and said he'd pick up Nikki later. She texted back that they'd drop her off after dinner. And then he headed for home because he was too angry to face Aster. How could she have done this?

16

The holiday weekend was over.
And it had been a smashing success in
so many ways.

Tuesday morning, Aster smiled as she headed for
city hall. The picnic and the tournament had been a huge
success. The council members had been impressed. She
had a good feeling that when the city council met in
October to vote on next year's budget that she would
have a full-time job and benefits come January first.

And best of all, the necessary money had been raised
to rebuild Sam's barn. Now he wouldn't have to work so
hard. He could relax a little and spend more time with
his daughter. As far as she was concerned, it was a win-
win.

And it was a short work week. Her smile broadened
as she entered city hall and made her way up the center
staircase to her desk in an alcove. Maybe along with a
full-time position, they could find space for her in an
actual office. It would be a lot less distracting than sitting
out there where most everyone that passed by her said

hello or engaged in a rather lengthy chat.

But even if her desk were to remain in the exact same spot, she would be happy; no, she'd be thrilled with a full-time position. She started listing all of the events she would plan from a Fourth of July parade to a Christmas celebration and definitely a bigger and better organized softball tournament at the Labor Day picnic. She even thought of making it a summer series starting with Memorial Day and then the Fourth and finally Labor Day. She tucked the idea in the back of her mind. She would have to give it some more thought.

"Aster, what are you doing here?" Mayor Banks wore a confused look on his face.

"Where else would I be on a workday?"

"With Ms. Birdie. She's going to tell Sam about the barn-raising. They're going to start delivering supplies today and the construction will get underway Thursday."

"That soon?" She forced her mouth closed so as not to gape at him.

"We felt it was an urgent situation. And with cooler weather on the way, it was best to get started as soon as possible."

"I understand."

"Have you mentioned any of this to Sam?" His gaze searched hers. "I know you two have gotten close, what with you watching his daughter."

"Um, no. You and Birdie asked me not to." And she was starting to wonder if that was a mistake. She'd learned what a proud man Sam was, and she worried he might misconstrue the town's kind gesture.

"I see." His brows drew together as though he was

worried about this surprise too. "Maybe it would be best if you were there today when he gets the news, you know, just in case the surprise is a little much for him."

She nodded. "I can do that."

"Good." He planted his hands on his trim waist. "There will be photographers there from the island's paper as well as some media from the mainland. Somehow the media got word of what the town was planning and insisted on covering it. This could be really good coverage for the island, so nothing can go wrong."

Media? Suddenly Aster sensed problems ahead. Maybe if she left right now, she could beat everyone to the farm and warn Sam about what was going to happen. And then she planned to leave before the photographers arrived. Yes, that sounded like a good idea. The last thing she wanted was her face in the news.

"Do you mind if I head to the farm now?" she asked.

"Not at all. Just make sure this goes well. I'll be along shortly."

She didn't know why it surprised her that the mayor would be visiting the Bell farm too. Of course, he'd want to be a part of a media event. He was, after all, a politician. But the bigger this announcement became, the more Sam would resist the offer.

And so, she set off on her bike. The ride was quiet. Not much traffic used the road now that the height of tourist season was over. Sometime she'd like to ride from one end of the island to the other, but she hadn't had the time as of yet. But she was sure once she had a permanent position at city hall that she would have more time on her hands. After all, she wouldn't need to work two jobs any longer.

It was the first time she'd let her thoughts go there. Her job at the Bell farm would be coming to an end. The thought saddened her. She was just starting to feel at home at the farm. She'd even come to make friends with Dash.

But her departure was still a ways off. After all, the council wasn't meeting until October. And the position wouldn't open up until January. It was plenty of time for Sam to find a replacement.

As she rode up the gravel lane to the farmhouse, she tucked her employment uncertainties in the back of her mind. She glanced over to the place where the new barn was to be built. This was going to be wonderful. She just hoped Sam agreed.

She raced up the back steps to the kitchen door. She rapped her knuckles on the screen door. "Sam? Sam, are you here?"

The other door was open so she assumed he was in the house and not out in the fields. She hoped. Because this was a big farm, and it would take her some time to track him down. Plus, it would be good if he was close to home when everyone arrived.

Knock-knock.

"Sam?" She raised her voice.

And then she heard footsteps. Sam appeared on the other side of the door. He was just settling his blue and white ball cap on his head. He didn't send her one of his usual friendly smiles. In fact, he looked as though he were frowning. "Aster, you shouldn't be here."

"I thought we could talk."

"I don't think so. I have work to do. I'm already late. I just dropped Nikki off at school."

"How did that go? Was she excited?"

"It went fine." He stepped out on the porch and pulled the door shut behind him.

Something was definitely wrong. When it came to Nikki, he liked to talk like a proud papa. "Was she nervous?"

He shrugged.

What was wrong with him? Everything had been fine yesterday at the picnic. He'd been smiling and talking. But then he'd disappeared after she'd talked with the mayor. And when she'd joined his family at The Lighthouse for dinner, he hadn't shown up.

Was he upset because she was going to take the full-time job at city hall? If so, he'd never said anything to her. It wasn't like she'd made it a secret.

Maybe she should try a little harder. "Did Nikki wear the pink dress? She couldn't decide between it or jeans and a purple top with a unicorn on the front."

"She wore jeans." He turned and started down the steps. "I really have to get to work."

She followed him. "Sam, what's wrong?"

When he looked at her, his brows were drawn together in a formidable line. "Why do you think something is wrong?"

She almost laughed at the ridiculousness of the question, but she erred on the side of caution. "Because you can't wait to get away from me. You've hardly said a word. And the look on your face is like you're mad at the whole world... Or maybe it's just me that you're mad at."

"Maybe." He turned to walk toward the old barn.

She continued to dog his steps. She practically had to take two steps for every one of his long strides. It didn't matter to her. She'd run if she had to. She needed to know what she'd done to upset him so much.

"Sam, I'm not leaving until you talk to me."

His steps slowed but he didn't stop. Nor did he speak.

"I mean it. I'll follow you into the field if I have to." She glanced down at her white canvas shoes. If she tromped around in the dirt, they'd never be the same again. So be it. She wasn't letting this end here. "Sam, stop. Talk to me."

He paused. His shoulders were rigid. When he turned, his normally sky-blue eyes had taken on a deep hue, much like a dark, stormy sea. He didn't say a word, but at least he was now facing her.

She planted her hands on her hips. "What in the world is going on? Does this have something to do with Nikki's first day of school? Did she say something that upset you?"

"This has nothing to do with Nikki, and you know it."

She knew it? How did he expect her to know anything when he wasn't getting to the point? At least now she knew he was in fact upset with her.

She searched her memory for anything she might have said or done wrong when she'd seen him at the picnic. Absolutely nothing came to mind except for her conversation with the mayor. That had to be it.

"Are you upset about me taking a full-time job working for the mayor if the city council approves the position?"

His gaze narrowed. "Do I really seem that shallow to you?"

Well... If that wasn't it, she was out of ideas. Unless he'd already found out about the barn-raising that was planned for him. Was that it? Her heart beat faster as she realized this could be a very big problem, especially with the media on the way.

Her gaze met his. "You know, don't you?"

A flicker of reaction showed in his eyes before he blinked it away. "You used me."

"I, what?" Surely, she hadn't heard him correctly.

"You used me to get ahead at city hall."

"I have no idea what you're talking about." She didn't really.

"I overheard you talking to someone after the ballgame yesterday." His words came fast. "You used my situation to guilt people into going to the picnic to donate their money—money I don't want. You made me the laughing stock of Bluestar." His face was red with anger or was it embarrassment or perhaps a little of both.

She took a step back. "That... That's not true. I... I didn't say anything about you to anyone."

His eyes widened upon realizing that his anger had made her quite uncomfortable. He sighed as though releasing his pent-up frustration.

When he spoke again, it was in a much softer tone. "I thought I could trust you, but now I know that isn't the case."

"Of course, you can trust me. I… I thought we were friends."

"Friends don't keep these things from each other. Friends have each other's backs. Friends don't knowingly hurt each other." He turned to walk away.

She grabbed his arm. "Don't you dare make those accusations and just walk away from me."

When he turned to her, she dropped her arm to her side. "I don't think we have anything left to say to each other."

"I do—"

"Sam!" A male voice called out.

They both paused and turned to find Mayor Banks waving to them from the side of the house. And he wasn't alone. Birdie along with her dog, Peaches, were standing next to him as well as photographers. Aster subdued a groan. Talk about bad timing.

Sam's gaze moved from the crowd forming in his yard to her. "It's not bad enough that the town pities me, but now it's going to be broadcast to the whole world."

"They are doing all of this because they care about you."

"And what about you? Why did you do it?" His accusing stare stabbed at her heart.

"Sam, come on over here." The mayor gestured for him to join them.

"Just be nice," she said. "They really did this out of the goodness of their hearts."

Without another word, he strode away.

She had no idea how this was going to turn out. Part of her wanted to get on her bike and ride away without a backward glance. She was angry that Sam thought so little of her that he would even entertain the thought of her using him to further her career. And another part of her hurt because she felt as if her time at the Bell farm was suddenly over.

She moved to the back of the crowd. She lingered in case her boss needed her for anything. She was surprised to find Sam put on a friendly face and played along. Though there were a couple of times she noticed the tick of his jaw muscle as though he'd clamped down his teeth, holding back his frustration. And when he smiled, it never reached his eyes.

Mayor Banks spotted her and made his way over to her. "You did good work today." He sent her an approving smile that she just couldn't bring herself to return. "I wasn't sure how Sam was going to take the news. It isn't every day that a town pulls together to help one of their own. But he took the news really well. Good job."

"I didn't really do anything." It was the truth, even if Sam didn't believe it.

"You did more than you think. You thought of the softball tournament that drew in more residents than we've ever had in attendance for the Labor Day picnic. And with the larger attendance, we were able to sell more items and raise more funds. I also heard that you were the one that baked the delicious apple cobbler. You're fitting right in."

"Thank you, sir."

"We'll talk more about the expansion of your duties next week. I have to get going. I have a meeting coming up." And with that the mayor moved to his golf cart, where a reporter approached him with a few more questions.

When the mayor and the press departed, Aster went with them. Maybe she should have stayed and tried to smooth things over with Sam, but she knew there was nothing she could say at this point to make things better between them. The knowledge weighed heavy on her chest.

17

e was in a perfectly foul mood.

Sam blamed it on being labeled a charity case by the town. Not even his own family seemed to think he could make it on his own. Didn't they see how hard he'd been working? How much progress he'd made on expanding the crops?

But the evidence of the town's doubt of his abilities was being delivered right then. Truckloads of supplies were being deposited near the future site of the barn. There was now a stack of lumber off in the distance. Followed by another truck with a special day pass in the window. It was hauling concrete block. People certainly weren't wasting any time getting this project off the ground.

The thought of a new barn sent a thrill of excitement through his body, but in the next breath, his bruised pride quelled the anticipation. He could have done this on his own. He just needed a little more time. But it appeared time was something he was out of.

After talking with one of the drivers, he learned the

barn they were going to erect was going to be the same
wood barn that he'd originally planned on building. It
was more expensive than its metal counterpart but in the
salty ocean air, he thought it would hold up better.

He still couldn't believe Aster had secretly gone
along with the plan. Maybe the town didn't have a clue
about what he'd been up to. It wasn't like he went in to
town and sat down at The Lighthouse to tell everyone in
listening distance his business. And maybe he hadn't
been so forthcoming with his family because he still
wasn't sure the expanded crops would grow—the
weather could be so fickle. And then there were the
market prices, up one moment and down the next. But
Aster was at the farm almost every day. He'd confided in
her. He'd thought she believed in him. He had never
been more wrong.

And now he had to deal with the fallout of blowing
up at Aster. He recalled the skittish look on her face. Had
he really been that intimidating? He didn't want to think
it was possible. Or had something horrible happened to
her in the past? Either way, he felt terrible for scaring
her. He'd do better in the future.

With the way things had ended with Aster, it meant
he was without a babysitter. He would have to stop
working in order to go into town and meet Nikki after
school. As it was, he was already behind in his work
after dealing with the mayor, Ms. Birdie, and the
reporters, who had far more questions than he'd been
prepared to answer.

He was standing in the middle of the pumpkin patch,
checking on their progress and hoping he'd have some

that were ready for sale at the end of the month. He'd made arrangements to have them for sale at the grocery store in town. It wouldn't be a lot of money but at this stage every little bit helped. Because now he felt obliged to pay back the town for the barn they were all determined to build. It just wasn't right taking all of their hard-earned money. He hadn't done anything to deserve such overwhelming generosity.

"Finally."

He glanced up from where he'd knelt down to peer under the large green leaves. "Hannah? What are you doing here?"

"I meant to get here this morning but one problem after another at the bakery delayed me."

He glanced at his watch. "Shouldn't you be at the bakery now?"

"Perhaps. But this is more important."

He straightened. "If you're here to lecture me about the pity donations for the new barn, you can save your time."

Her brows lifted. "I'm not here about that."

"I don't have much time. Nikki will be out of school soon." He realized he was inadvertently taking his bad mood out on his sister. "Sorry. It's been a long day. What did you need?"

"Isn't it Aster's job to pick up Nikki at school?"

He shrugged. The last thing he wanted to do was get into this conversation with his sister. "Am I not allowed to meet my own daughter after her first day of school?"

Hannah quietly studied him. "Something is going on with you and Aster. What is it?"

He had no idea how much she knew. "Why would you say that?"

"Because I saw Aster earlier in town."

"And what did she say?"

"Nothing. She walked right past me without saying a word. It was though she was totally lost in her thoughts and never heard a word I said to her. And by the look on her face, whatever she was thinking about wasn't good."

"And so, you naturally jumped to the conclusion that I'm to blame. You're my sister. Aren't you supposed to give me the benefit of the doubt?"

"I'm on your side when you're right. But I think I know what's going on."

He sighed. The last thing he wanted was for his sister to evaluate him. But he didn't see that he had a choice. If he walked away, she would follow—just like when they were kids. Hannah always needed to have the final word. It was best to get it over with as fast as possible.

He pulled off his work gloves and shoved them into his back pocket. "Say what you've got to say."

"I think you aren't happy about the town raising money to build you a new barn. Am I right so far?"

He hated how his sister knew him so well. As her gaze prodded him to answer, he finally nodded.

"And I think somehow you're blaming Aster for this. Right?"

He lowered his gaze and shrugged. "She lied to me."

"I highly doubt she lied to you—"

"She did." He struggled to keep his tone level. But he didn't want to scare his sister like he'd done with Aster. "Maybe she didn't make up lies to tell me but she lied by omission. She knew what was going on the whole time. And she never said a word to me. She did it so she could get a promotion at work." When he glanced at Hannah, her mouth was gaping.

It took her a moment to gather herself. "Are you serious?"

"Of course I am. How am I supposed to trust her with Nikki after this?"

"Whoa. Slow down, brother. Why is it that you're directing all of your anger at Aster?"

"Because she had every opportunity to tell me and she didn't."

"But then what about Mom and me. Why aren't you mad at us?"

He crossed his arms. "So, you knew too?"

"Everyone knew...except you."

"That's just great. So, the whole town has been talking about how pathetic I am that I can't keep the farm running without being bailed out." He'd heard enough. He was finished with this conversation. He started toward the house.

"Samuel Bell, don't you walk away. Not like this."

Since when did his sister start to sound so much like their mother? He stopped, straightened his shoulders, and then he turned to her. "What?"

Hannah was quiet, as though she were waiting for him to calm down. "I think your pride has been bruised."

He shook his head. "Stop analyzing me."

"I'm serious. I think you're too proud to ask for help, and now that the town has stepped up because they care about you, your pride can't take it."

"You don't know what you're talking about." She was hitting closer to the truth than he wanted to admit, even to himself.

"I think I do because I was in your position not so long ago." When he went to disagree, she held up her hand to stop him. "After the bakery was flooded, I was scared that everything I'd dreamed of had come to an end. I wouldn't admit it to anyone, but when I was alone at night I worried. People offered to help me but would I let them? No. I was too stubborn, perhaps too proud. I wanted to do it on my own. But I couldn't. It was impossible. In the end, a lot of people helped me and now looking back on it, I don't know what I was thinking. It's okay to ask for help or in your case, to accept the help that is offered."

He hated to admit it but his sister was actually making some sense. Maybe he was letting his pride stand between him and the ability to make the farm profitable again.

"See," she said, drawing him from his thoughts. "You know I'm right. And none of this was Aster's idea. She just got caught up in the middle of the whole thing. You owe her an apology. She's the best babysitter you've ever had. Not only is Nikki happy but I've noticed you smiling more than usual. Don't mess this up." Her phone buzzed and she pulled it from her pocket. She glanced at the screen. "Okay. I've got to go. And you have an apology to deliver. The sooner, the better. Good luck."

His sister walked away, once again having the final word. How did she manage it? Probably because a lot of times she was right. Not that he'd ever admit it to her. He would never hear the end of it.

But Hannah had him slow down long enough to realize that he was taking all of his frustrations out on Aster. And that wasn't fair to her because she'd done nothing but try to help them.

Just then another truck rumbled down the lane. Sam blinked to make sure he wasn't seeing things but on the back was at least a half dozen porta potties. Who all was planning to show up for this? The whole town?

He still wasn't happy about the town paying for his new barn, but he just didn't have it in him to fight the entire town. And perhaps he was letting his pride ruin this opportunity. In the end, it would be good for Nikki because he'd have more time to spend with her.

With him resigned to the fact that he was going to accept the town's help, it left him with one big problem—fixing things with Aster. He was ashamed of the hard time he'd given her.

But when he glanced at the time, he knew his apology was going to have to wait. It was time to pick Nikki up at school. And so off he went—all the while he tried to think of a way to make things up to Aster.

♥♥♥

She was fuming.

Aster had gone back to city hall but other than answering a few emails, she hadn't gotten much work done. All she could think about was the argument she'd had with Sam. She'd never seen him so worked up.

Was she wrong for thinking he might have been happy about the new barn? Perhaps it was a lot for a proud man, who worked hard to stand on his own two feet, to accept.

But why did he have to blame her for everything? It hadn't been her idea. The plans were well underway before she'd even stepped foot on Bluestar Island.

Maybe she should have clued him in but everyone had been counting on her to keep quiet. She'd thought she was doing the right thing. Obviously, she'd been wrong.

Needing to hear a friendly voice, she reached for her phone. She instinctively dialed Rosa. Talking to her always made her feel better.

It wasn't until she heard her friend's voice that she realized she shouldn't have phoned. She shouldn't have made it easier for Oz to find her. But what was done, was done. Now that Rosa was on the phone, she felt better.

They didn't talk about Sam. It wasn't that she didn't want to confide in her dear friend. It was that she didn't want to be overheard by her co-workers.

And so, they talked about general things such as Rosa's winnings at bingo last week and Bluestar's weather as well as a crime drama they used to watch together on Thursday evenings.

When the short conversation ended, Aster felt better. She glanced at the clock. It was almost time for Nikki to get out of school. Aster was anxious to hear how the girl's day went. But she had no idea if she was still Nikki's babysitter or not. That part of her conversation with Sam was still a bit fuzzy.

She shutdown her computer and grabbed her stuff.

She headed out the door and rode her bike to the elementary school. She glanced around for any sign of Sam or one of his family members, but she didn't see anyone. So, she settled herself on one of the large decorative rocks in front of the school.

She pulled a book out of her purse because she wasn't going to sit there and think about how disappointed she was that things had gone so poorly with Sam. Nor did she want to think about his comment about not trusting her. Because when Nikki stepped out of the school, Aster wanted to be genuinely happy for her, and she wanted to hear about her day instead of focusing on her own problems.

Aster always kept a book on hand because you never knew when you were going to have time on your hands. It was a mystery novel. The heroine had a cat and a dog that always made Aster smile with their antics. She liked how the cat was always outsmarting the dog. Talk about a bit of "cattitude."

"Aster?"

The breath caught in her lungs. She would know that male voice anywhere. It was Sam. Was he angry that she was there at the school? Was she supposed to have kept her distance? She wasn't sure how things stood between them right now.

He stepped around the rock and stopped in front of her. She wanted to keep reading and ignore his presence, but that wasn't the right thing to do—the adult thing to do. Sometimes being an adult was so hard.

And so, she closed her book and lifted her chin until her gaze met his. "I wasn't sure who was picking up

Nikki."

He nodded as he hitched his thumbs into the corner of his jean pockets. "About earlier, I didn't handle that very well."

"You made yourself clear." She got to her feet. Not wanting to rehash what had been said earlier, she knew it was time for her to make a quick exit. "Since you're here, I can leave. Tell Nikki I hope she had a good day."

"Wait. Stay. Tell her yourself."

Her brows drew together as she looked at him. "You want me to stay?"

He shrugged. "You don't have to, but I'd like a chance to apologize."

Now she really was confused. What had caused this sudden change in him? She wanted to ask but right then her mind and her mouth were at a complete disconnect. She hoped he'd continue to explain things.

He shifted his weight from one foot to the other. "I shouldn't have said what I did earlier. I was caught off guard and I... I let my pride do the talking."

"You're not mad at me?"

He shook his head. "I'm mad at myself for handling things so poorly. I shouldn't have taken everything out on you."

She couldn't help but wonder something. "What made you change your mind about this not being my fault and that I wasn't using you to get a promotion?"

His face took on a slight tinge of pink. "I shouldn't have said it. I was starting to come to that conclusion on my own when my sister stopped by the farm. Hannah let me know in no uncertain terms what a jerk I'd been."

A smile tugged at the corners of Aster's lips as she thought of Hannah laying into her brother. Aster wanted to tell him that he was lucky to have someone who cared enough about him to tell him when he was being a jerk. She'd always dreamed about being a part of that kind of loving family.

"Why are you smiling? It wasn't funny. She didn't hold back. And she got the final word."

"Which was what?"

"You know, I can't really remember now but she did tell me that I'd treated you poorly and I needed to apologize. It might be some of the best advice she's ever given me. But don't tell her I said that, or I'll never hear the end of it."

"Your secret is safe with me." It was as though the dark clouds had rolled away, and the sunshine was once more streaming down on her. She felt energized and happy. "So we're good?"

"If you want us to be." And when she didn't immediately respond, he asked, "You do want us to be, don't you?"

She nodded. "I was just wondering if this also means that you're willing to go along with building the new barn."

"My sister thinks I'd be a fool not to. She said I'm letting my pride get in the way."

"And what do you think?"

He sighed. "That she's probably right." He shifted his weight back to the other foot. "The thing is I just feel wrong about accepting this very generous gift. I feel like I need to give something back."

190

"You could thank everyone."

"It needs to be more."

"Like what?"

"That's just it. I don't know."

"Daddy! Daddy! You're here." Nikki came running up to them. She didn't stop running until she plowed into her father. Sam stood still as he absorbed her energy. Nikki wrapped her arms around him. And then she glanced at Aster. "And you came too. Does this mean we're going for ice cream?"

"Ice cream?" Sam asked. "Why would you think that?"

"Because we always go for ice cream when we're celebrating something special." She sent him a big smile.

"We do?" He forced a confused expression, but his eyes were smiling.

"Daddy, stop being silly."

"You think I'm silly?" He swung her up in his arms like she was as light as a rag doll.

Nikki smiled as she nodded her head.

"Was it a special day?" Aster asked, already knowing the answer.

Nikki once again grinned as she nodded. "I made a new friend. Her name's Amanda."

"That's great. It's fun to make new friends." Aster should know. She'd been making new friends since she stepped on this island. But it was the two friends standing in front of her that held a special place in her heart.

"I want chocolate," Nikki said. "No, I want vanilla. No chocolate. I don't know."

Sam lowered her to the ground. "Well, you have some time to think about it before we get to Dips."

"Dips?" Aster hadn't heard of it.

"It's really called Whippy Dippy, but the locals often refer to it as Dips. It's a summer island tradition. Have you been there yet?"

"No. But I think ice cream sounds perfect right about now."

"Let's go." Nikki took a hold of Sam's hand and then Aster's.

"But my bike," Aster said.

"My bike's here too," Nikki said. "We could ride them."

"We'll put them in the back of the golf cart." Sam pointed to his golf cart off in the distance.

And so, they loaded up the bikes and set off for Whippy Dippy. After a rocky start to the day, things were back to normal. Aster couldn't be happier. There was just something special about spending the afternoon with Sam and Nikki. She was starting to wonder if there would be a way to keep her job at the Bell farm after she got promoted to full time at city hall. Because now that she'd had a glimpse of this loving family, she didn't want to walk away.

18

ap-tap. Tap-tap-tap.

The sound of hammers filled the air Thursday morning as the sun slowly ascended in the sky. Sam couldn't deny the excitement pumping through his veins. Construction on the new barn had officially begun. Well, that wasn't quite true. Because on Tuesday while he'd been at Whippy Dippy with Aster and Nikki, his neighbors had been there laying a wall of concrete block around the foundation. When they'd finished, the wall stood close to four feet tall.

Sam couldn't believe all of the people who had turned out. Every one of his farming neighbors were there. In addition, he'd swear more than half of the town was there.

His mother and sister had orchestrated the food because what was a barn-raising without food. Tables were lined up with red and white check tablecloths. On top of those was a long line of slow cookers that were plugged into orange extension cords. The delicious aromas of Italian roast beef, rigatoni, enchiladas, mac and cheese and more food wafted through the air.

Large silver coffee pots were set up at the end of the tables with stacks of disposable cups. The men took turns grabbing lunch so the construction wasn't paused. There was lots of framing to be done. And Sam made sure he was right there doing as much as he could muster.

This wasn't the first barn-raising on the island. They might not be quite as fast as the Amish, but they came in a close second. Though it had been a while since they'd done one. The last one Sam could recall was when he was a teenager. But the older ones were teaching the younger men and women the way it was done from the framing to building the walls.

It was a busy day. His farm hadn't seen this many people on it at one time in his lifetime. And he felt really guilty for getting so bent out of shape over this generous act. Everyone was happy to be there—happy to help him. And he realized since he'd lost his wife that he'd been isolating himself far too much. He wouldn't let that happen again.

When evening rolled around, everyone went home. Even Nikki had left with his mother. They were off to do some baking for tomorrow. He didn't know where they found the energy because after almost eleven hours of work, he was worn out.

The barn wasn't done but the framing was up. The next day, they'd start at sun-up by adding the walls and roof. It was utterly amazing what could be accomplished when everyone lent a helping hand.

Jennifer Faye

"How do you think it went today?"

He turned to find Aster standing next to the folding table they'd left up to make tomorrow's breakfast easier. "I think it is amazing what can be achieved when everyone pulls together."

"I agree. Every time I looked up, it seemed like there was a whole new section completed."

He stepped up to her. "Thank you."

She tilted her chin upward. "For what?"

"For helping me to see that this is a good thing. Not just for me but for Nikki, who needs more of my time, and for my family, who I know worry about me."

She brushed off his words. "I didn't do that much."

"Yes, you did. And I'd hug you right now if I wasn't so dirty."

She moved in close and wrapped her arms around him as though she didn't care about the dirt and sawdust clinging to his clothes. She fit against him as though she were made to be there. He wrapped his arms tightly around her and held her close. For a while, he never thought they'd have a moment like this. He'd been such a fool.

He lowered his head and got a whiff of her strawberry shampoo. And then without giving it a thought, he pressed a kiss to the top of her head. He never thought he'd do this again. He never thought he'd let himself get close to another woman after he lost Beth.

He thought he'd feel guilty for caring for another woman, but he didn't. He still loved Beth—he always would. But he was finding he had the ability to care for someone else—someone like Aster.

He wasn't quite sure how Aster had worked her way past his defenses. Was it the way she was so good with Nikki? Or the way she stepped up without asking and helped out? Or the smaller things, like the way she smiled at him that filled his chest with a fuzzy warmth? Whatever it was, she'd become special to him.

The farm was never going to be the same when Aster left to work full time at city hall. He was tempted to ask her to come work full time for him just so he could see her every day. He knew Nikki would love the idea.

Still, it wasn't fair to Aster to ask her to give up her work. He'd seen the way she lit up when she was working on the softball tournament. She liked working with the community, and she was very good at it. The reality of his thoughts startled him. It wasn't just babysitting he wanted with Aster—he wanted something more meaningful.

He halted his thoughts. He wasn't thinking clearly. He reluctantly lowered his arms to his sides. When she glanced at him, a warm fuzzy sensation started in his chest.

"Why don't we have a seat on the porch?" she said.

He didn't think that was a good idea, not with his jumbled feelings. "But I'm all dirty."

She smiled at him. "Not that dirty." She grabbed his hand and drew him toward the back porch. Once on the porch, she said, "Stay here. I'll be right back."

He stood at the top of the steps and looked out over the farm in the last lingering rays of sunlight. For so long, he'd lost the vision—this beautiful vision. He'd let himself get caught up in the daily grind.

But right then, it all looked so peaceful. The goats were resting in their pen—even Dash was taking it easy instead of getting into trouble. Sam's gaze moved to the left, and he appreciated all the hard work his neighbors had done that day. Though it was just the framework, it was starting to take on the appearance of a barn.

And in the background was the old barn. Though parts of it were missing, it was still somehow standing. Sam saw himself in that barn. He'd weathered the storms in his life from losing his young wife to the unexpected death of his father that sent his entire family into a tailspin. Both deaths had taken their toll on him, but miraculously he was still standing.

"What has you in such deep thought?" Aster's voice drew him back to the present.

He turned to find her standing there with two tall lemonades in her hands. She offered him one and he took it. "Uh." He wasn't about to admit that he was comparing himself to an old dilapidated barn. "I was wrong about accepting the town's help."

"It takes a big man to acknowledge when he's wrong."

He nodded as he took a long, slow sip of the sweet but tart refreshment. "But there's something that's bothering me."

"What's that?"

He moved to the swing on the back porch. "How do I thank everyone?"

Aster sat down next to him. "You could do a big picnic."

He shrugged. "We just had the Labor Day picnic, and

everyone has basically been having a picnic with all of the food being laid out all day."

She nodded. "Then what about a party?"

"A party?" He leaned back on the swing as he rolled the idea around in his mind. He could honestly say his experience with parties centered around Nikki's birthday parties, and while Beth used to plan them with all of the extras including balloons and streamers, now his mother took over the duty. "What sort of party?"

Aster was quiet for a moment as though considering the idea. "What about something to celebrate the season. Like Octoberfest?"

"I was hoping to do something right away." He set the swing in motion. "Maybe not this weekend because the barn won't be finished in time but maybe next weekend while it's still on people's minds."

"I know. How about a Harvest Dance?"

He shook his head. "Not a dance."

"Why not?"

He hesitated. "Because…"

"Are you going to elaborate?"

He didn't want to make the admission, but he knew she'd press the subject until he explained. "I don't know how to dance."

"Well, that's no big deal. Just learn."

He remembered how Beth had gotten so frustrated with him for not dancing with her at weddings. At their own wedding, he'd stepped on her toes more than once. He was terrible at it.

He shook his head. "It'll have to be something else."

"Are you refusing to learn?" Her gaze searched his.

"There's no time." It was true.

"There's time. I can show you. As long as it's just the basics, I'll help you."

His gaze met hers. "You will?"

Why did that invitation sound appealing to him? He'd always gone out of his way to avoid dancing. But the thought of holding Aster in his arms certainly appealed to him.

"So, you'll do it."

"Trust me, you don't want me stepping on your toes. Beth would tell you how bad I am." He hadn't meant to mention her. He didn't talk about her much. "It... It just won't work."

"Did you and Beth dance much?"

He stared out into the long shadows settling over the farm. "You don't want to hear about her."

"I do, if you're willing to tell me about her."

He turned to Aster. "I don't talk about her much."

"Why not?" Genuine surprise mixed with curiosity reflected in her eyes.

"At first, I didn't talk about Beth because it was too painful. I felt like I'd been broken into a million pieces, and that the slightest thing would send those pieces scattering over the floor. And I couldn't fall apart. I had a daughter to raise on my own. Nikki needed me, and I couldn't let her down. Not like I'd let Beth down."

Now what had he gone and said that for? He hadn't meant to dredge up all of these painful memories. He'd been holding them in for so long that sometimes he felt as though they were suffocating him.

"We don't have to talk about this, if you don't want

to." Aster's voice was soft and comforting.

He got the feeling he could tell her anything and it wouldn't go any further. But would she look at him differently if he were to reveal his dark secret—the one that kept him up at night?

As though she read his mind, Aster reached out and placed her hand over his. Her fingers tightened around his hand. A zing of awareness raced up his arm and set his heart racing. How did she do that? Aster brought him to life with just a look or a touch. For so long, he thought he was dead on the inside. But being around her made him want to live again—to feel again.

And that worried him. What was he doing? He wasn't in any position to fall for anyone. He had Nikki to think of. How would she feel about someone else taking her mother's place in her life? How would he feel about it?

He withdrew his hand. He couldn't let himself be that vulnerable again. He couldn't love and lose again. When Beth died, he didn't know how he'd get through a single day much less an entire week. The pain had been so overwhelming. But somehow he had made it. To go through something like that again would be too much for him.

He stared out into the night. Maybe the way to put distance between them was to tell Aster the truth about what had happened to Beth. It wouldn't be easy, but he felt it was something he had to do. Aster had to know the reason there could never be anything between them.

"Beth and I were high school sweethearts. We both knew what we wanted. I wanted to take over my

grandparents' farm. I already worked there when I wasn't in class. And she wanted a family—a big family. Beth had been an only child, and she'd always wanted siblings."

He was stalling. He was telling Aster too much information that she didn't care about or need to know. He needed to get to the point.

"When my grandfather died and my grandmother found the farm to be too much for her to run on her own, she passed it on to me. I was out of school by then and working the farm full-time. There was no reason for Beth and I not to get married. So, we did. We didn't get pregnant right away. Beth had been worried that something was wrong and we wouldn't be able to have kids. And then one day, Nikki came along with pink cheeks and blue eyes. She was everything we'd hoped for and more."

There he went again, telling Aster a bunch of stuff she didn't want to know. It was just that every time he opened his mind to the memories, they all came flooding back to him.

He cleared his throat. "Things were going well. Nikki was just a few years old, and we were trying for another baby. I was trying to expand the farm. That day I had a business meeting in Boston." The breath caught in his throat as his memories were crystal clear about that very painful day.

He had to get through this. He had to keep going. He knew if he stopped now that he'd never say it. And he just needed to get it out there. He needed to say the words.

"I had a lot to do. Bad weather was in the forecast for several days, and if I didn't get the fields planted before then, I didn't know when I would be able to plant. But I couldn't cancel my appointment at the bank to expand the business. I didn't expect to be gone long. I thought I could work late when I got home." His voice cracked with emotion.

Maybe he shouldn't have made such a big deal of the rainy forecast. If he hadn't gone on about the upcoming two weeks of rain, then maybe Beth wouldn't have felt the need to act. Maybe things would have turned out differently.

"But Beth being Beth took matters into her own hands while I was gone. She dropped Nikki off with my parents. Her parents had died in an accident the first year of our marriage, so she'd become very close with my family."

Again he let himself get distracted. It was so much easier to talk about anything but what had happened. He just needed to get it out there. He got to his feet and moved to the railing. He blindly stared out at the night.

"Beth came home and took the tractor out." His voice grew rough with emotion. "She'd driven it before but... Not without me. No one knew she was trying to help me get the field ready for planting." He blinked repeatedly, trying to keep his emotions in check. "My meeting in Boston took longer than expected, and then I missed the ferry so I had to wait for the next one." He raked his fingers through his hair. "It's like everything that could have gone wrong, did go wrong that day."

The familiar ache in his chest stole the breath from

his lungs. Maybe peeling back the scabs on this very deep wound wasn't the best idea. But now that the door to these memories had been cracked open, he was helpless to close it again.

The very vivid scenes played in his mind. He was drawn back there as he had so many times in the past, especially at night when sleep evaded him. The memories played out like one long sad movie.

He'd told himself a million if-onlys—if only the forecast had been different, if only he'd rescheduled the meeting, if only he'd have persuaded Beth to go with him, if only the meeting hadn't run late, if only he hadn't missed the ferry. Just one of them might have saved Beth's life.

His vision blurred. Moisture dampened his cheek. How could he have not been able to save his first love? How could it have gone so terribly wrong in the blink of an eye?

And then there was a hand on his shoulder. It was a simple comforting touch that helped him gather his crumbling emotions. He needed to finish his story. He needed to make Aster understand why they could never be more than friends.

He cleared his throat. "When I got home, I called to Beth but she didn't answer. After searching the house both inside and outside, I called my parents. They told me they had Nikki and that Beth had gone back to the house to do some work. In that moment, I knew what she was up to. I took off for the fields…"

His voice died away. The vivid memories played in his mind. He blinked repeatedly, but it didn't stop the moisture from dampening his cheeks. He ran the back of his hand over his face.

"I knew she'd gone out to work the fields. She was trying to help me. She wanted to surprise me. I should have been there. I should have been the one out there. I should have been the one on the tractor." His voice was uneven as he fought to hold back his emotions. "I should have been the one that died... Not her."

His hands clenched the wood rail as his whole body went rigid, and he fought the wave of emotions that came over him. He should be past this huge emotional response. He should be able to remember this day without falling apart. He should be able to move on.

And yet he knew none of those things were ever going to be true for him. That day had changed him forever. He was not the same man that he had been before that moment—before he'd found his childhood sweetheart crushed beneath the tractor. The memory made him shudder.

Aster's hand was still on his shoulder. He could feel her presence and sense her compassion. Because she, too, had experienced something devastating—something that filled her eyes with pain when she didn't think anyone saw but he had.

He knew whatever Aster's trauma was that it wasn't the same as his. He sensed that though her pain was different from his, her wound cut deep. In that they had common ground. It was easier for someone who had been hurt deeply to understand. And perhaps that was why he was able to open up to her.

Aster didn't push him. She didn't prod him for the

details. She probably wouldn't say a word if he were to stop right there, leaving the rest of the nightmare unsaid.

But he couldn't leave it there. He couldn't let the memories do him in. He had to rise above. He knew it was the only way he was going to have a decent life. He owed that much to Nikki. He owed it to her to be the best person he could be.

"When I stood at the top of the rise, I... I saw the tractor. It... It was overturned." His voice failed him as he stared out into the darkness. He swallowed hard past the lump of emotion in his throat. "Beth... She was trapped under it."

On that very tragic day, as he'd stood at the top of the hill, there was a part of him that had known the stark reality of the situation, but the other part of him refused to accept the severity of the situation. The hopeful part of him had clung to the thought that the accident wasn't as severe as it seemed—that there would be a miracle—that Beth would survive.

As the memories overcame him, he stopped fighting the moisture as it tracked down his face. He barely noticed it as his thoughts spiraled back in time—little more than four years ago.

"The rest is a blur. I called for help as I ran to her. But when I reached the tractor, I knew I was too late. I tried to lift the tractor but I couldn't budge it. Not even a little." His throat felt raw as he fought back the sobs— for his long-lost wife, for his motherless daughter, for himself, for the long lonely years. "I... I held her hand until help arrived. I felt as though a part of me had died that day out in the field."

If it wasn't for his family, he wasn't sure he would have made it through those first dark days. They made him eat, even though he had no appetite. They made him get out of bed, even though he clung to the sleep where Beth still lived in his dreams. They made him put one foot in front of the other, even when he stumbled. They helped him stand again. Through it all, they'd loved him.

He wondered if Aster had a family like that—a family that was there even when he told them to go away—a family that refused to give up on him. Something told him she didn't because she never talked about them.

Aster leaned her head against his shoulder. It felt good to have her so close—to be able to share this moment. He leaned his head to the left, resting his cheek upon her silky hair. He breathed in the soft strawberry scent of her shampoo. It was like a balm upon his wounded heart.

He didn't know how long they stood there together, leaning on each other. He wasn't quite sure who was holding the other up. Not that it mattered on that September evening.

Much too soon Aster pulled away. The spot where her head had been quickly cooled. He missed the feel of her touch. He longed to draw her back to him but knew it wouldn't be right.

"Do you want me to stay for a while?" Her voice was soft and full of emotion.

Yes, he did. He wanted to sit on the porch swing with her as the darkness wrapped around them. He wanted to drape a blanket over them and count the stars. But he knew it was best for both of them if she left.

"You should probably get going. It's going to be a big day tomorrow."

"All right."

As she made her way down the steps, he called out to her. "It's getting late, let me give you a ride home."

He knew she'd be safe on the island. The crime rate was almost non-existent. But it was the gentlemanly thing to do. And perhaps it had something to do with him not being ready to say good night.

"I've got my bike. It has a light. And it isn't far. But thank you."

And then she was gone. He was left alone with the ghosts of his past. He took a seat on the swing and stared out at the stars glittering in the inky black sky.

What would Beth say if she were here? Would she approve of what he'd done with his life? Or would she be upset that he'd buried himself in his work instead of dealing with his feelings? And what would she say about Aster?

19

hree days came and went in a flurry of activity.

And by the end of the weekend, the barn was complete.

Monday afternoon, Aster biked to The Lighthouse Café. She had an important errand to run before she met Nikki at the school. She'd promised to help Sam do something special to thank all of the people who'd been so amazing and generous to him. And she'd immediately started planning the Harvest Dance. It had become her pet project. And it needed one more thing.

Something had changed between her and Sam since he'd opened up about his wife's death. It felt as though it had drawn them closer. Any tension surrounding the fundraiser had dissipated.

Since that emotional night on the porch, Sam smiled more. He didn't look as though he had the weight of the world on his shoulders. And he genuinely seemed happy about the new barn.

In turn, she was happy—the happiest she'd been

since leaving her home in L.A. She smiled and greeted some passersby. She didn't know their names. Not yet. But she'd seen them around the island.

Bluestar was really growing on her. When she'd first arrived on the island, she hadn't been sure what she would make of small-town life. For so long she'd told herself that she was a city girl through and through. Because in the big city you became basically anonymous, able to move about and only rarely run into someone you knew. She found comfort in her anonymity.

But life on Bluestar Island was a lot different. The locals all seemed to know each other. And they were getting to know her, which she'd been resistant to in the beginning. But it hadn't taken her long to start opening up. Not about her past. Never about that. Though she thought of sharing it with Sam, especially now that he'd shared the most painful moment in his life. She couldn't even imagine what it felt like to lose someone you loved that much. She'd never loved like that.

Since that night there'd never been a right time to talk. That wasn't necessarily true. She could have made the time. But what would he think of her story? Would he think less of her for letting Oz into her life? How could he not? She did.

With a sigh, she parked her bike outside of The Lighthouse and was about to open the door when Sam's mother and Chief Campbell exited the restaurant hand-in-hand. They both smiled when they saw her.

Sam's mother had always been so kind from the first time Aster had met her. It was impossible not to like her.

Aster could only imagine what it must have been like to have her as a mother. In that moment, she was jealous of Sam. She wondered if he knew how lucky he was to have such an amazing family.

"Aster, I've been meaning to catch up with you." Helen's green eyes radiated a warmth that immediately put Aster at ease. "I wanted to thank you for all you did for my son."

Aster wasn't quite sure what the woman was referring to. "Thank you but I... I didn't do much."

Helen's smile broadened. "You're too modest. We all know without you to convince my son to accept the help from the town that he never would have done it. He'd have let his pride get in the way and everyone's efforts would have gone to waste."

"It wasn't just me. Hannah helped convince him."

Helen nodded in understanding. "You're good for him. I haven't seen him this happy in a very long time."

Um... She wasn't quite sure what to say. "I'm glad things are going well for him. He's a great guy. And your granddaughter is the sweetest. But Dash, well, he's a handful."

Both Helen and Chief Campbell let out a laugh before agreeing with her. Just about everyone in Bluestar had heard about the little goat's skills with escaping his pen. The older he got, the farther he ventured.

"We don't want to keep you." Helen tucked a strand of her short auburn hair behind her ear. "I just wanted you to know that your efforts to help my son and granddaughter are appreciated."

And then Helen did something completely

unexpected. She reached out and hugged Aster. Not a barely there hug but a great big draw-you-in-and-squeeze type of hug. There was only one other person who hugged her this way—Rosa. Aster blinked back the rush of tears.

When they moved on down the sidewalk, Aster entered the café. She headed straight back to the counter. She noticed Darla off to the side refilling someone's coffee. So, she took a seat to wait for her.

A minute later, Darla placed the coffee pot on the warmer and turned with a smile. "What can I get you?" She blinked and shook her head. "Sorry. It's habit. Wait. Do you want something?"

"No." Aster felt bad about bothering her friend at work, so she decided to place an order. "On second thought, how about an iced tea and some advice?"

"Okay. Iced tea first. And then the advice." Darla rushed off to get the iced tea and top it with a wedge of lemon. When she placed it in front of Aster, she said, "So, what's this advice you need? Let me guess. It's about Sam." Aster nodded as she took a drink of tea, but before she could say a word, Darla continued. "I knew it. I knew you two would get together."

"Shh…" Aster glanced around to make sure no one had overheard her friend's exuberant voice. Then she said softly, "It's not like that. We're friends."

"Friends first and then dating. It's the natural progression of things."

Aster shook her head. "Not always."

Darla gave her a strange look. Why was she staring at her so strangely? She started to get paranoid. Was it her makeup? Had it come off?

Her fingers moved to her jaw. "Is something wrong with my makeup?"

"No. You look beautiful as always."

Aster expelled a pent-up breath as she lowered her hand. "Then why are you looking at me like that?"

"I just can't believe you don't see what everyone else does."

She had absolutely no idea what Darla was talking about. "Which is what?"

"It's the way he looks at you. It's like you are the only woman in the room. He's so into you."

"What? No, he's not!" Then realizing she'd raised her voice, heat rushed to her cheeks. She didn't dare glance over her shoulder at the nearby tables. Hopefully, no one had paid them any attention. She swallowed hard and then tried again in a softer voice. "You don't understand. He's not over his wife. He's not ready to start a new relationship." The acknowledgment deflated her. "And you know that I'm in no position to start anything."

Darla rolled her eyes. "That's just because you're afraid of taking a risk. You know, not everyone is like that creep."

"I know." She didn't think Sam was anything like Oz. "But that's not why I'm here. I wanted to ask you if you had any recommendations for a musical group for the Harvest Dance."

"Oh." Darla smiled as she lightly clapped her hands. "So, you're helping Sam plan it."

"Of course I am. And don't go making it more than it

is. I offered to help him with the dance if he went along with the barn-raising."

"I have a feeling he would have caved just because you asked him too."

"That's not true." Was it? No. Of course not. He knew how important the new barn was to his and Nikki's future. Her mouth grew dry and she sipped at her tea. "Darla, focus."

"Okay. But I have to say that you're no fun today."

"I have a lot to do. And not much time to get it done." It was the truth. "I just need some help getting a band—"

"Are you planning another special event?" The mayor's voice came from behind her.

Aster turned on the stool to find her boss standing there with curiosity reflected in his eyes. "Um, yes. But no."

The curiosity turned to confusion. "I don't understand. You are? Or you aren't?"

The last thing she wanted to do was get into this with the mayor. After all, it wasn't so long ago that Sam had accused her of using his situation in order to further her career. She didn't want to repeat that episode.

She swallowed hard. "I am. But it's a personal event."

"Must be a big event if you are booking a band." Mayor Banks' dark brow arched.

She had the feeling it would be easier and faster just to tell him what was going on. And so she laid it all out for him about the Harvest Dance. She'd planned out some finger foods and refreshments, as well as the decorations. The music was where she'd run into problems.

"That's a great idea," he said.

"But it isn't an island event. It's Sam's way of thanking everyone who helped with the barn."

"I understand but it's still good for the community. I like it. Feel free to work on it during work hours. Keep me updated on your progress."

"Uh… Yes, sir."

"You know this would make a good follow-up article for the paper."

"No, sir." When he frowned at her, she rushed on to say, "I mean Sam doesn't like publicity. His isn't doing this to gain attention. He just wants people to know how much he appreciates their generosity."

"I understand. No publicity. But keep me informed."

"I will."

After Mayor Banks turned and walked over to a table, Aster turned back to Darla. "How did that happen? This isn't good. Sam isn't going to like having the mayor involved. He's going to think I'm using this event to further my career… Again."

"Relax. He'll understand. Everyone knows the mayor is anxious to make his mark upon the island."

Aster didn't think it'd be that easy to explain. She was going to have to talk to Sam, the sooner, the better. She checked the time. It was almost time to pick Nikki up at school.

"Do you have any suggestions for a band?" she asked.

Darla started naming off some of the local bands that

played around the island. Most were all country bands and a couple were eighties cover bands. Aster wrote down all of their names.

"There's a possibility you could get a really big name for the party," Darla said.

"I don't know. We don't have a lot of money."

"You might be able to get her for free."

Excitement pulsed through Aster's veins. "Tell me more."

"You could call Sam's sister, Em Bell. She hasn't been back to the island to visit in a while, but she might be able to make it. I don't know for sure. From what I hear she's really busy making a name for herself. But if she knew it was for her brother, she might drop everything."

"I totally forgot about Sam mentioning her when he first hired me. But she's probably busy and this is so last minute."

"You won't know until you ask her."

"How? I don't have her number. And I don't want to ask Sam because if she's busy, which she probably is, I don't want him feeling let down."

"Good point. But I can solve one of your problems. I'll be right back." She rushed to the back of the restaurant.

Aster glanced toward the doorway to make sure no new customers came in while her friend was away from the counter. Luckily, it was a quiet afternoon. No one came in during those couple of minutes, and the few lingering customers seemed content with what they had been served.

Darla returned with a yellow sticky on the tip of her finger. "Now you have Em's number. Good luck!"

"Thanks. I think I'm going to need it."

"Sorry. Duty calls." Darla turned to grab the coffee pot from the warmer. "Fill me in later."

"I will. Thanks." Aster laid money on the counter to cover the tea and then she started for the door.

She'd spent a little more time in the café than she'd intended, and now she'd have to hurry so she wasn't late picking up Nikki. This meant the phone call would have to wait.

She hopped onto her bike and headed for the school. The elementary school was on the edge of town. It didn't take long to get there. Aster was pleased when she found she was seven minutes early.

She reached for her phone and placed the call. She couldn't believe she was calling a music star. She'd watched Emma Bell as she'd sung her way into stardom on *Songbird*. Boy, could she sing. Aster could only dream of singing that well.

And now the phone was ringing. Aster's stomach shivered with nerves. Would she answer a phone number she didn't recognize? Aster hoped so.

Ring-ring. Ring-ring.

She should hang up. But then she decided a voicemail might help the situation. However, she had friends who never bothered listening to their voicemails. So, it wasn't any guarantee that Emma would get the message. Still, she had to try.

"Hi, Emma. You don't know me, but I am a friend of your family's. I'm a new resident of Bluestar. Anyway, I don't know if you've heard but the town has built your brother a new barn. And now I'm helping him plan a big thank you party. It's going to be a harvest dance next weekend. I know this is short notice, but I was wondering if there's any chance you would be available to attend. I know your brother would love if you could sing a song or two."

And then Aster left her phone number and thanked her. Now the only thing she could do was sit and hope that Emma called her back. In the meantime, she phoned one of the local bands.

"Aster! You're here." Nikki smiled as she ran toward her. When she stopped in front of her, she gave Aster a great big hug.

"Where else would I be?"

Nikki pulled back and shrugged. "I don't know. Wait until you hear about my day."

"Was it that good?"

"Better. I made another friend."

With the sun shining overhead and a gentle sea breeze, they set off toward the farm. Nikki talked almost nonstop. Aster loved being a part of this family, but she couldn't forget what he'd told her the other night about losing his wife. Any random thoughts she'd had about him and her—about them—well, she knew it would never happen. He was still in love with his wife.

The knowledge weighed heavy on Aster's chest, but she knew it was the way it was meant to be. They were friends. That had to be enough.

They had just arrived at the Bell farm. In the distance sat the new red barn. It was beautiful. Well, as beautiful

as a barn could be with its deep red painted walls and the white metal roof. The front door was open and she wondered if she'd find Sam inside.

"Can we go see Dash?" Nikki asked.

"You know the rules. Homework first and then you can play." Aster gave her a look that meant business.

Nikki huffed in disappointment. "Okay."

"You go ahead inside and I'll be right there. I just want to have a word with your father."

Nikki groaned as she turned toward the house with her pretty pink backpack. As she trudged up the steps, her ponytail swished back and forth. Aster turned toward the barn. She made her way to it and found Sam inside. He had his arms crossed as he looked around.

"Is there a problem?" she asked.

He jerked around. "I didn't hear you come in."

"Sorry. I didn't mean to startle you. You seemed to be deep in thought."

"I was thinking about how exactly I want to use the barn."

"You mean besides storing your farm equipment?"

"I'm considering putting this section of the barn to better use." His eyes were bright with excitement.

She had no idea what he had on his mind, but whatever had put him in this good mood, she was all for it. "And what do you have in mind?"

"You know how Nikki loves the goats?" When Aster nodded, he continued. "Well, right now they are pets. I was thinking we could have a goat farm. I mean we already do but I was thinking we could start producing and selling the milk and cheese."

"That's a great idea."

"And it's all thanks to you and the town. Farming the land is great, but the bigger the fields get, the more I'm away from the house. If I turn more of the land back into grass fields for the goats, the less time I'll be out on the tractor. I'll be around more for Nikki."

Aster smiled. She was so happy for him. "I think that's a great idea."

"And I think Nikki will approve."

"I think you're right."

She swallowed hard. "There's something I need to talk to you about."

The light in his eyes extinguished. "This sounds serious. Please tell me you aren't quitting already, are you?"

She shook her head. "Nothing like that."

"Okay. But you have me worried, so out with it."

"You know how I volunteered to plan the Harvest Dance for you?"

"Yes. And I've also given that some thought. There's a lot of planning to be done. It's going to take a lot of your time, and I think it's only fair that I pay you."

Aster shook her head. Even though she could use the money, she refused to accept a cent. "I'm not doing this to make money. I'm doing this because friends help friends."

"Are you sure I can't change your mind?"

"I'm positive." When he didn't argue, she continued. "Anyway, I was discussing the plans for the dance with Darla at the café and well, the mayor overheard me."

"And he doesn't want you to do it?" When she shook

her head, he asked, "He thinks the dance is a bad idea?" When she shook her head again, he said. "Then I don't understand. What's the problem?"

"I was getting to that. He thinks it's a great idea. In fact, he said I could work on it while I'm at the office and he even offered to help."

Sam's eyebrows drew together. "I'm not seeing the problem."

"I don't want you to think that I'm using the event to further my career. Nothing could be further from the truth. I'm doing it because we're friends—at least I think we're friends. Right?" She stopped her nervous rambling.

Sam smiled. "Of course we're friends. And I know I jumped to the wrong conclusion before the barn-raising, and I'm very sorry about that. I just had a lot of emotions and I took it out on you, which I shouldn't have done. You don't have to worry. I know you're doing all of this because you're an amazingly kind and generous woman. And if the mayor has noticed all of your hard work, all the better. I hope it does help your career."

"You do?" She wasn't sure she'd heard him correctly.

He nodded. "I do. But it's for a selfish reason."

Now he had her full attention. "Which is what?"

"I want you to excel at your job because I want you to stay on the island. You've prodded me out of my shell that I've been stuck inside for far too long. You're good for me. You're good for Nikki. See, I told you it was a selfish reason."

It took her a second to realize she was smiling. A

great big, broad smile. And her eyes blurred with happy tears. She blinked them away.

"I have a confession," she said.

"What's that?"

"I hope I excel at my job, too, because I'm falling for—" She stopped before she said him and instead said, "The island. You and Nikki have been good for me too. When I came here, I was broken and trying to fit the pieces of my life back together. You have helped me be confident again and believe in myself and my decisions."

"I did all of that?" His warm gaze caressed her face.

"You did. Thank you. I have no plans to leave the island. I just have to find a place of my own so I can let Darla have her office back again."

"I can rent you a room. I have six of them."

"Thanks. But no. I need to do this all on my own." And she needed to forget about Oz and what he'd done to her, but she didn't think that was possible. She wasn't the same person she'd been before the stalking and attack. She had to learn to live with what happened and accept it was part of who she was now.

"I understand." Sam's deep voice drew her from her thoughts. "But just know the offer is always available."

"Thank you."

"Aster! Aster!" Nikki ran into the barn. They both turned to her as she said, "Are you coming to help me?"

"I'm coming now."

"Good. Because I'm stuck on my math. And you're good at it." Nikki took her hand. "Come on."

Aster couldn't help but smile. She liked being needed. She'd never realized that until then. And there was one other person that needed her—Rosa. Aster couldn't help but wonder if it was possible to convince her dear friend about the benefits of island life. It was worth a try.

20

hy exactly had he agreed to this? Sam inwardly groaned. He must be working too many hours in the hot sun and not getting enough sleep. He assured himself that was the reason he'd agreed to take dancing lessons from Aster. Because there was no way he would agree to such a thing if he was in his right mind.

It wasn't the dancing he was opposed to. It was the part where he'd make a fool of himself in front of Aster. He didn't want her to think less of him. The realization that he cared what Aster thought of him made the breath still in his lungs.

"Daddy, what's wrong?" Nikki's voice interrupted his thoughts. "Your face is all scrunched up like you do when dinner is burned."

He released the pent-up breath. "Everything is fine, sweetie." They walked up the sidewalk toward the dance studio where Nikki took her ballet lessons on Wednesday evenings. "Are you excited about your lesson tonight?"

She nodded her head. "I really wanted the tutu. Can I get a tutu? Please."

"When your teacher says you need one, we'll get you one. Don't you like your new pink skirt?"

Nikki shrugged her slim shoulders. "I guess so. It has a pretty pink ribbon just like Kelly's."

When Sam glanced up, he found they'd reached the dance studio. "Here we are. Now remember if you need me for anything, I'll have my phone. Just call me on yours. It's in your backpack, right?"

"Yes, Daddy. You checked twice now."

He nodded. "Of course. I just wanted to be sure."

"What are you going to do?"

"I don't know." His thoughts immediately turned to Aster. "I might go for a walk on the beach."

"That sounds boring. You could see if Aster wants to have dinner."

"Dinner? But we already ate." Was his seven-year-old practicing to be a matchmaker? He quickly dismissed the notion.

"You could take her for ice cream. Girls like ice cream." She smiled at him as her eyes filled with hope.

Hope? She was hopeful about him having ice cream with Aster? He swallowed hard. He should ignore it, but there was another part of him that worried his daughter was getting her hopes up only to have them dashed.

He cleared his throat. "Nikki, why do you want me to have ice cream with Aster?"

"So we'll be a family, silly." She skipped away into the dance studio, leaving him slack-jawed on the sidewalk.

He didn't remember anything about his walk to the beach. He was totally lost in his thoughts. Nikki wanted Aster to be a part of their family—a mother for her—a wife for him. His heart raced as his palms grew clammy at the thought.

He would have to set Nikki straight this evening. He couldn't let her imagination get away from her. Because he wasn't ready to move on. Even though it'd been more than four years, he wasn't ready to recreate the family they once had. Beth's image filled his mind. His heart swelled with love, but the excruciating pain he'd come to know since her death wasn't as piercing. It was still there but it was…duller. What did that mean?

"Sam! Over here!" The familiar voice had him seeking out Aster.

Aster waved her hand, and he headed straight for her. If she had any part in putting this idea in his daughter's head, he was going to make things clear to her. They weren't a couple. They never would be.

Her stomach shivered with nerves.

When she'd proposed dance lessons to Sam, Aster had been so sure it was a good idea—that it would give Sam the confidence he needed to enjoy himself at the harvest dance. But now that he was heading in her direction, her heart leapt into her throat.

Maybe this wasn't such a good idea. Maybe she should refer him to the dance studio in town. Surely someone there could help him better than she could.

But when he stopped in front of her, she said, "Hi. Are you ready to dance?"

"No." His brows drew together into a formidable line. Something was most definitely wrong. "We have to talk."

"Oh. Okay." She had no idea what had him frowning. She hoped he hadn't changed his mind about hosting the dance.

He rubbed the back of his neck. "Nikki has the idea that you and I...that we're going to be a family. She thinks if I take you out for ice cream that we'll get together, and she'll have a family again."

Aster looked shocked. "I never said anything like that to her." As his brows furrowed together, she grew even more nervous. "I didn't. You have to believe me."

"I do." He sighed. "I know Nikki wants a mother. I... I just can't give her one. And I feel so guilty."

Aster remembered as a child how she'd desperately longed for her own parents. Nothing and no one had ever filled that spot in her heart.

But Nikki's situation was thankfully different. She had a loving father, and she was open to letting someone in her life—someone to be a caring and devoted mother to her.

"Maybe you should consider dating." The words slipped past her lips before she considered Sam's reaction.

"What?" His eyes widened. "I can't believe you suggested such a thing. Wait. Are you saying we"—his hand waved between them—"should date?"

"No. The last thing I want is a relationship." As he stared at her with uncertainty reflected in his eyes, her blood pressure rose. "It's true. After my last nightmare of a relationship, why would I want another?"

It wasn't until the words were out of her mouth that she realized she'd once again said too much. It was Sam's presence that made her a bit excited and nervous, causing her to speak without thinking. But now that she'd said the words, there was no way to take them back.

In a blink, the look in his eyes changed to curiosity. "This bad breakup... Is it why you moved to Bluestar?"

She drew in an unsteady breath. This conversation was never supposed to happen, but how was a person supposed to lock up the past and pretend it didn't exist? That it hadn't changed them?

Not sure if she was making a mistake or not, she nodded. Maybe he'd just leave it there. Maybe he wouldn't ask any other questions. But then there was this part of her that wanted to talk about it—that wanted to get it out there once and for all.

She hadn't spoken the details of that fateful night since she'd talked to the police and then the DA. But all of that had been the stark facts and how she'd thought she'd die that night. She hadn't discussed the months where she almost jumped out of her skin when someone knocked at the door. Or how she couldn't return to her apartment—the scene of the attack—and instead stayed in Rosa's spare room.

"Aster, what is it?" Sam's deep voice was soft and comforting.

There were times when Sam reminded her of a great big teddy bear. She could imagine being wrapped up in his big muscular arms where nothing bad could ever happen to her again. If only that were true…

And then quite unexpectedly he reached out to her. Her initial reaction was to back away. But this was Sam—Nikki's dad—the gentleman farmer. And so, she stood her ground even as her heart raced.

And then his thumb gently swiped across her cheek. When he pulled his hand away, she noticed the moisture glistening on his fingertip. "Whatever it is"—his voice was barely more than a whisper—"you can talk to me. Maybe I can help."

She had tears on her cheeks? She hadn't even noticed because she had been so caught up in the memories that were now strands woven into the fabric that was her life.

"Can we walk?" It would be easier to say what she had to without watching the pity filter across his face.

"Sure." He fell into step beside her as she held her flip-flops and they made their way to the water's edge.

For a while, they walked in silence. She appreciated that he was letting her tell this story at her own pace. His quiet presence was comforting.

If she was truly going to move on with her life instead of hiding behind the shame she felt for allowing a monster into her life, she needed to say the words. Maybe if she admitted what had happened and confronted her feelings, they would leave her in peace. Was that possible? Or was it just wishful thinking?

But when she admitted everything, would Sam still want her to work for him? Would he allow her around his daughter? After all, she wasn't the poster girl for smart decisions.

Still, she had to get it out there. She had to tell the

truth. And then she had to let the chips fall where they may.

Before she lost her courage, she said, "My full name is Charlotte Aster Smith."

She noticed how his brows rose in surprise, but he didn't say anything. They kept walking. The water surged over her bare feet before receding back into the ocean.

"I'm from Los Angeles. I had to leave. Darla offered to take me in and give me a chance to figure out what came next. That's how I ended up here on Bluestar Island." She was rushing ahead. She had to slow down and fill in the awful details. She didn't want to. She wanted to forget about that awful time in her life, but she knew it was never going to be possible because now it was a part of her. She could only hope to lessen its power over her.

"I didn't leave California willingly. Not really." She'd thought when Oz's case hadn't gone to court that she would never have to recount one of the worst moments of her life, but she'd been wrong. By holding it all in, she was holding people at arm's length. "I had a job there. A good job. I worked on a college campus as an event coordinator. I loved it. I got to interact with the student body as well as a lot of artists." She smiled as she recalled her old job and how much she'd enjoyed it. This was yet another thing that Oz had robbed her of. "My friends talked me into trying one of those dating apps. I gave it a go. The first couple of guys were duds but the third one was impressive—at least that's what I thought in the beginning." Her voice faded away.

Sam reached out, taking her hand in his. "You don't have to tell me any of this."

"Yes, I do. I need to know that I have control over the ghosts of my past. Maybe then they will leave me alone."

"I understand."

"I don't think you do. No one could understand the nightmare I've been living with."

"It might not be the same but trust me, I have my own ghosts that keep me up at night."

She knew he was referring to his wife's death. And she immediately felt horrible for dismissing his pain. That wasn't what she'd meant—not at all.

She gave his hand a firm squeeze. "I'm sorry. Sometimes I forget that other people have ghosts of their own."

"It's okay. I'd like to hear about yours, if you still want to tell me."

In her mind, she went back in time. The memories were so vivid that it was almost like Oz was standing in front of her. "Oz was charming and complimentary. He was too good to be true. And I loved how he showered me with flowers and little gifts. But as the gifts grew in number and time went by, little by little he became more possessive. I... I don't have a lot of experience with relationships. Most were casual. So, when he would call to check up on me when I was out with friends or when I went shopping, I thought it was sweet. I foolishly thought it meant he cared."

"It wasn't foolish." Sam's voice took a firm tone. "You were trusting. There's a difference."

"He started insisting that I not hang out with my friends. I did anyway. And then he'd wait for me outside my apartment, and we would argue about who I could and couldn't spend time with. But when I caught him following me, it totally creeped me out. I ended things then and there. He didn't take no for an answer. He said we were destined to be together." A wave of goosebumps prickled her skin as she remembered the way he'd said the words. "When I still wouldn't go back to him, the threats started. I reported him to the police. They had a talk with him. When he roughed me up in a parking lot, I was able to get a restraining order."

Sam stopped walking and turned to her. "That's horrible. No one should have to go through something like this. I'm so glad you got away from him."

She gazed into Sam's eyes while their hands were still connected. He was such a good guy. Her instincts hadn't been wrong about the blue-eyed farmer.

She could stop the story here, but she knew it would be the easy way out. She forced herself to keep going. They continued walking down the beach as she recounted the final night in her apartment when Oz had ignored the restraining order, and she'd ended up battered, bruised, and broken by the time the police physically pulled him off her.

"In the end, they plea-bargained him down to house arrest because it was his first offense. I don't think that this was the first time he'd done something like this to a woman. I just think it's the first time he got caught."

"And that's why you left California and changed your name?"

"He has friends. And one of those friends secretly told me that he was trying to hire someone to kill me."

Shock reflected in Sam's eyes. "Surely this was enough to lock him away for a long time."

She shook her head. "After I reported it to the police, they tried to find the person that told me, but he had disappeared. So, it was my word against his. The DA told me if I had somewhere to go, far from L.A., that it was a good idea. They believed the threat, but they had no proof. I believe if he gets a chance, he'll kill me."

She stopped walking as she fought to hold back the sobs. She'd been holding them in for so long. She'd been telling herself that she'd been refusing to cry since she'd left California because that was giving Oz the power. But when Sam pulled her into his arms, she let loose with her emotions.

She cried on his shoulder for the trust that she'd lost in her own judgment, the friends she'd left behind, the fun job that was now nothing more than a memory and abandoning the one person she considered family, Rosa.

She'd been in fight-or-flight mode for so long she hadn't let herself deal with the grief of giving up so much. She didn't know how long he held her until her tears dried. She pulled back and swiped at her cheeks. She must look a mess now.

And her scar, was it still hidden beneath her heavy makeup? Her body tensed. She hoped so. She didn't tell him that part. She'd already said enough.

"I'm sorry. I didn't mean to fall apart on your shoulder." Her gaze moved to the place where she'd rested her cheek and noticed how her tears had dampened his shirt. She reached out and ran her fingers over the tear stains. "I made a mess of both of us."

His hand caught hers. "No, you didn't. I know how much it means that you confided in me."

"Please don't tell anyone. Only two other people on the island know what's going on and until I'm sure Oz has forgotten about me, I just want to lie low."

"I understand. And you don't have to worry. I won't tell a soul."

Ding. Ding. Ding.

Sam reached for his phone in his back pocket. "Sorry. It's my reminder to go pick up Nikki. Looks like we didn't get to dance."

"No, we didn't. When does Nikki have another lesson?"

"Friday."

Aster smiled. "Then it's a date." Then realizing how that sounded, she rushed to correct it. "I mean we'll meet here for a dance lesson."

"Relax. I know what you meant." He sent her a reassuring smile that made her heart flutter in her chest. "Are you ready to go?"

"I think I'll stay here for a little bit. I like walking on the sand."

He looked hesitant to leave her alone but finally he said, "Okay. I'll see you tomorrow." He started to walk away but then paused and turned back. "You should stay for dinner on Friday and then we can come into town together."

"But I'll have my bike."

"I'll throw it on the back of the golf cart."

"Okay." She smiled. "It's a plan."

And then he was gone, leaving her alone with her thoughts. Was she being paranoid? Would Oz give up on his promise of revenge when he learned she'd skipped town?

She liked it there in Bluestar. She was starting to see it as a definite part of her future. She glanced to the side to catch one last glance of Sam, but he'd already disappeared from view. This island definitely had a lot of reasons for her to stay on it. And he was one of them.

21

*S*he made dinner.

And he'd insisted on doing the dishes after the meal. It all felt so natural.

Sam hadn't expected Friday's meal to feel so comfortable—so routine. He realized over the past month the three of them had shared a number of meals together. And yet without his noticing, Aster had become a part of them—a welcome face at the table. She even had a certain seat where she sat for the meals—the chair to his right. The chair that had once been Beth's spot.

The pain of loss dug at his heart. And yet whether it was due to the passage of time or Aster's easy, unassuming company, it had felt natural for her to be there next to him.

No wonder his daughter had jumped to the wrong conclusion about the three of them becoming a family. But he'd had a heart-to-heart with Nikki and explained that wasn't going to happen. Nikki wasn't happy but she seemed to accept what he'd said.

"This was fun." Nikki smiled brightly.

Sam suspected his daughter was up to something. "Dinner was fun, huh?"

Nikki continued to smile as she nodded. Her gaze moved between him and Aster.

His gaze moved to her plate. "So much fun that you didn't finish your spaghetti and meatballs?"

Nikki glanced down. "Oh."

Even though both he and Aster had finished, his daughter had most of her food still on her plate. She used her fork to scoop up some pasta and shove it into her mouth, leaving a trail of sauce over her chin and lips. He sighed and shook his head. His little girl had a heart of gold but neatness wasn't one of her virtues. And yet he couldn't love her any more than he did right at this moment.

He reached over and picked up Nikki's napkin from the table. He held it out to her. "Here you go."

Her gaze moved from him to the napkin. She snatched it up and swiped it over her face. "That was the best meal ever."

"Ever?" Though it was an excellent meal, he wondered about his daughter's enthusiasm for it.

Nikki grinned and nodded. "Aster is the bestest cook. Right, Daddy?"

His attention turned to Aster, whose cheeks had taken on a rosy hue. "Yes, it was very good."

Her gaze lifted and met his. "Thank you."

They gazed at each other a little longer than was necessary and his pulse began to race. His gaze dipped to her pink lips. He wondered what it would be like to kiss her. He wondered if she ever had similar thoughts.

Maybe it was this domestic setting that had him seeing Aster as something much more than a babysitter. Or maybe it was Nikki's attempt at matchmaking. Did his daughter see something he didn't?

And then Aster turned away and moved to the sink. The moment had passed, and he was jarred by the direction of his thoughts. His mouth grew dry, and he reached for his glass of water. What was wrong with him?

With the meal finished, he insisted on clearing the table and placing the dishes in the dishwasher. They just fit in the full dishwasher. He put the bottle of dishwashing fluid on the counter to remind him to run it when they got home that evening.

And then just as Sam had promised, he placed Aster's bike into the back of his golf cart. Then they drove Nikki to her gymnastics lesson. Some people thought his daughter was enrolled in too many things, but he thought it was good for her to try different things so she could learn what she really liked. And he didn't make Nikki do any of it. They were all her ideas. Right now, he was following her lead.

Once they dropped Nikki off at her lesson, they were on their own. When they both climbed back into the golf cart, he realized it wouldn't be a big stretch to imagine this as a date. A date?

The thought reverberated in his mind. He tramped the accelerator too hard. They lurched forward. He immediately let off the pedal. "Sorry."

"Everything okay?" Aster asked.

"Um, yeah. Sorry about that. My foot slipped." The

jerk of the cart was nothing compared to the jolt of his thoughts.

And yet he continued onward toward the beach, even though his mind told him this evening was a mistake—that he shouldn't dance with her. Still, there was this other part of him that said everything would be all right. This other part was excited to spend more time with Aster—alone time with her.

As he found a parking spot near the beach, he realized he was going to be so busy stepping on her toes that he wouldn't have time to think of anything else. And she would be so unhappy with him that romance would be the last thing on either of their minds. The thought kept him moving forward.

"Is everything all right?" Aster's voice drew him from his thoughts. "You've been awfully quiet."

"I'm sorry. I didn't mean to be."

"If this was about dinner, you don't have to worry."

"Dinner?" He was confused.

"You know, with Nikki going on about the spaghetti. I'm sure she was just being nice and thinks *you're* the best cook in the world."

"She's right. It was delicious. Maybe you'll have to teach me your trick. Because right now, I just open a jar and dump it over the pasta."

"My secret is the internet. I don't have a lot of experience in the kitchen."

"You couldn't tell. Everything you've made us has been delicious, especially the apple cobbler."

The color bloomed in her cheeks. "Thank you. I'm learning as I go along."

They made their way down the beach to a place where there weren't any people. The last thing he wanted was an audience. If he was going to make a fool of himself, it was best to do it in private. He just hoped Aster didn't expect too much from him.

♥♥♥

What made her think this was a good idea?

Every time Sam gazed at her, her stomach dipped.

Even so Aster couldn't think of a legitimate excuse not to dance with him. In the beginning, dance lessons had seemed like a good idea. Maybe she hadn't considered the fact that she found him so very handsome.

And there was the way he stared into her eyes that made her feel as though she were being drawn in by his blue eyes. She could so easily drown in them. She wondered what it would be like to be loved by Sam. Not that she was in love with him. She assured herself that she was just curious.

But as she imagined Sam moving on with his life and building a family with another woman, she got an uneasy feeling in the pit of her stomach. She imagined him smiling as he came in the door from working in the fields and walking up to his new wife as she stood at the stove, stirring their dinner. And then Nikki would stroll in, all smiles now that she had the family she'd dreamed of.

"Shall we stop here?" Sam's voice stirred Aster from her daydream.

"Uh, sure." She wasn't sure how far down the beach they'd walked as she'd been caught up in her thoughts.

"Aster, if you changed your mind about this, I won't

be upset."

She shook her hear. "Why would you think that?"

"Because you're frowning."

She was? She quickly placed a smile on her face. "No frowning here."

He hesitated. "You do know you're a glutton for punishment, don't you?"

"We'll see about that." She kicked off her sandals.

"We're doing this barefoot?"

Her smile broadened. "We are."

So, he took off his shoes and set them next to hers as though they normally lined their shoes up next to each other. As soon as she realized the direction of her thoughts, she stopped them.

The sun was sinking low in the sky when he held his arms out to her. Her heart tumbled in her chest. She longed to walk into his embrace and stay there forever. She imagined pressing her head to his muscular chest and hearing the thumping of his heart.

"Aster?" His brows scrunched together.

She realized she was still standing in the same spot. So, with her heart pitter-pattering, she stepped forward. Leaving a respectable distance between them, she placed one hand on his shoulder while his arm snaked around her waist, sending her heart racing. Her other hand she placed within his. His long fingers wrapped around hers.

"Shouldn't we have some music?" he asked.

Heat swirled in her chest and rushed to her face. What was wrong with her? She was having problems remembering the most basic of things when she was around him.

"Um, yes." She quickly withdrew herself from his hold.

She retrieved her phone in her back pocket and immediately fumbled it. It landed in the sand. Sam picked it up and brushed it off. The heat in her face intensified.

She took the phone, and even though her fingers felt stiff and clumsy, she managed not to drop it again. She pulled up her music app, where she had a country music channel already selected. She turned it on and words of love emanated from her phone.

She inwardly groaned. Why had she picked this music? Did they have to sing of a love story and Romeo?

Her gaze didn't meet his as she turned up the volume and then returned her phone to her pocket. She wanted to change the music but she didn't dare for fear that Sam would read something into it. She just had to keep acting like this dance and the words of undying love were not getting to her. Not at all.

"Shall we?" He held his arms out to her.

Immediately she felt the magnetic draw. Once more his arm wrapped around her waist as she rested her palm against his shoulder. Her heart thump-thumped so loud it echoed in her ears. She could act like his close proximity had no effect over her. She could do this.

His mouth grew dry.

He hoped she didn't notice that his hands had grown clammy.

Sam took Aster's delicate hand into his and closed his fingers around hers. He immediately noticed how her skin was smooth and soft. His gaze moved to her face—everything about her was beautiful. And what she was doing dancing on the beach with him was beyond his comprehension.

But he had no idea how they were supposed to dance together when she was standing so far away. They could easily fit Nikki and his mother between them. He didn't know much about dancing, but he was pretty certain their stance was incorrect.

He tightened his hold on her waist, drawing Aster closer. He also noticed she kept her gaze averted. She had definitely changed her mind about this lesson. She just didn't want to hurt his feelings by telling him.

"Let's not do this," he said. "It was a mistake."

When he went to pull away, it was she who tightened her grip on his shoulder and hand, holding him in place. At last her gaze met his. "We can do this."

He sighed. It was best just to get it over with. "What do I do next?"

"How about we do something simple? We'll sway side to side. All right?"

"Whatever you say. You're the teacher here."

She nodded. "We'll go left and then right. Ready, set, go."

They went in opposite directions. But no toes were stepped upon so that was a plus. He apologized, but she said it was her fault for not being more specific. And so, they tried again. This time it worked. And he had to admit that it wasn't bad. Not bad at all. He could do this, especially with Aster in his arms.

It took them another try but they got it. This wasn't

so bad after all. Not that he'd admit it out loud or anything.

But there was something special about holding Aster in his arms. He lowered his head ever so slightly and inhaled the strawberry scent of her shampoo. It was gentle and sweet, much like her.

As though Aster sensed the shift in his thoughts, she pulled back slightly. She raised her chin until their gazes met. "I think you've got it."

"You think your toes are safe?"

"I do." She smiled at him. "Would you like to learn something a little more challenging?"

"I don't know." He wasn't so sure he wanted to push his luck. He didn't relish the idea of making a fool of himself in front of her.

"Oh, come on. You got this figured out. I'm sure you can do this next one."

"You have a lot more faith in me than I do." He smiled.

"Just trust me."

How could he resist her when she smiled at him? All of his arguments faded away. Right then, if she'd have told him she wanted him to walk on water, he would have tried it. He would have failed for sure, but it wouldn't have kept him from trying it for her.

"Okay. What do you have in mind?"

"Nothing fancy. I promise."

"Show me."

Aster didn't need to be told twice. She stepped back. "Okay. It's going to look like this."

He watched her bare feet and noticed that her

toenails were painted a light sparkly pink. Her feet were petite just like the rest of her barely more than five-foot frame. He was mesmerized as she moved so gracefully.

Then she stopped. "Now it's your turn."

"My turn?" He shook his head. "I don't think I can do that."

"Sure you can." She moved to stand beside him. "Okay now with your right foot step forward. Then with your left foot step to the side. Then bring your right foot over to your left."

He tripped over his own feet. He groaned. "This isn't going to work."

"Yes, it will. Just slow down and try again."

"I don't think so."

When he went to walk away, she reached out, taking his hand in her own. She drew him back to her. "Please."

Her eyes pleaded with him not to quit. How was he supposed to say no when she looked at him that way? And so, he tried again. And again. And again. He felt as though he truly understood what people meant when they said they had two left feet. But to Aster's credit, she was quite patient with him.

"Good!" She smiled. "You've got it."

He did? "I can't believe it."

"Now we have to dance together." Before he knew it, she was in his arms. She lifted her chin and gazed into his eyes. "Just repeat what you learned."

As he continued to stare into her beautiful eyes, his heart began to pound. He told himself it was due to the nervousness he felt over getting the dance steps right. And then he realized their gazes had held a little too long.

He glanced down at their feet, and it only took two steps for him to land on her toes. It was so confusing when he was looking down. He was having problems remembering how he was supposed to move.

"Don't think so hard," she said in a gentle voice. "Try and let your feet move from memory."

"That's so much easier for you to say than for me to do." And so, they tried it. He got the first couple of moves right, but then he ended up once more stepping on her toes. "Sorry."

"It's okay. Let's try again."

This time she said the moves out loud. That helped a lot. It would appear his memory wasn't as good as he wanted to believe. Again and again they went through the motions.

And then she didn't say anything, and they moved through the sequence of steps without him stepping on her toes or making a single mistake.

"I did it." He smiled at her. His gaze lowered to her lips. His heart pounded against his ribs. "Uh, I mean, uh, we did it."

Would it be so wrong to kiss her now? He wanted to press his lips to hers more than he'd wanted anything in a very, very long time. There was something about being with Aster that had him feeling that anything was possible.

His gaze rose to meet hers again. He wondered if she could hear the pounding of his heart. It was so loud it drowned out the crash of the ocean or the call of the birds overhead.

He gazed deeply into her eyes. There was a spark of excitement in them. His gaze dipped to her lips again. He started to lean forward.

Ding. Ding. Ding.

He jerked back. It was as though he'd just been startled out of a trance. He blinked. And then with a sigh, he reached for his phone in his back pocket and swiped off the alarm.

"It's the alarm I set so I wouldn't be late to pick Nikki up after her lesson."

Aster reached for her phone too. She turned off the music. "We should get going."

Together they quietly walked up the beach. He couldn't stop thinking of how close he'd come to kissing her. What had he been thinking?

Maybe it was because he'd been single longer than he wanted to admit. Still, that didn't mean he should go around just kissing anyone. But Aster wasn't just anyone. Not even close. But he didn't want to delve into exactly what that meant.

Instead, he decided that conversing was safer than the direction of his thoughts. As they climbed into the golf cart, he asked, "So how did you learn to dance?"

She shrugged. "I don't dance. Not really. I just know a few moves."

"A few more moves than I know."

"When I was a kid, my foster sisters would watch a dancing show on television. We challenged each other to see who could dance the best." She smiled as she recalled the memory. "We looked dancing up on the internet and learned some of the dance moves. I don't remember all of them."

"It's nice that you have those good memories."

"I'd forgotten about them until now. Thank you."

"For what?"

"Reminding me that even though those years weren't easy that there was some happiness sprinkled in between the challenges."

He pulled the golf cart into a parking spot near the studio. "In that case, you're welcome."

He climbed out and got her bike for her. "Thank you for the dance lesson. Sorry about smashing your toes. I hope they don't hurt too much."

She accepted the bike from him. "They're fine. And this is where we part because I'm going that way." She pointed in the direction of Darla's apartment. "Good night."

"Night."

His gaze followed her for a moment until he realized he was staring. He turned and headed in the opposite direction. The moment on the beach when they'd almost kissed replayed in his mind. Just the memory made his heart race.

And then he shoved the memory to the back of his mind. He couldn't dwell on it. It was a mistake to let his thoughts go there. Because he couldn't let it happen. He didn't deserve to find happiness again.

22

h, what a beautiful morning.
The sun shone brightly as a gentle ocean breeze rushed over Aster's skin. She smiled and resisted to break out in song. Instead, she lightly hummed a ditty.

She'd been in a great mood all weekend—ever since Sam almost kissed her on the beach. She may not have a lot of experience with men, but she was bright enough to know when she was about to be kissed.

Her heart fluttered in her chest at the memory. For so long she'd tried to convince herself that he didn't see her that way. But it wasn't true. He was interested, even if he was fighting it.

Her future on the island was looking rosier with every passing day. It would be perfect if Rosa was there. Soon she'd broach the subject with Rosa of her moving to the island too. Wouldn't it be perfect?

Her steps were light and bouncy as they barely touched the sidewalk. Today was going to be an awesome day. She could feel it.

First, she had her job at city hall, which was the perfect position for her. She'd never thought she'd find something she'd like doing as much as she'd enjoyed working on the college campus where there was a lot of positive energy that kept each day interesting.

But Bluestar had an energy of its own and so much potential. She was constantly adding to her list of potential events to plan for the town, including a baking competition, a music festival on the beach, and maybe a hot dog eating contest, but the more she thought about the last idea, the more she didn't care for it. Still, there were hundreds of other ideas. They didn't even have to do the same thing each year. They could go for some versatility. Maybe the town could vote on one of the events each year. As soon as she got to her desk, she'd start brainstorming ideas from the ones they'd used at the college to some more unique ones.

Just up ahead there was a crowd forming in the street. She wondered what it was because they were blocking the road for golf carts and bikes alike. Then there was a gasp and people started to back up.

Now that she worked at city hall, she supposed it was her duty to check on things just in case authorities needed to be called. Mayor Banks liked his town to run smoothly. His philosophy was that anything that disrupted Bluestar's calm serenity needed to be dealt with immediately.

And so, Aster quickened her steps toward the crowd. She pardoned her way to the front and then came to an abrupt stop. Dash stood there. And he wasn't alone.

This time he had brought along two of his buddies

for the adventure. Was that Billy? And Gruff?

Dash and his cohorts eyed the throng of people warily. Being they were used to farm life where there weren't many people, all of these strange faces must be startling.

"We should shoo them out of town!" a male voice called out from the crowd.

"I'm not touching them. You do it," shouted a woman.

"Everyone clap their hands—"

"No!" What was wrong with these people? Had they never seen goats before? Aster stepped forward and turned to the crowd. "The goats are fine where they are until their owner arrives. Do not scare them."

There was a murmur that rippled through the crowd. Aster didn't stop to listen to their opinions. She didn't care what these people thought. All she cared about was making sure the goats made it home safely.

She retrieved her phone from her back pocket. Thank goodness she'd decided to get a disposable phone. She dialed Sam's number. It rang. And rang. *Please answer. Please answer.*

"Hello."

"Thank goodness. Sam, you have to come to town right away. It's Dash. He's here and he's not alone. He's brought a couple of friends with him."

"How in the world did he manage that? Never mind. Can you keep them with you until I get there?"

"I'll try." And then she told him exactly where they were.

She turned her attention to Dash. She had a feeling

he was the ring leader. Wherever he went, his friends would go. So, if she could get ahold of his collar, she hoped she could keep them with her until Sam arrived.

"Hey, Dash, remember me?" She inched forward as a hush came over the crowd. She forgot about the audience and instead focused on the scared goats. "How did you get here, little guy? That must have been some adventure." With every word she spoke, she moved closer to Dash.

When there was a loud pop in the distance, Dash's head swung to the right. His eyes were big and round with fear. Poor little guy. His big adventure was more than he'd bargained for.

With him distracted, she moved closer and was able to grasp his collar. He swung his head around to look at her with a *what-are-you-doing* look.

"It's okay." She kept her voice soft and soothing. She ran her hand over his side the way Nikki had shown her to do. "Everything is going to be okay."

She just kept talking to Dash as the seconds slowly ticked by. She had no idea how much time passed as the crowd thinned out.

"Here you go." The female voice was familiar.

Aster turned her head to find Sam's mother standing there holding a rope. "Thanks."

She took the rope and tied it securely to Dash's red collar. He didn't seem to mind. He was too busy checking out all of the sights around him. Dash was certainly the curious sort.

"I'm sorry my son's goats have now become your problem," Helen said. "Did you call him?"

"I did. He'll be here shortly."

"Would you like me to watch them until he arrives?"

"Thanks. But Dash and I are friends now. I don't mind waiting." It wasn't until the words were out her mouth that she realized this delay would make her late for work—late for a job where she was anxious to make a good impression.

"Would you like me to wait with you?" Helen asked.

"That's okay," she said automatically. "We're good."

Helen worried her lip as though she wasn't sure if she should stay or go.

"It's okay," Aster said. "You can go. We'll be okay." She glanced at her charges. "Right, Dash?"

He glanced up at her as though he understood what she'd said.

Helen's brows knitted together as though she were torn. "I have to get to work, but I don't feel right about leaving you here alone."

"Go. I promise we're good. In fact, I'm going to move the goats over to the sidewalk so traffic can get through."

"Good idea. You lead Dash, and I'll make sure the other two follow. I should know their names but I always get them mixed up."

Aster pointed to the one on the left. "That one is Billy." She moved her finger to the one on the right. "And that one is Gruff." Then she glanced down. "Okay, Dash. Let's go."

She pulled on the rope but Dash didn't budge. It appeared he was starting to enjoy his trip to town. But then she glanced forward and realized that wasn't it.

There was a wall of people between them and the sidewalk.

It took a bit to disperse the crowd. Once that was done, Dash followed her to the sidewalk. And luckily Billy and Gruff followed suit.

Once on the sidewalk, traffic began to move again. Who knew there could be a traffic jam in Bluestar?

"Thank you for the help," Aster said to Helen. "We should be good here until Sam shows up."

"You're sure?"

"Positive."

Helen hesitated before she gave a little wave and then rushed off down the sidewalk. At least one of them would be on time for work. She wondered what the mayor would say when she provided her explanation for being late to work. Hopefully, Sam would be there soon, and she wouldn't be too late.

♥♥♥

He'd done it again.

Every time Sam thought he had the goat pen secure, Dash found another way out. That was one smart goat. This time Sam was certain the gate had been fully latched because he'd double checked it. Yet as he rushed out the back door, he noticed the gate was now hanging fully open. How had Dash opened it? At this rate, he was going to have to start padlocking the gate.

He rushed over and secured the gate before he had more escapees. Thankfully, Dash and his cohorts hadn't been injured while out on their sightseeing trip. But Sam was pretty certain Aster wasn't too happy about goat-sitting when she was supposed to be at work.

He hadn't seen Aster since their dance lesson on Friday—when he'd almost kissed her. He couldn't believe he'd almost lost control. It would have ruined their perfect arrangement.

Because in the end, he couldn't be the man Aster needed him to be. He'd already failed Beth. He couldn't fail Aster too. She'd already been through so much with that monster.

His pickup truck bounced down the country road as he headed into town. He didn't have a day pass as was required to drive into the heart of Bluestar. His pickup was for on the farm or making deliveries to the docks before 9:00 a.m. each morning. And yet he kept driving. If he were cited for not having a pass, he would just have to deal with it.

Making his way through town was very slow-going. There were people, carts, and bikes everywhere. When people saw him, they moved out of the way.

At last Aster and the goats came into sight. Dash was amusing himself by eating flowers in a wooden planter outside of a dress shop, and Aster was struggling to drag him away. Sam inwardly groaned. And then Billy and Gruff joined him by munching on the other flowers. Not only did he owe Aster a big apology but now he had to replace the flowers.

Sam pulled to a stop and jumped out. He rushed over to Aster.

His pulse raced just being near her. Perhaps he hadn't gotten as much perspective as he'd thought.

Aster struggled but finally got Dash and the other goats away from the planter that now just had bare green stems sticking up.

"I'm sorry." Sam reached for Dash's rope. "I got here as soon as I could."

"I tried to keep them out of trouble, but I failed."

"It's okay." He went to wrap an arm around her shoulders to show support but he hesitated. Physical contact might not be wise. His arm lowered to his side. "It's just some flowers. I'll make sure they're replaced."

She glanced past him to the pickup. "You can't drive that in town."

"I had no choice. Did you really think I'd be able to manage three goats on a golf cart?"

Aster laughed. "You do have a good point. I just hope you don't get caught, or you'll get fined."

He shrugged. "It is what it is." He tugged on Dash's rope. "Come on, boy. It's time to go home."

Luckily, Dash listened to him. Sometimes the stubborn goat pretended he was deaf when Sam talked to him, but it seemed Dash was growing bored with his visit to town. Billy and Gruff followed them. Those older goats should have known better than to follow Dash, who was the young one in the bunch. Sam sighed.

One by one he lifted the goats into the bed of the truck. When he turned around Aster was frowning at him. "What's wrong?"

"I'm just worried about leaving them alone in the back of the truck."

"There isn't enough room up front with me." Not that he would want them in the cab of the truck. Who knew what they'd find to munch on up there? "And I didn't have time to grab the crates. At least it's not far."

To be quite honest, he didn't like the idea either, but if he went really slow nothing bad should happen. He hoped.

"I could go with you."

He shook his head. "I couldn't ask you to do that. You have to get to work."

"You didn't ask. I offered."

It was the safest option. "Are you sure?"

She nodded.

"Do you want to drive or ride with the trio of trouble?"

She smiled at his name for the goats. "I'll drive. But I can't stay."

"I understand. And I appreciate this a lot."

He tossed her the keys, and then he climbed into the bed of the truck to make sure there weren't any more prison breaks. He didn't know what he'd do without Aster. She always seemed to be around when he needed her most.

23

Dark clouds gathered overhead.

Two days later, Sam gazed upward.

He knew whatever was coming their way wasn't going to be a typical rain. He could feel it in his bones. It was his grandmother's saying and when he was young, he thought it was a bunch of nonsense but now, not so much.

He'd checked the weather site periodically that morning, but they were still only reporting a light rain in the forecast. Rain he could deal with but anything more than that could be disastrous to his remaining crops. And so, he set off for the field.

The day moved quickly and so did he. He didn't stop for lunch. As the sun faded behind the dark clouds, the temperature dropped. He kept the tractor moving. He couldn't stop now.

He peered up at the sky, hoping the storm would hold out. But the wind was starting to get bad. The trees in the distance were leaning hard to the east.

Big rain drops splattered against the windshield.

Suddenly, the heavens opened up, and a torrential rain started. He couldn't so much as see out of the windshield. But he knew if he didn't keep going, the tractor would end up stuck in a mud pit. And so, he kept moving forward, squinting through the rain-splattered windshield and relying on his memory to reach the edge of the large field.

It was so slow going. But better safe than sorry. Another of his grandmother's sayings.

He wished he was back at the farmhouse all snug with Nikki and Aster. He imagined them in the warm kitchen, huddled around the table as Nikki completed her homework. The vision brought a smile to his face. A flash of lightning and the immediate crack of thunder vibrated through his entire being and made his smile very short lived.

♥♥♥

Thunder shook the windows.

It rattled Aster physically and emotionally.

It was so dark out outside it was like nighttime, even though it was the middle of the afternoon. And somewhere out there was Sam. She just hoped he was safe.

"Look!" Nikki stood beside her and pointed toward the gate on the goat pen.

Dash was standing at the gate. His head moved up and down, over and over. Then the gate swung open. Aster's mouth gaped. He must have used his mouth or tongue to work the latch. Luckily, most of the goats had decided to climb into their houses, seeking shelter from the rain. But there was Dash headed out the gate. Where was he going?

Another crack of thunder must have scared him, as he started running. Worry coiled up in Aster's gut. That little goat got himself into more trouble than she could imagine. And it appeared even a storm wasn't going to stop him.

Small limbs started to break off the trees and blow across the yard. One limb hit Dash. He fell over. Nikki screamed and ran for the door.

Aster was hot on her trail and grabbed her arm before she could step outside. "You can't go out there."

"I have to. Dash is in trouble."

"He'll be fine." She had to believe that because to think anything else was just too painful.

"No, he won't. He needs me."

Aster glanced out the door. The little goat was once again standing in the wind—in the middle of the yard, where debris was likely to hit him again. She couldn't stand there and do nothing. But she also had Nikki to think of.

"If I go out and help Dash, will you promise to stay here in the house?"

"Yes. I promise." The worried look in Nikki's eyes dug at Aster's heart.

"I mean it. I won't go unless I'm sure you'll stay here, no matter what."

"I cross my heart." Her little finger swiped across her chest.

If she was going to help Dash, she had no choice but to believe Nikki. After all, Nikki was very well-behaved, much better than Aster had been at that age.

"Okay. I'll be right back."

Aster rushed out the door but found that the strong winds were pushing on the screen. When she let it go, the door banged hard against the house. As she moved down the steps, her hair was pressed back against her head. She couldn't remember the last time she was in such fierce winds.

When she glanced back to the last place she'd seen Dash, he was still standing there. She called out to him, but her voice was carried away in the wind. There wasn't a chance he could hear her. She couldn't even hear herself think.

Moving in the strong wind took more determination than normal. She also had to keep an eye out for any blowing debris because leaves and limbs would periodically blow by her.

When she was within several feet of Dash, she called out to him. He must have heard her that time but lightning spooked him. He took off running away from her. The boom of thunder shook the earth as the rolling crescendo continued to play.

Aster considered leaving him, but she couldn't do it. Dash had a lot of personality and even though she hadn't wanted to, she'd grown quite fond of him. And then there was Nikki, who was beside herself with worry.

Aster set off after the goat. Her thoughts turned to Sam. He was out in this weather. He was probably used to it, but that didn't make it any less dangerous. She'd feel a lot better if she saw his tractor drive up right about now.

She raised her hand to shield her eyes from the

blowing wind, and then she squinted into the direction she'd last seen him drive off. There was no sign of headlights or the big green tractor. Her heart clenched with worry.

Right now, there was nothing she could do to help Sam. She wasn't even sure where exactly he was at the moment. But she could help Dash, and so she kept moving. Every now and then, she caught a glimpse of the goat. He was headed for the old barn. What was it about the barn that kept drawing him back again?

Aster glanced back toward the farmhouse, but it was lost in the sheets of rain that poured down. She might as well keep going. The old barn was her best chance for shelter until the worst of the storm passed over.

2 4

This was one of the worst storms in ages.

With a relieved sigh to be home, Sam drove the tractor into the backyard and parked it. He'd worry about the damage to the grass another time. He just wanted to get inside. He imagined settling down at the table with Nikki and Aster to enjoy a nice hot cup of coffee.

He climbed out of the tractor. The wind was blowing the rain with such force that the raindrops stung his face. The fierce wind pressed his clothes flush to his body while the unrelenting rain instantly soaked him.

He moved slower than he'd like, but when you were walking into a strong wind, it wasn't easy going.

At last he reached the steps and made his way to the door. It opened before he touched the handle. Nikki stood there with tears on her cheeks.

He stepped inside and pushed the door closed. He glanced around for Aster, but she was nowhere to be seen. A cold chill of apprehension raced up his spine.

Aster was in trouble. He could sense it. He couldn't let anything happen to her. The past couldn't repeat itself. Adrenaline sent his heart racing. If anything happened to her, he'd never forgive himself.

He knelt down in front of Nikki. "What's the matter? Where's Aster?"

Nikki pointed to the door. "She made me promise to stay here. I'm so scared."

She reached out and hugged her father. He hugged her back. Neither paid attention to the fact he was dripping wet.

He was so relieved to find Nikki safe, but where had Aster gone? What would drive her out into the storm? And then it came to him.

He pulled back from his daughter's hug. "It was Dash, wasn't it? Did he get out again?"

Nikki nodded. "He got hit by a limb and then he ran off. Aster went after him, but she never came back."

His chest tightened. "How long has she been gone?"

Nikki shrugged. "A long time."

Sam's worry escalated, though he hid it from his daughter. "I have to go make sure she's all right. Can you stay here for me?"

Nikki nodded. "I tried to call Gran but the phones aren't working."

"It'll be okay." He was surprised the house still had power. Just then a flash of lightning and a crack of thunder sent the lights flickering.

Tears rolled down Nikki's pale cheeks. "I didn't know what to do."

He hugged her again. "You did the right thing. You

stayed in the house and waited for me. Now I need you
to wait again. Do you know where we keep the
flashlights?"

Nikki nodded. "In the pantry."

"Right. I need you to get those and bring them to the
kitchen."

"But the lights still work."

"They won't for long and we need to be prepared."

"Okay. I can do it."

He kissed the top of her head. "That's my big girl.
I'll be back. I love you."

"I love you too."

And then he headed back outside. He ran toward the
goat pen. The gate was slightly ajar. He thought he'd
finally fixed the latch so Dash couldn't get free, but
apparently the little goat was smarter than Sam had given
him credit for.

"Aster!" The roar of the storm drowned out his
voice.

Sam closed and secured the gate so no other goats
could escape. And then he glanced around, trying to
decide which direction they'd gone.

It wasn't hard to guess where Dash would head. The
old barn was his favorite place to explore with all of the
discarded wood and old tires. Sam wasn't sure how
much of this pounding wind and rain the old building
could handle. His body tensed. If they were in there, it
could be dangerous for both of them.

Sam fought the ferocious wind as he made his way
toward the barn. He didn't see any sign of them, but his
gut told him to keep going—they were inside. And he

needed to get them out of there before the rest of the roof caved in or worse.

When he reached the barn, it emitted an ominous creak under the strain of the unrelenting wind. Boards were being worked loose.

"Aster!" He wasn't sure she would be able to hear him with all of the noise. "Aster, I'm here!"

And then he tried to open the door. It wouldn't budge. He tried again, putting all of his strength into it. Again the door refused to move.

He stepped back and glanced at the door. It was then that he noticed the entire building had shifted. The door was at an angle with one corner smashed down into the wet ground. The barn was collapsing.

"Sam! Sam, is that you?"

The sound of Aster's voice brought tears to his eyes or was that just more rain? He moved as close to the door as possible and yelled, "I'm here. Can you hear me?"

"Yes. I can't move the door. I think the barn is leaning to the side."

"Can you get out another way?"

"I tried but we're pinned in here. The boards keep falling."

This was his worst nightmare come to life. Aster was in danger and he blamed himself. Just like he'd blamed himself when Beth had her accident.

But this time there was something he could do. Adrenaline pumped through his veins. This time he wasn't too late. He would save Aster.

The only way to reach them was to open the door. He

tried again. It still wouldn't move.

"We need to open the door!" He planted his feet firmly on the ground. "Can you push while I pull?"

"I'll try!"

"On my count... One. Two. Three."

He gave it his all, groaning as he used every muscle in his body. Nothing. Aster and Dash were trapped. His heart pounded in his chest as he gulped down the cool air.

"I'm going to walk the perimeter!"

"Don't! It's not safe! Things are flying around in the back of the barn!"

And one of those things could hit Aster. His body tensed. Either he found another exit or he had to get this door opened. His mind raced with scenarios to free them.

"I've got an idea! Hang on!" He set off moving as fast as he could in the storm.

Each second felt like a minute. And each minute dragged on like it was an hour. But Sam wasn't deterred. He dodged debris that flew through the air. In the morning, there would be a lot of clean up to do, not only there on the farm but across the island. But, that was the least of his worries.

When he reached the house, he headed straight for the tractor. The large rubber tires kept him from getting stuck in the mud and debris. He drove it to the new barn where he'd placed some supplies in the office. He grabbed a chain and climbed back into the tractor.

Rain pelted the windshield, making it difficult to see. The wind pushed against the tractor, rocking it from side to side. The storm wasn't letting up. It was as though it had stalled over the island.

When he reached the old barn, he backed the tractor up to it. He climbed out and approached the doors.

"Aster!"

Nothing.

With as much force as he could muster, he cried out, "Aster, can you hear me?"

He pressed his ear to the door, trying to hear her over the pounding of his heart. In that moment, he sent up a little prayer. He could use all of the help he could get.

"Sam, I'm here."

He released a pent-up breath before murmuring a thank you that his prayer had been answered. "I'm going to pull the door open! Stand back!"

"Okay!"

He hooked the heavy chain through the door handles and then attached it to the tractor. He hoped it would open the door without bringing down the whole building.

He started the engine and then slowly pressed on the accelerator. Perhaps the wood would splinter and break. He could only hope. After all, it was a very old barn, probably a hundred years old... Maybe more.

But as luck would have it, the wood wasn't going to budge, not without a lot of horse-power. And so, he increased the force on the door. More. And more.

Crack. Crack.

And suddenly the door gave way, pulled from the rusty hinges. It fell in a heap. Sam climbed out of the tractor and ran back to the barn that miraculously was still standing.

He peered into the darkness. "Aster?"

"We're here." She stepped forward, holding a feisty black goat.

"Dash." What was he going to do with the escape-artist goat? He took Dash from her. The little goat's wiggling ceased when Sam took ahold of him. "Can you get out on your own?"

"Yes."

He stepped back, giving her room to get out. And when she was free of the barn. He took his first easy breath.

All three of them squeezed into the tractor. It was cramped with Aster on his lap, holding Dash. But somehow they managed to get back to the house without incident. Sam carried Dash to a goat house and then secured the gate. He would have to work on a better closure to keep the little goat from pulling another disappearing act.

Once he stepped inside the house, Nikki ran to him. She wrapped her little arms tightly around him. And for a moment they stood there hugging. No words were needed.

Then he rubbed her back. "Everything is okay now. You don't have to worry."

Nikki pulled back and with big eyes she stared up at him. "Is Dash okay?"

"He's fine and probably already plotting his next adventure."

"We watched him open the gate with his mouth."

"His mouth?" Had he heard her correctly? When both Nikki and Aster nodded, he said, "I guess I need to get a better latch on that gate."

"Can I go see him?" Nikki clasped her hands together. "Please."

"Not while the storm is raging outside. You can see him tomorrow."

"But Daddy…"

"No." He said it gently but firmly. "Did you get your homework finished?"

She shook her head.

"Go finish."

She frowned at him. "But it's storming."

"And it'll soon pass. You need to have your homework done for school tomorrow."

She sighed. "Do I have to?"

"Afraid so."

Nikki huffed and then moved to the kitchen table.

He turned to Aster, who was shivering. "You need some dry clothes. Come on."

He led her upstairs. The only thing he had to offer her were some sweats and a T-shirt. He handed her a towel as well.

While she changed in the bathroom, he moved to his bedroom. No sooner had he stepped into the room than a flash of lightning followed by the rumble of thunder zapped the power. He waited in the darkness, hoping like other times that the power would come back on. It didn't.

He stepped back out into the hallway. "Aster, are you okay?"

"Yes. I'll be out in a minute."

"No rush." He headed back to his room.

Sam didn't rush to change his clothes. He needed a

moment alone—a chance to work through what had just happened. His hand rubbed the back of his neck as he paced the floor. He was still shaken by how close Aster had come to getting severely injured.

After he'd finally changed into dry clothes, he went downstairs. By the light of a battery-operated lantern, he spotted Aster knelt down in front of the fireplace in the living room. He stood there for a moment, taking in the sight.

Tonight, he'd thought he was going to lose her too. The thought stabbed at his heart. And he couldn't ignore the similarities between what had happened to Beth and what had almost happened to Aster.

She straightened and then turned. When her gaze reached him, she jumped. She pressed a hand to her chest. "I didn't hear you enter the room."

"Sorry. I didn't mean to startle you."

"It's the storm. It has me on edge. I hope you don't mind that I started a fire. It's a little chilly in here."

"Not at all." He couldn't think of what else to say. All he could think was how much he wanted to keep her safe.

He went to Aster as though drawn by a magnetic force. His gaze scanned her to make sure she was all right. And that's when he noticed the ugly redness on her jaw. He reached out to her. "You're hurt."

"What?" She looked confused.

He gestured toward her face. "Did you get hit by something?"

Her fingers automatically moved to the right spot as though it must hurt her. "I'm fine. It's an old scar."

The scar wasn't that old. It took him a moment to put the pieces together. "Is that where he hurt you?"

She nodded as her eyes grew misty.

His fingers lightly caressed the uneven skin. "I'm so sorry."

"Don't be. It's over and done with."

"Is it?" His gaze searched hers.

She glanced down as she nodded.

He couldn't believe someone had hurt her—someone who was supposed to care about her. His body tensed. How could a man do that to a woman? How?

Aster deserved to have someone treat her with tenderness. And then he did what he'd been wanting to do since he'd learned she'd been in danger. He reached out to her.

Her eyes widened with surprise. He hesitated, waiting to see if she would step away. She didn't.

His hands gripped her shoulders as he slowly drew her close. He didn't want to scare her away. She wrapped her arms around his chest. Her head came to rest just below his shoulder.

He wondered if she could hear the pounding of his heart. He tried to tell himself it was a reaction to the scare they'd just experienced, but he couldn't bring himself to believe it. His heart was pounding because of her.

Aster had this way about her. She was bubbly at times. Serious at other times. But always caring and thoughtful. He was drawn to her—wanting to know her better—to understand the reason she sometimes got a faraway look in her eyes. She was like a book, and he wanted to read every word on every page.

The fact he'd come so close to losing her in that fierce storm had him pulling her closer. He didn't want to let her go. Not ever.

But as soon as that thought settled over him, Aster pulled back. And when she raised her chin and stared into his eyes, his heart slammed into his chest.

The moment felt so right, like they were meant to be doing this all along. And then his gaze dipped to her lips. They were full and pink. They were so tempting.

All of the reasons this was a bad idea slipped from his mind. All he could think about was how Aster had brought him back to life. She was like a bright ray of autumn sunshine reflecting off the dew on the grass and bringing light to his dark, stormy soul.

He lowered his head, pressing his lips to hers. They were soft and smooth. At first, she didn't move. Had he caught her off guard? Had he totally misread the moment?

His body tensed. This was a mistake. Just as he was ready to pull away, her lips moved beneath his. The tension eased from his body.

It had been so very long since he'd held someone close. And Aster definitely wasn't just anyone. She was amazing—amazing with Nikki—amazing with the farm—amazing with him.

In the background, the storm continued to rage outside. But inside, the battle had been won. Sam gave into his desires as he continued to kiss Aster.

He didn't want this moment to end. It felt so right to have her in his arms. In that moment, the reason he'd fought kissing her totally escaped him.

As their kiss deepened, a moan swelled in the back of his throat. He didn't ever want to let her go.

"Daddy, I have a question," Nikki called from the kitchen.

He inwardly groaned. This moment had ended much too soon.

Aster stirred at his side. With great reluctance, he let her go. His heart continued to pound in his chest as though he'd just run a marathon. How did Aster do it? How did she break down his barriers like they were paper-thin?

He thought of the last time he'd let a woman get this close to him and how horrifically it had ended. Not that he would ever want to go back and change his life with Beth. They'd shared a beautiful life and from it they'd had Nikki—the light of his life.

But to do it all over again... His defenses went back up around his heart. He thought of the way Aster had put herself in harm's way today. He thought of all the ways it could have gone so wrong, from flying debris to the remainder of the barn collapsing. Cold fingers of apprehension trailed up his spine.

Aster traced her fingers around her mouth. As he glanced at her rosy lips, he knew this moment, whatever you wanted to call it, couldn't happen again. He couldn't let himself get close to her. With time his feelings for her would fade away. They had to.

He cleared his throat. "Aster—"

"Daddy! I'm stuck. I don't know how to do this."

"You should go help her," Aster said, "unless you'd

like me to."

He shook his head. "I'll go."

Their talk would have to wait for later. Until then he'd be sure to keep a safe distance between them. Because he knew no matter what he told himself, there was this draw between them that defied logic. It was too strong. And when he was within her circumference, his brain had a complete disconnect.

And he couldn't risk continuing to care about her—drawing her further into his life. Because in the end, he didn't deserve her. He'd failed to protect Beth—to be there for her when she needed him most. He didn't deserve to move on and be happy.

He gave Aster one last glance before he moved from the room. Even if Aster was everything he could ever imagine wanting in a partner. He wasn't worthy.

25

ad that kiss really happened?

Aster ran her fingers over her lips, remembering the tingling sensation of his kiss. It most certainly had happened. But what did it mean?

Aster had rolled that question around in her mind as they'd huddled together in the farmhouse as the storm continued to rage outside. Sometimes there was lightning and thunder with the rain, and other times it was just the pounding rain and wind.

Aster kept to the shadows, not wanting to scare Nikki with the ugliness of her scar. She must have accidentally rubbed off her makeup when she'd been drying off with the towel. The fact Sam had seen it in the firelight had made her self-conscious. But when he'd kissed her, she forgot about everything but being in his arms.

The power never came back on, so they had to make due with some crackers and warming cans of soup over the fire for dinner. Both she and Sam worked to make it fun for Nikki so she wouldn't worry about the weather.

They rearranged the living room furniture and put out sleeping bags. Because as much as Aster wanted to go home to her room in Darla's apartment, it was too dangerous out there in the dark with the strong winds. Power lines were obviously down as well as the phone lines, and even cell service was out. She could only imagine it was the same all over the island.

Luckily, Nikki liked the idea of camping out in the living room. Nikki's spot was in the center. Aster occupied her by reading an adventure/fantasy book. Meanwhile Sam periodically went outside to check on the goats. She couldn't help but wonder if he was worried about Dash escaping again.

When Nikki finally gave in to the sleep that claimed her, Aster closed the book and set it aside. She envied the little girl's ability to fall asleep so easily. Even though Aster was tired, she knew sleep was a long way off for her.

And so, she stood up and quietly tiptoed out of the living room to go see what Sam was doing. He wasn't in the kitchen. She moved to the back door. She stared out into the dark night. She couldn't make out much but every now and then, there was a flash of light, probably from Sam's flashlight. He was in the goat pen, making sure they were all safe. The wind had started to calm down. Maybe the worst of it had passed. Could they be that lucky? She hoped so.

She continued to stand near the window as the rain tap-tapped on the windows. Finally, Sam returned to the house. She turned on the lantern to help him see what he was doing. He kicked off his boots and then shrugged off his yellow rain slicker. He hung it on a hook in the mud room.

"Is everything all right?" Aster asked.

"Uh. Yeah." His gaze didn't meet hers.

"You were out there for a long time. I was worried something had happened to the goats."

"They're fine. I was just securing things. I temporarily chained the gate so Dash can't open it." He skirted around her, leaving a lot of distance between them. "Is Nikki sleeping?"

"She just dozed off." She swallowed hard, not sure what to say. "Sam, we should talk."

"Maybe tomorrow. I need to get some shut-eye. Tomorrow is going to be a big day." He walked away without giving her a chance to say a word.

She followed him into the living room. Why was he acting so strange around her? Her fingers moved to her scar. Was that it?

Her defenses closed in around her. It was an ugly scar. She'd be the first to admit it. All she wanted to do was go home—the sooner, the better. But until the morning came, she was stuck there.

Sam stepped over to her and whispered, "I'll take the couch. You can have my bed. It's at the top of the stairs."

She liked the thought of having some distance. "Are you sure?"

He nodded. "I'd rather be down here where I can periodically check on things."

With a heavy heart, she climbed the stairs. She knew where Sam's room was because Nikki had previously

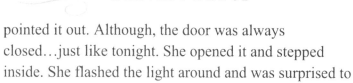

pointed it out. Although, the door was always closed…just like tonight. She opened it and stepped inside. She flashed the light around and was surprised to find the room neat and tidy.

She didn't know why that surprised her. Even though Sam was single, he kept things orderly. Why should his bedroom be any different?

But as she swept the flashlight around the room, she noticed the room lacked any photos or personal items that hinted at the gentleman farmer, who slept there each night. How strange. Almost as strange as him kissing her and then being repulsed by her scar.

Tears stung the backs of her eyes. She lay down on the bed. When her head came to rest on his pillow, she detected the faint scent of his aftershave. She inhaled the spicy scent and her thoughts were drawn back to that kiss. A tear slipped down her cheek. She swiped it away. Another tear tracked down her other cheek. How was she ever going to get to sleep that night—or what was left of the night? She was so miserable.

What had he been thinking?

The answer was obvious. He hadn't been thinking.

Sam hadn't slept much during the night. It was though the storm had torn back the scabs on his tattered heart, and the torturous old memories mingled with new ones of Aster being trapped in the old barn. They'd come so close to another catastrophe.

But this time the "ifs" were all about Aster. If he had stuck closer to home with the storm brewing. If he'd slowed down and figured out how Dash was escaping. If he had told Aster not to go to the old barn for any reason.

The "if" statements were intermingled with him berating himself for letting things get so out of control with Aster. The kiss had stirred up a tsunami of feelings in him. And now he had no idea how to calm the tumultuous emotions.

He poured himself a cup of coffee. He didn't have an appetite. He made sure to be quiet, as Nikki and Aster were still asleep. The power had been restored but apparently that wasn't the case for the whole island.

Birdie, with Peaches by her side, had driven out to check on them. She'd informed him that half of the island was still without power, and the landline phones were still down. Cell service was spotty at best.

As such, school was canceled for the day, perhaps the rest of the week. With all of the damage, they were calling in support from the mainland. They were allowing vehicles immediate access to the island for the remainder of the week. They needed the larger vehicles to help haul away the debris and assist with the repairs. Once he'd been updated, Birdie moved on.

He moved to the back porch. The sun had returned and the sky was a beautiful blue with only a couple of white, puffy clouds floating by. But on the ground, well, that was quite a different story. There were fallen tree limbs and broken twigs. It was going to take quite some time to get the farm back to its prior condition.

Luckily, the new barn stood untouched. The old barn was leaning as though another gust of wind would knock it completely over. Sam wasn't going to wait for that to happen. He'd already placed a call to a company that was interested in purchasing the reclaimed wood. With the old barn being a hazard, Sam was able to convince the lumber people to send out a crew the following day. Soon the barn would be history.

"Are the roads open?"

At the sound of Aster's voice, he turned. She stepped onto the porch and quietly closed the screen door. The sight of her with her hair a bit mussed up was endearing. But the dark shadows under her eyes worried him. He wanted to go to her and comfort her. And just as soon as that thought came to him, he shoved it aside. He wouldn't—he couldn't—change his mind at keeping his distance.

He cleared his throat. "Birdie was just here. She said the roads are open, but there's been a lot of damage." He glanced down at the half-full mug in his hands. "Can I get you some coffee?"

He gaze didn't meet his as she shook her head.

And so, for a few moments, they stood there in an awkward silence. He longed to hold her in his arms, and yet he resisted the urge. He couldn't let himself care about someone that deeply again. When he'd lost Beth, he'd lost a piece of himself. He never thought he was going to be able to climb out of the black depths of grief that clutched him in utter darkness. But somehow he had.

Nikki's sweet innocent love gave him the strength to claw his way back to some semblance of the man he'd once been. Though he knew no amount of time or love would ever make him that man he'd once been—the man who had been Beth's loving and devoted husband. He was a different person now.

She lifted her chin. Her gaze at last met his. "We can't go back to the way things used to be."

He shifted his weight from one foot to the other. "I suppose not."

He knew what was coming next—she was quitting. He wanted to stop her. He wanted to fix things. But he knew he couldn't do any of those things. It wouldn't be right for either of them.

"You regret kissing me, don't you?"

"It was a mistake." He was shutting down on the inside, pushing her further away. "It can't ever happen again."

For a moment Aster was silent, as though his words had stunned her. Surely, she couldn't have thought that they would have some sort of future. It was one single kiss, nothing more.

"I agree."

She did? Those two little words stabbed deeply into his heart. He didn't know she felt the same way.

The enormity of the situation hung between them. All it had taken was one moment that had totally gotten out of control, and now their ideal situation was ruined. And he had no one to blame but himself.

Aster blinked repeatedly. "I… I should go. I don't want to see Nikki looking like this. I'll stop back to explain things to her."

Part of him wanted to beg her to stay, but he knew it would only make things worse. He was certain she would have an easy time finding another job. However, he would never find anyone that would come close to replacing her. Among Aster's many attributes was her

brilliant smile that glowed like the sun, warming him from the inside out.

He halted his thoughts before he talked himself out of doing what needed to be done. "Don't worry. I'll talk to Nikki." He had no idea how he'd explain any of this to his daughter. He was having a hard time explaining it to himself. "But you can stop by and see her whenever you want."

Pain reflected in her eyes. "I'll do that."

And then she turned and walked away. He noticed the stiff line of her slim shoulders and the quick sway of her hips as she moved to her bike, which was on the side of the house.

He forced himself to turn and walk inside the house. He didn't trust himself to watch her ride away. Because if she were to turn back and look at him with pain reflected in her big hazel eyes and her bottom lip sticking out ever so slightly, it'd be far too tempting for him to go to her. He'd pull her into his arms and kiss away her unhappiness.

He stepped into the kitchen. The screen door closed gently. He didn't want to wake Nikki. And then he stood there in the silence. Already the house seemed so empty without Aster.

26

ow had everything gone so terribly wrong?

The question circled around in Aster's mind as she made her way into town. Her thoughts rewound to last night and the earth-moving kiss. It had been filled with such emotion. At least it had been on her end.

When he had looked at her, she had felt like she was the only woman in the world. Without words, he'd made her feel beautiful—made her forget about the jagged scar trailing down her jaw. And when he'd kissed her, it was as though he'd cared deeply for her.

She vividly recalled the gentle touch of his lips on hers. Her heart had pounded so loudly. He must have heard it too. She'd never been kissed quite like that—like there was no tomorrow.

And yet it'd been nothing more than a fleeting moment.

Love wasn't meant for her. Her parents had been torn from her life much too soon. She'd been searching for

love ever since. And she'd failed at every turn. Why did she think things with Sam would be different?

It was fine. She would be fine on her own. Everything would be fine when she focused on her job at city hall and forgot about the gentleman farmer.

And what about the kiss? Well, that was simple. She'd just overthought it. It had been nothing more than a reaction to a turbulent evening for both of them—an outpouring of their emotions. At least that was what she tried to tell herself.

And to make a bad situation worse, Nikki had been caught in the middle. Aster's heart ached at the thought of not spending time with the little girl anymore except for the occasional run-in on the sidewalk. And she wasn't going to understand Aster's sudden absence. How could she when Aster barely understood how things had fallen apart so suddenly.

She felt as though she'd lost something very precious—something she would never get back. She blinked back the tears. How had she let this happen?

Needing to hear Rosa's calm, reassuring voice, Aster reached for her phone. There was no signal. With a resigned sigh, Aster slipped her phone back into her purse.

Mayor Banks was standing on the steps of city hall, speaking with the sheriff. She stood off to the side and waited until they'd finished their business. She needed to keep busy—to stop thinking of everything she'd lost during the storm.

When the sheriff moved on, she approached the mayor. "What can I do to help?"

The mayor blinked as though he'd been lost in thought. "Do you have your bike?"

"I do."

"With the whole phone system being down, could you deliver some messages?"

"That I can do."

And so that's how she spent her day, delivering messages to vital workers as they strived to restore power and phone service to the entire island. It wasn't like she was in there getting her hands dirty, but she knew how important communication was in times like these. And the tasks kept her from focusing on the ache in her heart. It was as though a piece of it were missing.

"Where's Aster?"

The little girl's voice came from behind him. Sam paused from gathering the debris in the yard to turn to his daughter. Nikki's hair was all mussed up. She was still in her pink pajamas and stood there in her bare feet. She rubbed her eyes but still looked as though she were half-asleep.

Now what was he supposed to tell her? That he'd driven Aster away for her own good? That Aster didn't really belong there on the farm? It didn't matter what he said, Nikki wasn't going to like it.

"She had to go." Short and to the point.

"Go? But we were supposed to make pancakes and eggs." Her face scrunched up into a frown. "When will she be back?"

He should have known his daughter wouldn't let the subject go easily. "She won't be back."

Nikki's eyes widened. "Yes, she will."

He approached his daughter, hoping to comfort her. "Aster wasn't here to stay. It was just temporary until her job at city hall became full time."

"She can't quit. We have plans."

"I'm sorry." When he reached out to his daughter, she jerked back out of his reach. "Nikki, it'll be okay."

"No, it won't. Why'd she leave?"

"Because..." How did he explain this to a seven-year-old? He had no clue. But he'd give it his best shot. "Aster deserves a chance to make a life for herself—to be happy."

"She was happy here with us." Nikki huffed as she crossed her arms and glared at him.

He couldn't take that belief from her daughter. "You're right. She was happy." He recalled the many dinners they'd shared. And the way Aster had smiled while helping Nikki feed the goats. "But she's excited about her other job. And now with the clean-up from the storm, her other responsibilities will keep her busy."

Nikki's face crumpled into a frown. "She didn't say anything about leaving."

"She would have but you slept in this morning." The hurt reflected in his daughter's eyes only added to his guilt for letting things get out of hand last night.

"I thought she'd have stayed." Nikki's eyes filled with tears.

He searched for a way to distract his daughter. "I can make pancakes with you."

"No! I don't want them now." She turned and ran back to the house.

He started after her. The door slammed shut. When he reached the back steps, he hesitated. Maybe it'd be best to give her a few minutes to calm down. He expelled a frustrated groan as he sank down on the steps. What had he done?

He was miserable. Nikki was heartbroken. And Aster, well, he was pretty certain she would never speak to him again. Not that he could blame her. He hadn't handled this well at all.

She had been on her feet quite literally all day.

Aster stared at her fitness watch and wasn't the least bit surprised when it showed she had taken more than seventeen thousand steps that day. With the phone system up and down sporadically throughout the day, there had been a lot of communications to deliver around town as everyone pitched in to clean up the storm's mess.

She'd tried calling Rosa a couple of more times throughout the day and got no answer. She found it strange for Rosa to be gone for so long, but she was happy her friend was getting out and about.

And now Aster was exhausted. She walked into the apartment she shared with Darla. She found her friend sitting at the kitchen counter with her laptop open.

"Hi." Aster closed the door behind her. "I didn't expect to find you here."

"The café is closed. They had to throw out a lot of food due to the power outage. So, they're waiting for a fresh shipment in the morning. Since I have the evening off, I thought I'd put it to good use."

Aster sank down on the couch and kicked off her shoes. She glanced over at Darla, who had resumed hunching over her laptop, with her fingers rap-tap-tapping on the keyboard. For the past month, Aster hadn't prodded Darla about what she did on her computer. And Darla never shared. But the curiosity was getting to Aster, and she needed a distraction from thinking about how things had gone so wrong with Sam.

"What are you working on?"

"Nothing important."

"That's what you say every time I find you working on your computer. So, what gives?"

Darla shrugged. "Nothing you'd be interested in."

"Try me."

Darla closed her laptop and turned to Aster. "Promise you won't tell anyone?"

"I promise. But I have to admit that you have me really curious now."

Darla hesitated so long that Aster didn't think she was going to share her secret. Then in a soft voice, Darla said, "I'm writing a book."

"A book?" Aster sat up straight. "That's awesome."

"I don't know about that. I'm pretty certain it's terrible."

"I doubt that. You used to do really well in your creative writing class in college. I remember reading some of your short stories. They were very good."

"This is a lot harder than those and a lot longer."

"What genre is it?"

"A thriller."

"Well, if you ever need some input, I'm your girl. I'd

love to read it."

"You would?"

Aster sent her a reassuring smile, even though on the inside her heart was breaking. "Definitely. You could send what you have to my phone or you could print it out."

Darla shook her head. "Thanks. But it's not ready for anyone else to look at yet."

"Okay. I understand. Just know the offer is there. You know someday I'll be able to walk into a bookstore and point to your book and say that I knew you before you were a bestselling author."

"I don't know about all of that. Right now I'd just be happy to finish the book. It just keeps going on and on. But enough about me. What are you doing here? Aren't you supposed to be at the farm?"

It was Aster's turn to shrug her shoulders. Saying the words out loud would make it all too real. She no longer worked at the Bell farm. Sam and Nikki were no longer part of her life.

For someone who had come to Bluestar Island intent on keeping to herself and not letting anyone past her barriers, she had failed miserably. Because whether she liked it or not, Sam had gotten to her. And she already missed him a lot—a whole lot.

"Aster, what is it?" Darla moved from the bar stool to sit by her on the couch. "Was it the storm? Did something happen at the farm?"

"Sort of." She paused, not sure she should say more. It was best just to forget about the kiss and Sam. But she knew that wasn't going to happen. Not anytime soon,

that was.

"Wait. Does this have something to do with the creep?"

Aster shook her head. "This is about Sam. Sam and me."

"Oh." Darla's face lit up with a smile. "I knew you two were meant to be."

"That's just it. We aren't meant to be. Not at all. One kiss and he's back pedaling so fast."

Darla gasped. "Wait. Back up. You guys kissed?"

Aster nodded. "It was during the storm. Right after he rescued me and Dash."

"Rescued you? And you were with Dash? Girl, I never thought I'd hear you were hanging out with a goat. Give me the details."

Needing someone to talk to, Aster started back at the beginning of the storm and how Dash had gotten loose. She told Darla everything, straight up to the kiss. And then followed it up with what was said that morning.

"It just doesn't make sense." Aster grabbed a throw pillow and hugged it to her chest. "Why would he kiss me one moment and then act like he couldn't wait to get away from me?"

"I know. He's falling in love with you."

"No. Absolutely not." She shook her head, refusing to even entertain the idea.

"You have to understand that he lost his wife a few years ago. And then you getting stuck in that old barn probably brought back some of those memories."

Aster hated to admit it but Darla made some sense. She just wasn't so sure Sam felt as deeply for her as

Darla thought he did. But then there was that kiss. It wasn't a light peck on the lips. There were real emotions attached to it. But love? No. Definitely not.

"It's not like that," Aster said. "Besides, ending things now is for the best. I'm not ready for a new relationship."

"Are you sure about that?" Darla arched a brow.

Aster, feeling uncomfortable under her friend's expectant stare, got up from the couch. "Is there any leftover pizza from last night?"

"In the fridge."

She didn't have an appetite, but she knew after the long day that she should eat something. And it was a good excuse to end this conversation. Because there was no way Sam was falling in love with her. People didn't love somebody like her.

27

riday morning, Sam kept finding himself glancing down the lane, looking for Aster on her bike. And then he'd have to remind himself she wouldn't be coming, not today and not any other day.

With Nikki spending the day with his mother, he set to work tearing down the rest of the old barn. With the tractor, he was able to hook up a chain to the unstable structure and pull a lot of it down by the time the reclamation crew showed up.

It was early in the afternoon when he'd made his way to the house for a cup of coffee. With help, the work had gone quicker than he'd ever imagined possible. It was quite possible they would have the site cleared by the end of the day. In part that made him happy because it would be safer, and he wouldn't have to worry about someone else getting hurt. It also made him sad because that barn was a piece of his past—a piece of his family's past. But one too many storms had made it a danger. It's what had to be done.

He stood out on the back porch with his cup of coffee in hand. He stared out at the goat pen. Dash was there, but he wasn't up to his usual antics. Instead, he was just standing on one of the bridges, staring back at him, as though trying to tell him that he'd really messed up with Aster.

Sam blinked. Had that thought really crossed his mind? He gave himself a mental shake. He needed to get back to work.

He gulped down the rest of his coffee and placed his cup inside. Then he headed down the steps. Just as he was crossing from the house to the field, he heard the sound of an approaching vehicle.

He paused and glanced to the side. He immediately recognized the flamingo pink golf cart. There was only one of that shade on the island. And it belonged to Ms. Birdie. But he recalled Aster driving it to his farm the first time she'd visited. Was it her?

He squinted down the long gravel lane. There were two people and a dog in the golf cart. As they drew closer, he realized it was Ms. Birdie driving. And wait, was that his sister? Emma was here?

He started toward the golf cart. Worry pumped through his veins. His youngest sister hadn't been back to the island in a long time. She was always too busy with her singing career in Nashville. What could have happened to bring her home?

The golf cart pulled to a stop. Both women and Peaches got out. Ms. Birdie was frowning at him. Oh no. She knows about Aster. He inwardly groaned.

He turned to his sister. "Welcome home."

She rushed up to him and threw her arms around his neck. After a tight squeeze, she pulled back. "I've missed you, big brother."

"Maybe you should come home more often." His response came out gruffer than he'd intended. He tried again. "We'd like to see you for birthdays and holidays. I know Nikki really misses you."

Emma glanced around. "Where is my niece?"

"She's with Mom. I take it you haven't seen her yet?"

Emma shook her head. "I came straight here." She moved to the back of the golf cart to retrieve her bags. He beat her to them and lifted them off. Emma smiled at him. "Thanks. I heard you've had a lot going on lately." She turned her gaze to the new barn. "Very nice."

"Thanks." He placed her bags on the ground next to him. "But I can't take the credit. The town pooled their resources together and built it."

"Looks great."

He turned his attention to Ms. Birdie, who was staring at him with a narrowed gaze just over the rim of her glasses. He swallowed hard. "Thank you for bringing my sister out here."

"You're welcome." There was no friendly smile as she continued to stare at him, making him feel uncomfortable like he had in school when he'd done something wrong.

He'd give it another try. "The barn is great. I can't thank you enough."

"And yet you went and fired Aster." Ms. Birdie clucked her tongue.

"I did not." Is that what the whole town was saying? Was that what Aster was telling them? Because it wasn't the truth. She was a great babysitter—the best he'd ever hired.

"Funny. It sure seems like it. Why isn't she here with Nikki?" Ms. Birdie's unwavering gaze had him shifting his stance from one leg to the other.

And when he lowered his gaze, even the dog appeared to be frowning at him. Sam inwardly groaned. "It wasn't working out."

"Hmpf!" When Ms. Birdie did that, it was never a good sign. "I think you made a big mistake. I think you let go of someone that made you happy. I just hope you come to your senses before she leaves the island."

Wait. What? Had he heard her clearly? But before he could formulate words, Ms. Birdie, spry as she was, had already climbed back into her golf cart with Peaches taking a seat beside her. Ms. Birdie started the engine.

"She's leaving?" His voice got drowned out by the sound of Ms. Birdie pressing on the accelerator.

He couldn't tell if Ms. Birdie hadn't heard him or merely was too upset with him to answer, but either way he didn't get an answer. And he supposed with the current circumstances it wasn't really his business. Still, the thought of Aster leaving the island because of something he'd said or done didn't sit well with him.

"So, brother, who's this Aster I keep hearing about?" He blinked and turned to his sister. "Um... No one."

Emma's smile broadened. "Oh, I think she is someone all right—someone important."

His chest tightened as he grew warm beneath his

sister's stare. What was it with everyone nosing into his relationship—erm, his association—with Aster? Why did people keep making such a big deal of it? Couldn't they just leave it alone?

He reached for Emma's suitcases. There wasn't just one or two but four. Who needed that much stuff? Unless she was moving home.

"How long are you staying?" The thought of having two sisters on the island to butt into his life made him worry a bit.

"I don't know. How long would you like me to stay?"

Well, he didn't have an answer for her because in one way he wanted her to stay indefinitely, but when it came to her butting into his personal life, a few days would be more than enough. He had to know so he could prepare himself. "Are you moving home?"

Emma let out a laugh. "You can wipe that worried look off your face. I won't be staying that long."

He didn't know his thoughts had translated to his facial expression. He'd have to work on it. "But you'll be here for a few days, right?"

"Long enough for the harvest dance."

He turned to her. "You heard about that?"

"Of course. Why do you think I'm here?"

"I... I don't know. I guess Mom or Hannah would have said something."

"Actually, it was Aster who called me."

"Aster? But why?"

"She asked if I would perform at the dance."

"She shouldn't have done that. You have more

important things to do with your time."

The smile slipped from Emma's face and was quickly replaced with a frown. "Is that what you think? What everyone thinks?" When he shrugged, she continued. "It's not true. You don't understand."

He carried her luggage to the back porch. "You're right, I don't. You've never explained it to me."

"Maybe I will but later. Right now, I want to know all about the harvest dance. Is it going to be in your new barn?"

He'd had so much on his mind with Aster's sudden departure and tearing down the old barn that he'd totally forgotten about the dance. It was in two days. No. Wait. It was tomorrow.

"Um... Yes, it is."

"So, where's Aster? I thought she'd be here setting things up for the dance?" And then a worried look came over her face. "You didn't fire her from that, too, did you?"

"No. Of course not." He hadn't thought about it until now. Still, if he were to keep his distance, everything would be fine. "I've got to get back to work."

Emma reached out, grabbing his arm. "Not so fast. We haven't even had a chance to catch up. Weren't you going to offer me something to drink after my long trip?"

His shoulders drooped. He should have thought of that. He wasn't being a good host because ever since Aster had left, he hadn't been himself. And so, he carried her luggage into the house before pouring some lemonade. Then they sat on the back porch.

"So, how's life in Nashville?" He was genuinely

curious. It was rather impressive that he was related to a country music star.

Emma shrugged as she stared off into the distance at the goat pen. "It's busy. There's always a song to be written, a meeting with someone, or a song to be recorded, and that's when I'm in town. A lot of the time, I'm out on the road touring."

"Did you meet Dolly yet?" It was their mother's favorite singer. They'd grown up with Dolly's voice playing in the house.

"I wish." She glanced at him. "And how are you doing? Really doing?"

"Well, now with the new barn—"

"No. I'm not asking how the farm is doing. I want to know how you as a human, a single-father, a widower is doing."

He shrugged. "I don't know what you want me to tell you."

"Okay. I'll tell you what I see. I think you're tired— the kind of tired that doesn't go away with a good night's sleep."

"Gee, thanks." He rubbed the back of his neck. "Do I look that bad?"

"Well, you do have bags under your eyes and frown lines. You need to lighten up and enjoy life."

"This from the person that never takes time off from her career to come home and see her family." He noticed how Emma glanced away, avoiding his gaze. "Why is that? Why have you been avoiding your family?"

"It's not you. It's not the family."

"Oh." It dawned on him what the problem was or

rather who was the problem. "You're avoiding Bryan."

She shrugged. "I guess."

"But he's not here. He's in New York."

"I know. But his parents are still here and well, it's just easier."

"Oh, Emma, when have you ever done things the easy way? You picked a very challenging career. You moved away from home without knowing a soul in Nashville."

"But I had to. I had to give singing a chance. How else would I know if I have what it takes?"

"You definitely have what it takes. You have the voice of an angel."

Color bloomed in her cheeks. "Thanks. But we were talking about you. And I know there's something going on between you and Aster. Mom told me. And Hannah told me."

"You mean the whole family has been talking about me?"

She shrugged. "They're worried about you."

"Don't be. I'm fine. I've got Nikki and the farm. That's all I need."

"Do you really believe that? Because I don't." Her direct gaze poked and prodded him in all of the wrong places.

Why did his sister have to keep pushing this? No wonder she'd gotten so far in Nashville. She wasn't one to give up when something was important to her.

He raked his fingers through his hair. "You don't understand."

"Maybe I would if you'd explain."

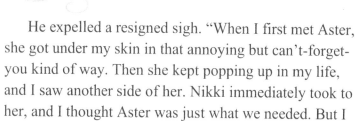

He expelled a resigned sigh. "When I first met Aster, she got under my skin in that annoying but can't-forget-you kind of way. Then she kept popping up in my life, and I saw another side of her. Nikki immediately took to her, and I thought Aster was just what we needed. But I didn't expect to start caring about her."

"Why not? Is she married? A criminal?"

He frowned at his sister. "Emma, get real. You know why I don't want to get involved. There's Beth and everything that happened with her."

"You mean the accident?"

His shoulders drooped as he lowered his head. "It was my fault."

"What?"

It was the first time he'd vocalized his guilt to his family. "The accident was my fault. Beth would still be here if it wasn't for me. If I had been here, she wouldn't have felt the need to go out on the tractor and it wouldn't have overturned." His vision blurred. He blinked repeatedly. "I should have been able to protect her."

"You mean you've been blaming yourself all of this time?" When he nodded, she said, "Sam, it was an accident. You didn't make Beth go out on that tractor. She wanted to do it. She wanted to do her part. And as for you protecting her, it wasn't what she wanted. Beth was strong and independent. She wouldn't want you going around punishing yourself. She'd want you to create a life for yourself that makes you happy with someone like Aster."

He shook his head. "I can't do it. I can't take the risk again."

"The risk of losing Aster?"

He nodded.

"I have news for you. You care about her more than you're willing to let on, or you wouldn't have been dancing on the beach with her."

His head lifted. "You know that too?"

"The whole town knows. They can see what you refuse to acknowledge. You're in love with Aster, or you wouldn't be this tied up in knots. And you're about to lose her for good unless you do something about it."

He ran his hands over his face. "I think it's too late for that. I don't think she'll give me another chance after the way I freaked out when she got trapped in the old barn during the storm."

"I think you might be surprised if you're honest with yourself and with her."

Sam was left with that thought as Emma entered the house. Would Beth want him to move on? Would Aster forgive him and give him another chance? Did he want a future with Aster?

The answers felt as though they had all been there just waiting for him to reach for them. He knew sweet, loving, caring Beth wouldn't want him hiding from life. In his head, he could hear her lecturing him about not moving on.

Her being on the tractor that fateful day had been her way to step in and surprise him. Beth was being Beth, and he had to accept that it was her time to go...even if it had been much too soon. He would forever love her, but perhaps his heart was big enough to love someone else too.

His thoughts turned to Aster. He loved the way her face lit up when she smiled. It wasn't just her rosy lips that lifted but her cheeks that puffed up and her eyes twinkled. She was kind and thoughtful. And then there was the closeness between Aster and Nikki. He'd refused to admit it until now, but they had grown so close he could see the lifelong bond forming between them.

The love he felt for her was the reason he'd overreacted when she'd gotten trapped in the barn. He couldn't bear to lose her. But wasn't that exactly what he was doing by pushing her away?

He had to take a risk if he was ever going to find true happiness again—not only for himself but for Nikki. Because Aster fit into their family. But would she feel the same way?

28

he harvest dance was the next day.
Aster wasn't sure what to do about
setting up for the dance. The thought
of facing Sam so soon didn't sit well with her. She'd
promised to go back to the farm to visit with Nikki, but
she hadn't planned to return so soon. She still didn't
understand how it had all gone so wrong. Not that it
would matter if she did understand. It still wouldn't
change anything.

It was just after noon. Work was done for the day,
and she was curled up on Darla's couch with a mug of
coffee cradled in her hands. If she was going to hand off
the party preparations to someone else, she had to do it
sooner rather than later.

But first she wanted to speak to Rosa. She'd been
trying to call her for the past couple of days, but her dear
friend never picked up the phone. Aster was really
starting to worry about her. It wasn't like her to be away
from home so much.

And today she'd had two hang up calls from a

blocked number. Each time she'd worried it might be
Oz, but she told herself it was a disposable phone
number, and the call could be for the prior owner of the
number.

She was about to dial Rosa's number when Darla
strolled out of her room in a pair of loose blue shorts and
a tank top. Her hair was mussed up and she was
yawning.

"Late night?" Aster asked.

"It seems the storm did more than take out the power
at the café. There was some flooding in the back, and
there was a surge of electricity that fried some of the
appliances. So, the boss called everyone in last night to
give the entire place a good going over from floor to
ceiling and everything in between." She yawned again.
"We didn't get done until after midnight."

"Oh." Now she wasn't so sure about asking Darla if
she'd take over coordinating the dance today.

Darla moved to the counter and poured herself a cup
of coffee. "What's on your mind?"

Aster shook her head. "Nothing."

"Uh-huh." Darla moved toward the overstuffed
armchair and sat down. She took a long sip of coffee.
"Okay, let's try this again. What do you have on your
mind?"

Aster sighed. "It's the dance. I'm supposed to be
overseeing the setup this afternoon and, well, I'm not
sure I should be doing it. Not with the way things ended
with Sam."

"Did he tell you to never speak to him again?"

"Of course not."

"Did he tell you to stay off his property?"

"No, but—"

"But nothing. People are counting on you to organize this dance. It's what's getting them through all of this storm damage and cleanup. I've heard them talking at the café about buying new dresses and new shoes. It's a big deal for the locals. There was even talk about making it a permanent thing on the social calendar. You can't let them down."

Knock-knock.

"Are you expecting anyone?" Aster asked.

"No. But that doesn't mean anything." Darla set aside her coffee and went to answer the door. "Hi. Come on in."

Hannah stepped inside with someone else. It took Aster a second to place the other face and then it came to her. It was Em Bell—*Songbird's* winner from last season and now Nashville's newest sweetheart.

She didn't think Em had gotten her voicemail since she hadn't heard back from her, but obviously that wasn't the case. They both stepped into the room.

Hannah's gaze locked with Aster's. "Just the person we wanted to see. I hope we aren't bothering you."

"Um, no," Aster said. "I just got home from the office."

"We wanted to volunteer to help with the party preparations," Em said.

"About that," Aster said, "I'm not sure I should be the one to coordinate it."

"If this is about my brother," Em said, "don't worry about it. He didn't mean what he said. He was just rattled

about the whole barn thing."

"What barn thing?" Hannah asked.

"I'll tell you later," Em said to her sister before turning back to Aster. "So will you come with us?"

Aster wasn't convinced Sam had changed his mind about things between them. He certainly hadn't made any effort to phone her. Not that she'd reached out to him either. She didn't know what to say to him.

"I don't think so," Aster said.

Hannah frowned. "Please don't let our brother ruin this for you. You worked so hard to pull it together on short notice, and you even got my sister to attend, which is a major accomplishment."

"Hey!" Em frowned at her sister. "I'm not that bad."

Hannah grinned at her sister. "Maybe you should come home more often, and then I couldn't say things like that."

"Maybe I will."

"Okay," Hannah said. "Enough about us. This is about the town and the dance that everyone is so excited about."

Darla reached for her coffee. "I was just telling Char...erm, Aster that everyone at the café was talking about the dance. People got new dresses and shoes, and I heard the hair salon is booked solid today and tomorrow."

Hannah turned to Aster. "And this excitement is all thanks to you. So, you can't back out now."

"But it's not my dance; it's Sam's." She felt awkward taking the credit.

Em rolled her eyes. "Like my brother could come up

with this on his own. I'll bet my next concert tour that you came up with it. Didn't you?"

"Well, uh, kind of." Aster's cheeks grew warm. "But you have to understand that I had to come up with a way to get Sam to agree to the new barn. Once he found a way to say thank you to the town, he was willing to let the building begin."

Hannah elbowed her sister. "See. She was instrumental in not only orchestrating the dance but also in helping to convince our stubborn brother to accept the new barn that he so desperately needed."

"I didn't know that our brother ever listened to anyone but himself." Em smiled at Aster. "You're good for him."

Darla sipped at her coffee. "That's what I've been telling her, but she won't believe me. Maybe you two can convince her that they make a good couple."

"We're not a couple." Aster said it with more force than she'd been intending. Her face grew even warmer.

"We're sorry," Hannah said. "We'll stop with the matchmaking if you'll go with us to start the setup because none of us know where things belong. And to be honest, I bet my brother won't even be around. Decorating isn't exactly his thing."

"The last I saw him, he was working on the old barn," Em said.

"And you'll both be helping?" Aster didn't want to go by herself.

When both Hannah and Em nodded, Darla said, "And me too. I took the day off so I could help."

How could she turn all three of them down? The

answer was that she couldn't. It looked like she had a dance to plan. The thought of running into Sam made her stomach shiver with nerves. What would he say? Would he say anything at all?

♥♥♥

Sam pulled his phone from his pocket. He gazed at the screen. No missed calls. No texts.

He shoved it back into his pocket. He wanted to talk to Aster, but he didn't know what to say to keep her from hanging the phone up on him. He'd been an utter jerk, and now he didn't know how to undo the damage.

He wasn't good at romance. Thank goodness he hadn't had to romance Beth, because it seemed like they'd always been together—first as classmates and then friends before they became high school sweethearts. Getting married had been the natural progression of their relationship.

But things weren't that simple with Aster. They both came to the relationship with their own baggage— baggage he was going to have to move out of the way if they had any chance of a future. But how did he fix what he had broken?

He recalled some of those romantic comedies that Beth had made him sit through and tried to recall some of the romantic gestures. The first thing that came to mind was flowers. He could do flowers. That didn't seem too hard.

It was mid-morning when he reached for his phone again. He searched for Bea's Posie Patch's phone number. He could honestly say he'd never called and placed a flower order to be delivered. When he had gotten Beth flowers, he'd picked them up in person and brought them home. Usually, flowers were reserved for birthdays and anniversaries, but in this case flowers seemed appropriate.

Once the flowers were ordered, he went back to work. The site of the old barn was a bit rough. It'd take removing the remainder of the debris as well as moving a bit of earth around before he could plant it and turn the area back into a green field, but that was exactly what he planned to do.

He'd also had some thoughts about expanding the number of goats he owned. If he were to cut back on his crops and shift his focus to the goats, he could begin producing milk and cheese.

In order to do that, he'd need to fence in more fields. He knew Nikki would love the idea. He wondered what Aster would think of his plan. He began to reach for his phone to call her, but he realized he couldn't do that...at least not yet. But he hoped her attitude toward him might soften after she received the flowers. And best of all the shop had assured him that they'd deliver the bouquet right away.

And so, he got the little Tomcat that he'd borrowed from a neighbor farm, and he began moving the dirt around, filling in holes, and smoothing out other areas. He might need some topsoil. He'd get on that tomorrow.

A few hours later, he noticed a string of golf carts coming down his lane. He realized the harvest dance was tomorrow. The topsoil would have to wait a bit longer.

His visitors were undoubtedly there to set up for the dance. He didn't see why he couldn't help. He may not be good with bows and streamers, but he could set up chairs and tables.

And so, he shut down the Tomcat and headed toward the new barn. By the time he got there, the place was a hub of activity. He looked for Aster. His gaze briefly caught hers. She didn't smile. She didn't do anything. *Oh, no.* Did that mean the flowers hadn't done the trick?

"Sam, what are you doing here?" Hannah asked.

He turned to his sister. "I live here. Remember?"

She laughed. "I know that but I meant what are you doing here, in the barn, where we're setting up for the dance?"

He swallowed. "I thought I'd help."

Her eyes widened. "Really?"

"Yes, is that so hard to believe?"

She planted her hands on her hips. "Actually, after everything you've done to sabotage the event, yes it is."

"Sabotage? What are you talking about?"

"Don't go acting innocent. We all know how you fired Aster."

"I didn't fire her. Why does everyone keep saying that?"

"It's how it seems. And it took a lot for us to talk her into showing up today so the least you could do is back off and give her some room so she doesn't feel quite so uncomfortable."

"Uncomfortable?" He hadn't even said a word to Aster.

"Well, that frown of yours is certainly a bit intimidating. Don't you have some tractoring to do? We have this under control."

He hesitated. He didn't want to head out to the field. He wanted to stay right there and straighten things out with Aster. But she appeared to be ignoring him because after that first meeting of their gazes, she'd made sure not to look in his direction.

He turned his attention back to Hannah. "Do you really think it's a bad idea for me to be here?"

"I do. Now go." She shooed him toward the door.

He'd never felt so unwanted in his life. And it wasn't his sister's prodding that made him feel unwelcome. He'd grown immune to his sisters' forcible ejection many years ago when they were doing each other's hair or nails and especially when they wanted to talk about boys.

It was Aster who was making him feel unwanted. It appeared his flowers hadn't helped the situation. She was still angry with him. And he had no one to blame for that except himself.

He walked away, only to pause at the doorway. He glanced back at Aster, who had her back to him. He sighed. Perhaps he was better off elsewhere. He kept going.

29

oday was the harvest dance.

Normally, Aster would be excited but not so today. She'd noticed how Sam hadn't been happy to see her at the farm. He'd frowned at her, and then he'd walked away, not willing to be in the same place as her. He couldn't have made his feelings any clearer.

Aster spent the morning in her room. Darla tried to get her to go out for a coffee, but Aster wasn't budging. It was Saturday so she didn't have to go to work. She had nowhere she had to be, and she intended to spend the day reading a book in her room. Alone.

The only problem was she kept rereading the same page. She sighed. She wondered what Sam thought of the barn all decorated with hay bales, corn stalks, and pumpkins. She'd loved what they'd done with the place. It no longer looked like a barn as much as it resembled a country dance hall.

Knock-knock.

Aster restrained another sigh. She knew Darla was

worried about her. But she needed to figure out what came next for her life. Like it or not, she'd fallen hard for Sam. And now she had to decide if this island was big enough for both of them.

Because at every social event, he would be there—all six-foot-plus of him with his tanned face and dreamy blue eyes she felt as though she could drown in. Could she deal with that on a regular basis?

And then there was Nikki. That little girl had Aster wrapped around her little finger with her cute smiles and her sweet laughter. She had a big heart and a love for animals that was contagious.

Knock-knock.

"Aster, there's a delivery for you." Darla's voice came through the closed door.

A delivery? She wasn't expecting anything. Curiosity had her rushing out of bed and opening the door. There stood Darla with a bouquet of red roses in a white vase. What in the world?

"Those aren't mine," Aster said.

"Yes, they are. Your name is on the little card."

"It is?" When Darla smiled and nodded, Aster said, "But I don't understand. Who would send me flowers?"

Darla shrugged. "Open the card and find out."

Maybe it was from the mayor. Maybe it was his way of saying her promotion had come through. But red roses? Still, it must be it because she couldn't think of any other reason for flowers. No one had ever sent her flowers in her life.

She reached for the envelope. She didn't recognize the handwriting but she did recognize the name of the florist. Bea's Posie Patch was a small shop in town with the most beautiful window displays.

Aster pulled the card from the envelope.

Aster, I'm sorry. Can we talk?
Sam

She read it twice just to make sure she'd read it correctly. What did it mean? What was he sorry about? Ending her employment? Or the kiss?

"Who's it from?" Darla's voice interrupted her thoughts.

"Sam. He wants to talk." Her heart beat quickly at the thought. But there was another more cautious part of her that wondered if it was a good idea.

"That's good. Right?"

"I don't know." Her heart told her to go to him. But her brain said some things couldn't be undone.

"By the way"—Darla's voice distracted her from her escape plan—"these were delivered yesterday but they were mistakenly left at the neighbor's."

Was that the reason Sam had been giving her strange looks at the barn? Maybe he was expecting her to approach him and thank him for the flowers. That was something she could do.

She turned her attention back to the big beautiful bouquet. They were really pretty. As she took them to the kitchen and placed them on the breakfast bar, Aster was rethinking her plans to skip the dance tonight. Perhaps she would go after all. It would give her a chance to thank Sam for the flowers.

And then she could tell him she was leaving the island. But was that what she really wanted? If there was a chance for happiness with Sam, should she take it? Her heart pitter-pattered at the thought. Was it what Sam wanted?

30

er stomach shivered with nerves. Aster entered the barn in a peachish-pink dress. It was the first time she'd dressed up since arriving in Bluestar. It felt strange to be in heels, but it was a good feeling. Being all done up gave her the boost of confidence she needed to face Sam.

She scanned the crowd of people for any sign of Sam. She didn't notice him anywhere. Was it possible he was skipping out on the dance? Impossible. He was the host.

Before she could locate him, people approached her to praise her decorating skills. Aster refused to take all of the credit. She explained that it took a small army of volunteers to turn the barn into a dance hall.

"Congratulations." Birdie approached her. And for once, she was without her sweet puppy-dog. "You did it."

"Did what?"

"Made this event a success. I have to admit that when

I first heard Sam was going to host a dance on his property, I had my doubts about its success. But to be fair, I didn't know you'd be helping him." Birdie glanced around. "Where is the host?"

"Um..." Aster's gaze darted around the room. "You know, I'm not sure."

Birdie leaned in closer. "You know he's a really good man who's had to deal with a lot of loss in his life. Don't give up on him."

"Birdie, did you see this food?" Agnes Dewey waved her toward the buffet that was setup on the far wall. "I'm not sure there's enough."

"I've got to go. Just keep what I said in mind about Sam. He's been through more than most his age." And then Birdie moved in the direction of Agnes. "There's plenty of food."

"I don't know." Agnes frowned. "What if we run out?"

Aster didn't hear Birdie's response as a microphone buzzed through the speakers. She turned toward the stage to find a band member adjusting the speaker system. Where was Sam? He was supposed to give the introduction.

She scanned the audience, and at last her gaze strayed across him. Her heart fluttered in her chest. He was busy talking with someone, but she could only see the back of their heads. Sam didn't notice her standing off to the side. She didn't mind. It gave her a chance to take in his appearance.

He looked so handsome in a pair of dark jeans, a nice shirt, and a dark-brown sport coat. His hair was combed with each strand in its proper place. And he was clean-shaven. She wasn't the only one who'd worked hard to look good for this evening. His efforts had definitely paid off.

The band member leaned down from the stage to speak with Sam. With a nod of his head, Sam spoke briefly to his companion and then made his way onto the stage. He retrieved the microphone from the stand. He looked uncomfortable standing on the stage in front of everyone.

"Hi." Sam shifted his weight from one foot to the other. "I wanted to thank you all for not only coming tonight but for, well, for creating this great big beautiful barn that we're standing in. I… I wasn't expecting this, and I wish I knew how to thank you all."

"You already did," shouted a voice from the audience.

"I guess I did." Sam offered an awkward smile. "It just doesn't feel like enough."

"It will once the music starts and the food is served," shouted another voice.

"It sounds like I'm holding up the fun." Sam smiled. "I hope you have a great evening." And with that he returned the microphone to its holder and made his way off the stage.

Aster's gaze followed him until he disappeared into the crowd. She knew standing up on the stage hadn't been easy for him. He was a man who didn't like a crowd and who took great pleasure in his solitude.

The music started to play. It was a slow tune, and couples were making their way onto the dance floor,

including Sam's mother and the fire chief as well as
Hannah and Ethan.

"May I have this dance?"

Aster turned to find Sam standing behind her. He
held his hand out to her. She hesitated for just a moment,
wondering if this was really happening or if she was just
imagining things.

She placed her hand in his, and then they moved to
the crowded dance floor. It would appear the people of
Bluestar enjoyed dancing. Aster made a mental note of it
and would figure out how to introduce more public
dances onto the Bluestar social calendar. The thought of
being paid to do something she loved for the people
she'd come to care about was like a dream come true.

There was one person in particular she cared about.
Her gaze moved to Sam. He wrapped his arm around her
waist. The motion sent her heart tumbling. She never
thought they'd be this close again. What did it mean?
Did Sam want to give their relationship a real chance?
She hoped so.

"You look beautiful tonight," Sam said.

Her heart just skipped a beat. "Th...thank you. You
look really good too." She was quite certain she wasn't
the only one to notice how he'd dressed up. A lot of
single women were staring in their direction.
"Everyone's checking you out."

His body tensed. "They're probably just surprised to
see me in something besides work clothes."

"Or they're checking out your dance moves." She
offered him a hesitant smile. Were they at the smiling
stage again? She swallowed hard. "You're doing really

well."

"Thanks to you. If you hadn't showed me the moves, I'd be stepping all over your toes."

"I think you would have managed just fine." She still wasn't so sure he was as bad of a dancer as he let on. Was it possible he'd just wanted to spend more time with her? She'd never know the answer because she couldn't work up the courage to ask him.

"You know I've been meaning to talk to you—"

"Wait." She suddenly realized in her nervousness that she never thanked him for the flowers. "I need to, erm, I mean I want to thank you for the flowers. They're so pretty. I would have said something yesterday, but there was a mix-up, and the florist dropped them off at the neighbor's apartment."

His eyes widened in surprise. "I'm sorry they took so long to reach you, but I'm glad you like them. I'm sorry I handled things between us so poorly."

"And I'm sorry I got defensive and walked away."

Her heart was pounding in her chest. She had no idea where this conversation was headed. Was this the beginning? Or the end?

♥♥♥

Holding Aster in his arms felt so right.

Sam hoped she'd give him another chance. His heart was beating so loud it echoed in his ears. He wasn't good at talking about his feelings. In fact, he avoided the subject as much as possible.

But if he wanted to win Aster over, he knew he had to let down his guard with her. He had to tell her how much she meant to him. And then he had to hope she'd feel the same way for him.

"Aster, I—"

The music abruptly stopped. A loud gasp brought them to a stop on the dance floor.

With great regret he let go of Aster, and his chance to speak from the heart slipped away. When the crowd parted, there stood his mother with her hand pressed to her mouth. What in the world?

He went to step toward her when Aster reached out and grasped his arm. "Don't."

He paused and took in the full scene. In front of his mother, Chief Campbell was on bended knee. When Sam glanced back at his mother, he saw tears slip down her cheeks. Was this what he thought it was?

And then someone handed the chief the microphone. "Helen, we've known each other since we were kids, but it's only recently that we've really gotten to know each other so much better. You've become my best friend, and I'm so blessed to have found love a second time. I can't imagine my life without you. Will you marry me?"

His mother was full-on crying now as she nodded her head.

"Give her the ring," someone in the crowd called out.

The chief's face grew red as he reached into his pocket and pulled out a ring box. He opened it and held it out to Helen. She in turn held out her left hand to him.

All the while Sam's head was spinning. Sure, he knew his mother was dating the chief. Hannah had made sure he knew what was going on. But he never thought it had gotten this serious, this quickly.

As he watched the chief slip the diamond ring on his

mother's finger, he wasn't sure how he felt about his mother moving on. He'd never pictured his mother with anyone but his father. Was that a bit childish? Perhaps. But it was the way it had always been.

But then he thought of his daughter. Nikki could have thrown a fit about him growing closer with Aster, but she had always been in favor of their relationship. Maybe he could take some lessons from his daughter.

This was going to take some time to get used to. But when his mother smiled at the chief, Sam could see the happiness radiating off her. In that moment, he knew this was a good thing and with time, he'd get used to his mother moving on. After all, he wanted her to be happy.

As people started to congratulate the happy couple, Aster propelled him forward. Part of him wanted to stay with her and tell her that he was falling for her but the other part—the dutiful son part—moved toward his mother, who was positively radiant.

When he stepped in front of her, he gazed into her eyes. And he knew this was the right thing for her. "I'm happy for you, Mom."

"You are?" Her gaze searched his.

He knew she couldn't be truly happy unless all of her children approved of the union. "Yes, I'm really happy for you."

"Thank you, Son." She reached out and hugged him.

When they went to part, he placed a feathery kiss upon her cheek. And then he turned to the chief to shake his hand. "Welcome to the family."

The chief beamed. "I couldn't think of a better family to join. Thank you."

And then to Sam's surprise, the chief pulled him in for a quick hug and a clap on the back. It was the closest contact he'd ever had with the man—the man who would soon be his stepdad. Sam had a feeling there would be more hugs in his future.

Sam moved away, letting his sisters have their turn with the hugs. Right now, he wanted to get back to Aster but he had no idea where she'd gone.

31

*S*miles filled the room.

Aster was so happy for the couple. If anyone deserved to be happy, it was Sam's mom. Helen was so kind and generous.

Aster watched as Sam hugged his mother and then the chief. She was happy for all of them. She'd always wanted a family like that—well, she'd had one many, many years ago, but they'd been stolen away before they could make memories like these.

A deep sadness came over her at times like these. She missed having her mother to offer advice—like what she was supposed to do about her feelings for Sam. She missed having her father around to encourage her to follow her heart. And her heart was right there on Bluestar.

Sam approached her. "Sorry for the interruption."

"No problem. I'm so happy for your mother and the chief. They look so happy together."

"They do. Although between you and me, it's going to take some time to get used to him being my stepdad."

"I understand. But think of it this way. Your family is growing and that is a good thing."

He nodded. "You're right. It's just different."

"It's your new normal. And soon, it'll all be natural for you."

"I know you're right. It's just going to take some time." His gaze held hers. "Can we finish our prior conversation?"

Her heart leapt in her chest. What was he going to say? Not trusting her voice, she nodded.

He took her hand and led her outside where it was much quieter. The moonlight was so bright you could see into the distant fields.

He lifted his head and pointed to the full moon. "Check out the harvest moon."

"It's so big. It's almost like you could reach out and touch it." She turned to him. "What did you want to say?"

He stared deep into her eyes. "This isn't easy for me. As you've already noticed, I'm not good with change. I get stuck in ruts, and that's where I stay until someone comes along and knocks some sense into me."

She wanted to rush him along and get to the point of this conversation because she thought she knew what he was about to say—what she hoped he'd say. But she resisted the urge. It was important for him to get this all out there. And so, she remained quiet as she listened to every word.

"I've been in a deep rut ever since Beth died. I'd convinced myself that I was to blame for her death. If I had been there—if I hadn't gone to the mainland—"

"It's not your fault." Aster's gaze searched his. "I'm so sorry for your loss—for Nikki's loss—but it wasn't your fault."

"I'm figuring that out now. Emma has pounded that into my mind. She's worried after Nikki grows up that I'll grow old all alone on this farm."

Aster's gaze searched his. "Is that what you want?"

He shook his head. "I think I'm finally ready to share my life with someone. I don't know when it happened. Maybe way back on that day when you double-parked and blocked me in."

Her heart pitter-pattered faster. Did he feel the same way for her as she felt for him? She gazed deeply into his eyes, willing him to say the words she longed to hear.

He cleared his throat. "But somewhere along the way, I started to fall for you. I fought it but I can't fight it any longer. I—"

"Daddy! Daddy!" Nikki ran up to him. "I'm so excited."

Aster's heart sank. *No. Finish what you were going to say.*

Sam cleared his throat as he knelt down by his daughter. "About what?"

"Grandma's wedding. She said I could be the flower girl. I get a new dress and everything." Nikki beamed with happiness.

Ding. Ding.

A text message. She stifled a sigh. She never thought she would grow so tired of hearing her phone go off, but that's all it seemed to do in the past few days. She remembered the calm peacefulness of not having one when she'd first shown up on the island.

Of course, back then she'd ditched her phone in an effort to stay hidden. But she was finding that hiding just wasn't a part of her. She was so much stronger than she'd given herself credit.

But who would be texting her now? Everyone that she'd given her number to was there at the dance. At least she thought they were. Maybe someone was running late and just wanted to let her know.

Ding. Ding.

She withdrew her phone from her sparkly little cross-body purse. She'd considered leaving her phone at home this evening, seeing as everything for the dance had been checked and double-checked. And yet she'd brought it in case the mayor needed to reach her.

I'm coming for you, Char. We're meant to be together.

Even though it was a warm evening, a chill raced through her. In its wake, there was a trail of goosebumps. She read the message again.

No. No. No. It can't be him. Oz couldn't have found her on the other side of the country. She'd been so careful. She thought of her calls to Rosa. But perhaps not careful enough.

The message came from a blocked number. She didn't have to see the number to know that it was from Oz, who was trying to torment her. But he was in California under house arrest so he wouldn't be coming to get her any time soon.

But how had he gotten this number? There was only one person in California that had it—Rosa. And Rosa hadn't been answering her phone for the past few days.

Aster's heart leapt into her throat. She moved toward the door, away from the commotion so she could make a phone call. She tried phoning Rosa again. And once more her dear friend didn't pick up.

Her worry mounted as she thought through what this meant. Had Oz sent someone to Rosa's house to find out the information for him? Had they done something to Rosa?

Aster knew she couldn't stand by and do nothing. She surprised herself by recalling the number for the police in California. She'd called it enough times when she'd been dealing with Oz. She never thought she'd be calling the number to have a welfare check done on Rosa.

She asked for the detective who had been in charge of her case. Thankfully, he'd been at his desk.

"Detective Garcia." His voice sound all too familiar.

"Detective, it's Aster, I mean Charlotte Smith. I just got a message from Oz. At least I think it's from him. It sounded like him. But the number was blocked. But how could that be? I thought he didn't have access to the internet."

"Ms. Smith, I've been trying to reach you. There have been some developments you need to be aware of."

Her blood ran cold as a chill of apprehension worked through her body. He went on to explain that Oz had skipped out on his house arrest. If that wasn't bad enough, he'd assaulted Rosa. Aster knew why he'd done it. He'd wanted information on her. And he'd do whatever it took to get what he wanted.

"How... How is Rosa?" The breath caught in Aster's throat as she waited for his answer.

"She's in the hospital. She took a hit on the head that had her out of it for a while. But her confusion is clearing, and she should be released in a day or two."

The pent-up breath rushed from Aster's lungs. "Thank goodness."

"But the thing is, now Oz is on the run."

Aster gasped. Her fight-or-flight mode immediately kicked in. She tightened her grip on the phone as she felt the earth move beneath her feet. Oz was on the move. And she'd gotten a threatening text. Could he track this number to her? She wasn't sure. She wasn't a tech expert. But it had the area code that was unique to Bluestar.

When the detective wrapped up the conversation, Aster didn't move. Her mind raced but her body didn't move.

A hand touched her shoulder. She jumped. The phone clattered to the ground.

"Aster, what's wrong?" It was Sam's calm, soothing voice. He bent over and picked up the phone.

Any other time she would have found comfort in having him so close, but right now all she could think about was leaving—leaving this island, leaving this amazing small town, leaving sweet, wonderful Sam— and just when things were finally coming together for them.

"I have to go."

His hand caught her arm. "Wait. What's going on?"

"I... I can't talk. I don't have time." She wrenched her arm away. "He's coming."

"Who?"

"Oz."

"He knows where you are?"

Tears spilled onto her cheeks as she nodded her head. "I have to leave Bluestar."

She didn't want to go. She didn't want to leave now when Sam was ready for a relationship. She wanted to stay there on that beautiful island with the people she'd come to care about.

But it wasn't safe—not for her—not for those closest to her. Oz had already hurt Rosa. She couldn't put anyone else she cared about in danger.

32

She was in danger.

Every muscle in Sam's body tensed.

He knew this time he could do something to protect the woman he loved. He wasn't just going to stand aside and let Aster deal with this monster on her own. Not a chance.

It was in this moment he realized just how much he loved her because if she insisted on leaving the island, he would go with her. The three of them would start over someplace else. It wouldn't be the same as island life, but he'd adjust. Nikki would miss his family but he'd make sure to bring her back regularly.

But before all of that he wasn't giving up on changing Aster's mind about leaving the island. If she stayed here, she'd be safer than out there on her own with a stalker bent on revenge.

"Sam, I'm sorry." She swiped at her damp cheeks. "I never meant for any of this to happen. Please tell Nikki goodbye for me."

"No. You have to tell her yourself. Just wait here and

I'll get her." He didn't give her a chance to change her mind.

He wasn't going to get his daughter. He was going to get help. If he couldn't convince Aster to stay all by himself, surely an army of people who cared about her would sway her to stay.

His strides were long and fast. He didn't have time to waste. First, he told his mother there was an emergency and asked her to watch Nikki until he returned. Then he found both of his sisters and let them know that Aster was in trouble. On their way to the door, they were joined by Darla, Birdie, and the mayor.

Darla filled in everyone on the seriousness of the situation. While she did that, he was on the phone with the sheriff, who told him that Los Angeles police had already been in contact with the local authorities. There was a sighting of Oz in New York earlier that day. He was getting close. But how close?

When they all stepped outside, Aster was gone. Sam knew where she'd gone—to the apartment she'd been sharing with Darla to grab her things.

"I'll go after her," he said to no one in particular.

"Not without me," Darla said.

"Or me."

"Or me."

They all agreed that they were going as a group to reason with Aster. If she stayed on the island, they would do everything possible to keep her safe. And so, they set off in their golf carts.

Soon we'll be together.

Aster read the message again. Cold fingers of fear inched up her spine. She could just imagine Oz laughing in that sick and twisted way he'd done when she'd last seen him at the courthouse. She shoved aside the unwanted memory.

She was leaving but she would never forget her time on Bluestar. Because even though she didn't have a family of her own, these people had quickly embraced her and made her feel like part of a family. They'd filled a hole in her heart that she hadn't even known existed. They let her know what it was like to be a part of a great big loving family. And for that she would always be grateful. She swiped at the tears on her cheeks. She would miss them all—even Agnes Dewey.

Aster raced to her room. She grabbed her suitcase from the closet and opened the small dresser drawer. Unceremoniously, she scooped up her underwear and bras and threw them in the bag, followed by her socks, shirts, and pants. These days she traveled quite light. That is what Oz had done to her life.

She paused as she saw a picture Nikki had drawn of the three of them. Tears blurred her vision as she stared at it and realized the gravity of what she was giving up. But she couldn't stay and put them in danger. She loved them too much to let something happen to them.

She took the picture and folded it up. She placed it in a side pocket where it wouldn't get ruined. She gave a last look around the room. She grabbed a swizzle stick from The Lighthouse Café. It was small enough to carry with her, though she didn't need the tiny plastic stick to remind her of all the good times she'd spent in that

restaurant. Those memories were locked up safe and sound in her mind. And there was nothing Oz could do to take them away from her.

Her laptop from work was sitting on the desk. She knew Darla would see that it made its way back to the mayor's office. And then with her bag in hand, she headed for the door.

Before she reached it, the door swung open. There stood Darla and she wasn't alone. There was a small crowd of people standing behind her. What were they doing there?

Sam stepped past Darla. "Aster, please don't go."

"I... I have to. I told you."

"I heard your fear talking, but I, um, we"—he gestured to the people behind him—"will do everything to keep you safe."

Her heart swelled with love for him—for them. She was so touched by this gesture. Tears splashed onto her cheeks. "I can't ask you, any of you, to do that. He already hurt someone I care about in L.A. in order to find me. I can't let him hurt any of you."

"He won't," Sam said. "I talked to the sheriff. He's calling in extra men. They're going to catch him."

She wanted to believe him. She really did. "But he'll just keep coming back."

"Not this time." There was certainty in his voice.

"You don't understand. I've already done this. I've gone to the police for help. The first time he was given a warning that he ignored. When I was granted a restraining order, that didn't stop him. And then when I thought he was finally going to be locked up, they gave him house arrest. He'll just keep slipping through the cracks, and he'll never leave me alone."

"That was then but things are much more serious now." Sam gazed into her eyes. "He has all sorts of warrants for his arrest now. He's going away for a very long time."

"If they catch him," she said more to herself than anyone else.

Sam stepped forward and wrapped his arms around her. She dropped her bag and leaned into him, resting her face on his shoulder. It was there she felt safe and…loved. At last she felt as though she were truly home. And she didn't want to go anywhere.

"As a romantic, I hate to ruin this moment," Birdie said. "But out of an abundance of caution, I don't think we should stay here. We need to go someplace this thug won't think to look for you."

Sam eased up his hold on Aster, but his arm still lingered around her waist, holding her to his side. "Where do you have in mind?"

"My place." Birdie gestured for everyone to follow her.

Aster wasn't sure this was a good idea, but no one was willing to let her head off into the night on her own. And she had to admit that in this group, she felt a lot safer. And so, she went with them to Birdie's house.

♥♥♥

He loved her.

From the top of her head with her silky hair down to her now-bare feet.

Sam didn't know it was possible to love so greatly

not once but twice. He felt as though it were a special blessing and to let Aster slip away would be the greatest tragedy of his life.

And he still hadn't been able to tell her how he felt. He needed to do that—the sooner, the better. But as he looked around Birdie's crowded bungalow, he knew this wasn't the spot to declare his love for Aster. He needed someplace more private. Not that he minded telling the whole world, but he wasn't sure Aster would appreciate a big public announcement.

"Why don't you take her out on the back deck?" Birdie winked at him like she knew what he was thinking. "I'll keep the crowd in here."

"But how did you know?"

Birdie smiled broadly. "I have my ways."

He wondered if she could read minds, but he wasn't taking the time to ask her. He had more important matters on his mind. He approached Aster, who was pacing in the small confines of the kitchen.

He caught her hand with his. "Come with me."

"We can't leave."

"We aren't. Just trust me."

Without another word, she placed her hand in his and followed him onto the deck. She moved to the rail and stared out at the ocean as the moonlight reflected off the rolling tide.

"I'm sorry," she said. "I never meant to draw you into my nightmare."

He placed his finger under her chin and lifted until her gaze met his. "What happens to you, happens to me. I love you, Aster. You aren't alone."

She didn't say anything for a moment, as though she wasn't sure she'd heard him correctly. "You love me?"

He smiled and nodded. "Very much so."

"I love you too."

He drew her into his arms and kissed her. The thought that there would be countless kisses in the future filled his soul with a joy and happiness that he'd never felt before. This was just the beginning. Perhaps not the ideal beginning, but he knew this was just a hurdle they had to get past together.

33

He'd never tire of kissing her.

The creak of the door and then someone clearing their throat had them pulling apart. The kiss had been much too short, but Sam was reassured that there would be more.

"Aster, I have news." Mayor Banks stepped onto the deck. "They've caught Oz."

She gasped. "They did?"

Mayor Banks nodded. "The sheriff has him, and they are preparing to transport him back to the mainland where he'll be extradited back to California."

Sam breathed an easy breath. This nightmare was over. Aster was safe. He wanted to wrap his arms around her and swing her around in a circle, but when he turned to her, he saw the frown on her face.

"What's wrong?" he asked.

"I want to see him."

"What? Why would you want to do that?" He thought it was the worst idea ever.

"Because he's had me on the run for months now. I

let him rule me with fear."

"But you had a right to be afraid after the way he hurt you."

"I can't let him hold that power over me. I have to show him that I'm stronger now. This island and all of you have helped me heal. I'm not the broken person who ran away from L.A. I need to do this."

Sam's gaze moved to the mayor, who shrugged his shoulders. Aster made good points, but he still didn't feel good about this idea. "Where is he?"

The mayor held up a finger and then placed a quick call. "He's still at the docks. I asked the sheriff to keep him there until we arrive."

Sam's gaze met Aster's. "Are you sure about this?"

Steely determination shone in her eyes. "I am."

♥♥♥

There was strength in numbers.

And there was strength in love.

Aster felt stronger now than she'd ever felt. Knowing how much the people of Bluestar cared about her, especially Sam, had given her the determination to stay on the island. And if she was going to make a new start, it meant she had to make an ending. She was done running.

Her stomach shivered with nerves as they neared the docks. Flashing lights guided them to the right spot. She was nervous about facing Oz once more, but her determination didn't fail her.

Even though she'd held Sam's hand with both of hers the whole way to the dock, she'd now pulled away. She needed to do this on her own without leaning on anyone.

Oz was being removed from the back of a cop car when she stepped past a number of uniformed officers. And then he was there, glaring at her with murderous rage written all over his face. How could she have ever thought he was handsome? Hate marred his face. Darkness radiated from his eyes, sending goosebumps cascading down her arms.

Her instinct was to back up—to get away as fast as possible. But she didn't allow herself that option. This had to be done or she would regret it for the rest of her life.

"I almost had you," he hissed.

"But you didn't get me." Her stomach shivered with nerves. She ignored the sensation. "You'll never get me. You're going away for a very long time. And when you come up for parole, I'll be there to tell them the sort of criminal you really are."

"I'll get you. You can't run away."

"I'm done running. I'm not afraid of you. You can't hurt me because I'm stronger than you." With her shoulders level and her head held high, she turned and walked away.

In the background, Oz spewed empty threats, and that was all they were because he'd left a string of crimes from coast to coast including the murder of a police officer that had tried to apprehend him at the New York-Connecticut border. Another shiver raced over her skin but she refused to rub her upper arms. She wouldn't let him see that he got to her. He was her past.

And there waiting for her was Sam. He was her future. She knew their life might not always be easy, but as long as they were together, there would be love. Their love would see them through the good and bad times.

She walked straight into Sam's embrace and wrapped her arms around him. "I love you."

"I love you too."

She didn't let go of him, but she did lift her head to meet his gaze. "Do you think the dance is still going on?"

"Why? Would you like to dance?"

"Yes, I would."

"Then let's go to the harvest dance. Even if it's over, I have music on my phone, and I can't think of anything I'd like better than to hold you in my arms."

"You know this is just the beginning."

"The beginning of us?"

"That and the fact we'll be dancing every chance we get for the rest of our lives."

"It's a date." He kissed her.

Hand-in-hand they walked away. Aster smiled. Her heart was complete. Bluestar was her home now and for always.

EPILOGUE

Three months later…

"We've arrived!"

It was a sunny December day as Aster stared from the deck of the ferry to Bluestar Island. Sam had helped her drive Rosa across the country. The moving van was on the ferry, and Darla was waiting for them at the dock with a special day pass to move the van through the town and get Rosa set up in her very own ocean view apartment.

Now all of the people that Aster dearly loved would be on this small island—most especially Sam. As he stood at the rail next to her, she reached out and laced her fingers with his.

He turned his head and smiled at her. "Are you happy to be home?"

"Home. It sounds so nice. Yes, I'm thrilled to be home." She smiled back at him.

"Everything is almost perfect."

Her heart stilled. Almost didn't sound good. In fact, it sounded worrisome. "What's wrong? Are you having second thoughts about us?"

He gave her hand a reassuring squeeze. "Not at all."

"Then what is it?"

"I was planning to hold off on this until Christmas, but I can't wait any longer."

Now her pulse thrummed in her veins. It surely couldn't be what she was imagining. Because for weeks now, they'd been talking about the future and what they both wanted for it. But that was all talk, right? They weren't ready for something more, were they?

Oh, who was she kidding? She would marry Sam in a heartbeat. With her spending most every day at the farm, they'd gotten to know each other better than she'd ever known another human. She'd let down her guard and found a happiness that she'd never known before.

She knew they still had so much more to learn about each other but it would take a lifetime to learn that much about another human. She couldn't think of a more delightful journey.

She smiled at him. "Well, now you've got me curious, what won't wait?"

He glanced over his shoulder at Nikki, who was sitting on a bench next to Rosa. Aster's gaze followed his to Nikki as she grinned and nodded. "Do it, Daddy."

"So, she knows about this surprise?" Aster couldn't stop smiling.

He looked a bit flustered. "She kind of helped with it."

"Then I'm sure I'm going to like it."

He shifted his weight from one foot to the other and then back again. He pulled off his gloves. "I want you to know that since you came into our lives, you've changed everything for the better. Before meeting you, I was just a shell of myself walking around. You brought me back to life. You showed me that my life didn't have to be over. You showed me that I was still capable of love. And I love you with all of my heart."

She blinked back tears of happiness. "I love you too."

He reached into his jacket pocket and pulled out a blue velvet box. Aster gasped. Was that a ring box? She blinked but it was still there. And it sure looked like a ring box. Her heart lodged in her throat.

Sam knelt down on one knee. In that moment, the whole world faded away. It was just him and her and the possibility of a happily ever after.

He opened the box and held it out to her. "Charlotte Aster Smith, I love you with all of my heart. You bring out the best in me. Will you be my best friend for the rest of our lives?"

She pressed a hand to her chest where her heart was beating wildly. Was this really happening? Were her dreams all coming true?"

She stared into Sam's loving, hopeful eyes. "Yes! Yes, I will!"

He straightened and then reached for her left hand. He slid the diamond solitaire onto her finger. "I hope you like it."

Tears of joy streamed down her cheeks. "I love it. I love you. I love Nikki. I love the farm. I love Dash. I love the island—"

"Slow down." He smiled at her. "What was that part about me?"

"You mean the part of about me loving you with all of my heart?" When he nodded, she lifted up on her tiptoes and wrapped her arms around his neck. "Sam Bell, I'd be honored to be your wife and your best friend from now until forever."

He pulled her close and they kissed. She'd never been so happy in her whole life. Her heart overflowed with love.

A tug on her jacket had her pulling back to glance down and find Nikki smiling up at them. "Are we a family now?"

Sam bent over and picked up Nikki. "Is that what you want?"

Nikki smiled and nodded. Her gaze settled on Aster. "Can I call you Mommy?"

The dam broke, and happy tears spilled onto her cheeks. She swiped them away. "I couldn't think of anything I'd like better. I'll do my best to be a good mother to you."

"My other mommy would like that and she'd like you, too," Nikki said with sincerity.

"You think so?" The child's words meant so much to her.

Nikki nodded. "You make Daddy happy."

They all hugged. Her heart was at last full. And this was just the beginning.

Aster's Amazing Apple Cobbler

INGREDIENTS

Filling:
3 lbs Gala apples
5 cups cold water
2 Tbsp lemon juice
3 Tbsp granulated sugar
½ cup light brown sugar
4 Tbsp flour
2 tsp vanilla extract
2 tsp ground cinnamon
½ tsp ground nutmeg

Batter:
2 cups flour
1 cup granulated sugar
2 tsp baking powder
¼ tsp salt
¾ cup milk
2 tsp vanilla
12 Tbsp unsalted butter, melted

*a sprinkling of cinnamon
** vanilla ice cream

- Preheat oven to 350°F.
- Grease a 9x13 pan. Set aside.
- In a large bowl, add cold water plus lemon juice.

- Wash, peel, core and slice apples. Add to water.
- Once all apples are peeled, drain off the water.
- Add granulated sugar, light brown sugar, flour, vanilla, cinnamon, and nutmeg. Mix well.
- Place apple mixture in prepared pan.
- In clean large bowl, mix together flower, sugar, salt and baking powder. Mix well.
- Add milk and butter. Stir well.
- Spread over the top of the apples.
- Dust lightly with cinnamon.
- Bake 40-45 minutes until golden brown.
- Let cool for 20 minutes before serving with vanilla ice cream.
- Enjoy.

Thanks so much for reading Aster and Sam's story. I hope their journey made your heart smile. If you did enjoy the book, please consider...

- Help spreading the word about Harvest Dance by writing a review.

- Subscribe to my newsletter in order to receive information about my next release as well as find out about giveaways and special sales.

- You can like my author page on Facebook or follow me on Twitter.

I hope you'll come back to Bluestar Island and read the continuing adventures of its residents. In upcoming books, there will be updates on Aster and Sam as well as the addition of some new islanders.

Coming next will be Darla's story!

Thanks again for your support! It is **HUGELY** appreciated.

Happy reading,

Jennifer

Other titles available by Jennifer Faye include:

WHISTLE STOP ROMANCE SERIES:
A Moment to Love
A Moment to Dance
A Moment on the Lips
A Moment to Cherish
A Moment at Christmas

WEDDING BELLS IN LAKE COMO:
Bound by a Ring & a Secret
Falling for Her Convenient Groom

ONCE UPON A FAIRYTALE:
Beauty & Her Boss
Miss White & the Seventh Heir
Fairytale Christmas with the Millionaire

THE BARTOLINI LEGACY:
The Prince and the Wedding Planner
The CEO, the Puppy & Me
The Italian's Unexpected Heir

GREEK ISLAND BRIDES:
Carrying the Greek Tycoon's Baby
Claiming the Drakos Heir
Wearing the Greek Millionaire's Ring

Click here to find all of Jennifer's titles and buy links.

About the Author

Award-winning author, Jennifer Faye pens fun, heartwarming contemporary romances with rugged cowboys, sexy billionaires and enchanting royalty. With more than a million books sold, she is internationally published with books translated into more than a dozen languages. She is a two-time winner of the RT Book Reviews Reviewers' Choice Award, the CataRomance Reviewers' Choice Award, named a TOP PICK author, and been nominated for numerous other awards.

Now living her dream, she resides with her very patient husband and two spoiled cats. When she's not plotting out her next romance, you can find her curled up with a mug of tea and a book. You can learn more about Jennifer at www.JenniferFaye.com

Subscribe to Jennifer's periodic newsletter for news about upcoming releases and other special offers.

You can also join her on Twitter, Facebook, or Goodreads.